The Atropine Tree

SARAH READ

Bad Hand Books
www.badhandbooks.com

For the Scratchlings. We're everywhere.

CHAPTER ONE

Alrick had arrived in time, but only just. The collar of his shirt strained against his throat; his cuffs pinched his wrists like ropes binding him to his dying father's bedside.

Lord Drummond's chest rose with a sound like chalk on slate, like plough on stone—each exhalation a surrender.

Alrick's uncle Tredan leaned in and held a blue orb jar to the old lord's slack mouth. The fog of his breath that had clouded the glass only an hour ago now barely reached past the rim.

Tredan stood poised with the lid.

Alrick counted the breaths. Counted the beads of perspiration gathered in his uncle's beard, counted the coarse ridges of his father's knuckles that he held between his hands. The lord's cold, dry skin seemed to wick the moisture from Alrick's hot palms. He spun the ring that hung loose on his father's finger. Those hands had once been thick with callous, rough with half-healed tears, but now the skin draped from his fingerbones like drawn curtains. Like the end of an act. The end of everything.

Twelve. Thirteen. Fourteen. Alrick counted, wondering if his school had somehow been frozen in time. If in his six years there, a hundred years had passed at House Aldane. His heart twisted to think of how much he'd missed. He was a boy when he'd left home. Now, a young gentleman. Within minutes, he'd be a lord.

"Thirteen. Twelve. Eleven." His half-sister, Nelda, counted, too. Whispered, so that the fine veil across her face barely stirred. Her ragged black dog, Fray, lay as if asleep at her feet, though his pert ears twitched.

"Three. Two." Nelda's voice faded.

His father wore at least a hundred years across his brow. The rim of the jar pressed into the greying skin, burrowed in thinning whiskers. Covered the lines Alrick had watched as a child, searching for that rare trace of humor. The lines that had disappeared after his mother died.

The lid of the jar snapped into place—and that was how Alrick Aldane knew his father, Lord Drummond Aldane, was dead.

Uncle Tredan held the jar up to the candlelight. The mist of Alrick's father's last breath reached like a ghost down the side of the glass.

Light played over the droplets condensing in Tredan's bottle. Alrick felt the other eyes in the room watching him.

He had come home to bid his father farewell, but he would not be returning to school.

The gold signet ring stuck at his father's knuckle. He feared he'd tear the soft crepe skin if he twisted or pulled too hard. Alrick looked to Tredan.

"I'll take care of it," Tredan Said. "I'll have it back to you this evening." He slid the blue glass orb into the pocket of his long coat, and for a moment, Alrick thought the bulge it formed moved as if it were breathing.

Alrick nodded and laid the slack hand on the sheet.

"Best to wait," a dry voice spoke from the shadows.

Alrick turned to the voice, to his half-brother, Aemon, who sat in the far corner beyond the reach of the candlelight save for its glow off his eyes and teeth.

"And why is that?" asked Alrick. If a hundred years had passed at House Aldane, a thousand had passed since he'd seen his brother. Not since Alrick's mother had sent Nelda and Aemon away to live with their mother's family. Just before she had died. Their return to House Aldane was a special exception. Alrick himself had granted it. Lord Drummond had been their father, too, and now the four of them—Alrick, Aemon, Nelda, and Tredan—were all that remained of the ancient Aldane family.

"Father's will hasn't been read, yet." The candlelight caught in Aemon's smile as it stretched wide.

"Let's not speak of such things now," Tredan said. He waved the housekeeper Merewyn over and she began to see to Lord Drummond, a half-hitch in her breath that stirred Alrick's own grief. The powder smell of her apron pulled at his heart like a chain yanking him back to his childhood, to her lap, the soft cushion from which he had learned his home—the whole world. His whole world.

He reached up and ran his fingers over the wood of the wide beam that spanned the low ceiling. It had seemed so high when he was young. How he had leapt, in this very spot, to reach these distant beams. Landed there on the bed where his father now lay—fallen. Already sinking through the linens into the straw, as if life itself had buoyancy, and death was leaden.

Merewyn rolled a bit of blanket under the lord's chin to hold his mouth closed. A sliver of rheumy yellow flashed from beneath his eyelids, the stillness of those soft folds uncanny. It sent cold down the back of Alrick's neck. No living eyes could ever be so still.

"He's with Mother, now," Nelda said.

"With Burgrune." Aemon put his hand on his sister's shoulder.

Tredan nodded. "Yes, and Eleanor. He loved them both."

"I know," Aemon said, "I saw."

"So you did," agreed Tredan. "We should go. Give Merewyn room."

Three young children entered the room. All wore undyed linen smocks, their heads shaved close, their faces scarred with the ravages of old pox that left their skin like masks. They were urchins from London—orphans that Tredan had claimed and cured.

I'm an orphan now, too. The thought came unbidden to Alrick's mind.

No, I'm a young man. Not a child. A Lord.

The children set to helping Merewyn—cleaning the room and folding clothes. Alrick almost wished himself in one of those smocks. Something to do. A duty. A place in the world, instead of spinning uncertainty.

Tredan's hand rested on his shoulder and steered him toward the door. Alrick stole a final glimpse back at his father. The dead lord's eyelids had slid further back. His pale eyes stared out into the room, each rolling to the opposite side. Perhaps there was a wife at each bedside and he greeted them both. Perhaps one eye looked to the past and one to the future. Or perhaps he was roving, surrounded by devils.

CHAPTER TWO

The halls had narrowed. The ceilings had lowered. Wherever Alrick walked, his childhood home had diminished. The air felt thick with all that misplaced density, weighing in on him from every side.

As he walked, the floor bucked and tilted as the old boards gave way against the foundation. He grew dizzy and sat on a bench beneath a dusty window. The bench rocked, legs tottering over uneven planks. He stood again, mind swaying with the sloping floor. He counted his paces, making his way to the long table in the hall. Tarnished candlesticks sat upon it, stuck into melted candle wax so that they stayed when the table rocked.

Even the smoothest, most seasoned beams of the walls had split—long gaping seams now filled with bandages of gauzy web. The cracks stretched long and straight like Aemon's smile.

Alrick pressed his fingertips into plaster fissures that crumbled away from the ice-cold limestone that had been piled up centuries ago. He dragged his sleeve over the wood trestle in the hall, collecting a furrow of dust that must have been accumulating in geologic layers since his mother's death.

He could still hear her voice circle the hall—calling out for Merewyn—sending her after a chambermaid to tidy a patch of floor left un-scrubbed. She didn't want her young Lord Alrick to catch a fever, to put a dirty hand to his mouth and leave her lord husband without an heir.

"Did you call me, m'lord?"

Alrick jumped. Merewyn stood at his elbow, her hands ready at her apron pockets.

"Call you? No. I don't think I did. I certainly didn't mean to."

Her brow raised—unsure if she should console him or scold his prank.

"I was thinking about Mother. How she used to call you."

"Used to, eh?"

"It was so long ago."

Merewyn laughed then and broke his confusion. "Not that long, dear boy. You're still a child, to me. Always will be the boy with the biscuits hidden in his socks till I had to scrub the crumbs from between your toes!" Her apron bounced with her laugh, and Alrick had to employ all his will to keep from going to her—to bury his face in her neck and let her dry his tears on the corner of her pocket.

I'm Father, now. Father never wept into Merewyn's apron. Did he?

He'd forgotten to respond. Again. Like at school—odd and quiet.

"Sorry, m'lord, I don't mean to tease. I've finished laying your father out for the doctor, bless him. Have you found something you'd like me to do?" She eyed his dusty coat sleeve.

"Merewyn, I don't mean to scold. But the house hasn't been kept well."

Her smile melted as she shook her head. "It hasn't m'lord. That's a fact. I've been busy with your father's care, and there's none other on house staff now, save the scratchlings what master Tredan brings back from London."

"I understand." He couldn't picture those children's thin limbs and small hands scouring the splintered floorboards. "Please, tell me what you need to bring it back. To get the house in shape."

Her smile firmed up again. "I will, m'lord. I'll make a list. You make one, too, of what it is you need. I daresay we're likely not equipped to meet the needs of a young lord. We'll bring it back, though. There's life in these old walls yet. Will that be all? Is there anything I can get you now?"

Alrick couldn't begin to count his needs. He felt them heavy on his back—keeping him small. A child forever. He felt tired, young, and worn all at once. "Where shall I sleep?"

"The scratchlings are opening a room in the west hall, above your uncle. We'll have m'lord's chambers ready in a few days, but till then, I hope that'll do."

The thought of sleeping in his father's room terrified him. *My room. They're all my rooms.* "Thank you, Merewyn."

Out the front hall window, he saw a rider speed away.

"Who's that?" Alrick asked.

"That'll be Mister Bellows. A tenant farmer does a bit o' work 'round here. He's been sent to fetch the doctor, and your father's solicitor."

Alrick watched puffs of dirt from the horse's hooves drift and settle.

"Could you please show me to the room you've prepared? I need to rest a while, I think."

"Of course, m'lord, this way."

Alrick followed the swish and sway of her hem over the uneven floor.

As they passed from the old keep into the newer expansion of the house, the air grew warmer. He became more conscious of his chilled cheeks—knew that they must be ruddy.

"*Rosebud*" his schoolmates had chanted, their own cheeks just as chapped.

The floors of the expanded corridor groaned and squeaked—oak against oak still enraged these hundred years after the indignity of becoming lumber. Drummond had said his own father had felled those trees and drove the nails to expand the house. The stone cube of the original keep was now framed by two incongruent halls, like overlarge ears—the Lady's wing to the east, where his mother's chambers had been, and Aemon and Nelda's mother before her. The west wing had always belonged to Uncle Tredan.

"I'm afraid you're up in the gables—just take the stairs till there aren't any more. Roof's low, but it's one o' the warmest spots in the house. More so for being over Tredan's study. Keeps his fires going, for all his weird ministrations."

"Thank you, Merewyn."

"Forgive me for not escorting you, but these old knees, m'lord. Should be a girl up there scrubbing. Send her for aught that you need."

Alrick nodded. Merewyn swished away.

He stood in a threadbare parlor with a low ceiling and a warm fire but few other comforts. The carpets and chairs looked older than the oak boards beneath his feet. Books and empty glasses were strewn across the tables. Papers drifted everywhere. In front of the glowing hearth sat a chair with stuffing spilling from it toward the tattered carpet. A waistcoat hung draped over the chair's back. He had no memory of the staircase before him. He did remember the chair. The rug. Curling up in front of the fire and listening to his uncle think aloud. Not understanding any of it but taking comfort in his voice.

But he didn't remember those stairs.

The way up was a narrow tunnel of plaster, the white walls greyed with the rubbing of broad shoulders. The steps bowed in the middle as if an unseen person stood on every step. He could almost feel their eyes on him.

A face materialized on the staircase and startled him from his imaginings.

"Alrick?"

"Uncle Tredan." His breath of relief echoed against the close plaster walls.

"I hear we're to be neighbors. So sorry about the mess. I'm afraid I'm set in my ways."

"It's no worry, Uncle. It's only for a few days."

Tredan's brow flinched. "Quite so. Of course."

Alrick began to climb. Tredan's face disappeared behind the curve of a landing.

As Alrick approached, he peered around the corner.

Tredan's chambers were even less presentable than his parlor. There were so many clothes strewn about the room that when he stood among them, his face seemed to hover as it had on the stairs.

"I don't permit the scratchlings to clean in here, you understand. It isn't safe for children."

Alrick nodded. "That must be why I have no memory of this part of the house."

"Quite so! You've never been here before, have you?"

Alrick shook his head as he took in the details of his uncle's room. The ceilings were higher, and the windows longer than they were in the keep. The wide windows were crossed with lattice and opened to the back of the house, overlooking the gardens.

"Seeing as you're a man now, and a lord, would you like a tour?"

Alrick smiled, nodded, and stepped into the room, gingerly avoiding anything that looked fragile or important. Or dangerous.

His tiredness evaporated when he saw the brass telescope poised by the window. He strode over to it, forgetting to walk carefully, feet rolling over debris. "We had one of these at school," he said, running his fingers over the brass tube.

"So, you know how it works?"

Alrick shook his head. "I was meant to study it next year. I'd looked forward to it."

"Easily solved. Join me anytime."

"Thank you, Uncle. I'd like that very much."

"Your father joined me once. But his eyes were so bad then that he couldn't understand what all the fuss was about."

Alrick had forgotten his grief again. It came crashing back in a cruel, cold wave.

Tredan must have seen it in his face.

"Come—through here is the fun part," He placed his hands on Alrick's shoulders and steered him through the mess and under a thick beam archway. The wood was stained in splotches of unnatural colors, the surrounding plaster absorbing the hues—purples, reds, yellows fading out from the doorway as if it were a portal to another world.

That was not so far from the truth, Alrick found.

The long, wood trestle tables that had once sat in the hall for feast days now lined the walls of Tredan's antechamber. Atop them sat rows of glass and crystal vials filled with dark and milky liquids. Pipes and tubing crisscrossed the wall behind the tables. Steam puffed from loose joints. A faint sound of bubbling filled the room. And quiet coughing.

To the right of a chest of drawers as tall as Alrick was a small door. It stood ajar and through it, Alrick could see—in what would have been a closet or maid's chamber—a cot upon which lay a small child. Pale and glassy-eyed, soaked in sweat.

"Who is that?"

"That is Edyta. She'll be working for us, once she's better."

"Another scratchling?"

"That's Merry's word for them, yes. I prefer 'employee'."

"They're only children, Uncle."

"They're orphans. They are dying all over the streets and slums of London. If I have the means to cure them, I feel I should do so, don't you agree? And I can't very well send them back to the city to sicken once more and most likely die."

"I'm sure, Uncle. But isn't there somewhere they could go and not have to work? To be children?"

"I'm afraid your view of the world may have been sheltered, my dear boy. There are more orphans in this world than there are kind places to put them."

Orphan.

"Don't worry. They don't work too hard. You may have noticed."

Alrick nodded and brushed more dust from his sleeve. "Yes, I saw. Merewyn isn't too pleased."

"No," Tredan smiled. "That's my fault, I'll own. Though now there's a young lord in the house, I foresee some changes. After all, there shall have to be a young lady at some point, shan't there?" Tredan winked.

Alrick felt his cheeks flare again. *Rosebud.* He wasn't certain there ever would be. He'd failed to develop the obsession that had seemed the sole motivation of his peers.

"No need to think of that now. Go, get some rest. You'll need your strength for dinner."

"Dinner?"

"For Aemon. I'm sure he's been rehearsing his speech these fifteen years. Should be quite a show."

Alrick felt the roses drain from his face.

Aemon and Nelda. His siblings—his family. All the Aldanes around one table. Surely he could heal their divide. They could stay at the house. Take the east hall for their own. Aemon could help manage the lands. Nelda could…do whatever it is young ladies do.

They'd be a family, here in the family seat.

He ran his fingers over the plaster on the stained wall as he ascended the narrow stairs, leaving trails in the dust—a path to lead him back to the house from this room that felt so set apart.

He looked through the low doorway at the top of the stairs.

The gabled attic room stretched the length of the extended hall. It had not been divided into apartments like the floor below. In his grandfather's time, it would have held a long row of beds for maids. Now, one area was set apart as a parlor. Several bookshelves, mostly empty, sat in the corner with some stuffed spindle chairs still shrouded in white sheets.

In the far corner sat a four-post bed with two of its posts sawn off to accommodate the low slope of the ceiling.

A scratchling stood on the washstand, securing a heavy curtain to the side of the bed that still had its posts.

"Hello," Alrick said.

The child continued to reach awkwardly from beside the ewer and basin.

"I can get that. Let me help you." Alrick reached up to the child, and the child reached back, allowing him to lift her back to the floor.

He handed her the ewer. "Could you fill this for me? And I'd like some tea as well."

The girl curtsied and hurried away.

Alrick finished hanging the curtain. He sat on the bed to remove his shoes, but after glancing at the floor, decided against it. The filthy carpet had worn straight through to splintered planks.

It's only for a few days.

He crossed to his small sitting area and pulled sheets from the chairs. The dust that rose from the cloth stuck in his throat. He coughed, choked, made his way to the small windows only to find that they had been nailed shut.

Perhaps the best place to begin would be his list for Merewyn. It was growing so long in his mind already that he was in danger of forgetting things.

The scratchling returned, carrying a steaming pitcher.

Alrick's spirit lifted at the thought of hot water over his hands, his face, his neck.

She handed it to him, curtsied, and disappeared down the stairs.

Perhaps she's gone for the tea.

The scent of bergamot and lavender hit him, and he realized he was holding an ewer full of tea. He sighed and set the pitcher on the table.

He pulled his pen and a sheet of paper from his pack.

Service would top the list. *What would Father have needed?* For a household of four—assuming Aemon and Nelda chose to stay. A butler. A valet. A footman. A ladies' maid. A house maid. A cook and scullery maid.

Alrick glanced out the window. A gardener. Perhaps a stable hand, once those were running again. Perhaps one now—to get them running.

Could he afford all this? Had Father the means for this but not the energy? He supposed he'd find out when the solicitor arrived.

He slipped the list into a desk pocket, embarrassed already at its extravagance.

"Best to wait," he whispered to the window. To the tangled, neglected garden below.

There is much you can do yourself.

He remembered white-washing walls and polishing shoes at school. Things a lord should not do, but could, if he must.

He lifted the ewer to his lips and drank.

CHAPTER THREE

Tall candlesticks stood at one end of the long table in the keep hall. Four high-backed chairs, two on each side, were set at places that sparkled with freshly washed crystal. Gossamer web still clung in the crevices of the carved wood, where a hasty clean could not reach. At the head of the table, the tallest chair was draped in a black shroud.

"It seems Merewyn has already dusted off the finery a bit," Tredan said. He led Alrick to the table. "Sit here. To the right of your father's chair. Placement is important. It means something."

Alrick sat.

"Remember to stand when your sister enters."

"Thank you, Uncle." There had been no ladies to rise for at school. His etiquette had rusted.

Tredan smiled and began examining a cut crystal glass—holding it to the light at angles and watching the refracted flashes dance across the table.

Finally, Aemon and Nelda arrived.

Alrick and Tredan stood as Nelda took the place to the left of Lord Aldane's chair, across from Alrick. Tredan frowned.

Aemon pulled Father's chair out and sat in it. He dragged a place setting in front of him. The shroud fell from the back of the chair and settled around Aemon's shoulders like a cape.

Alrick felt heat rise in his face.

Tredan cleared his throat to speak, but Aemon spoke first. "I hope you're not too distressed for a proper dinner, little brother." He waved his hand to two scratchlings that stood in the shadows beyond the reach of candlelight. One carried a wide tureen of soup rocking between her small hands. Steam shrouded her face. A boy carried a pitcher of wine.

Alrick's throat felt tight. "You're in Father's place."

"Father's place is the grave." He held his cup out to the scratchling and it was filled with wine as dark as the shroud across his shoulders.

"He means your seat," Tredan said. "I understand your frustration, but have some respect, nephew."

A stirring came from behind Nelda's veil. It danced softly in the current of her breath. "Sit aside, Aemon. For now. You're upsetting Mother."

The candles guttered. The light cast through their glasses glowed red from the wine, red like Alrick knew his cheeks must be.

Aemon stood, a growl buried deep in his throat. The shroud slipped from his shoulders and pooled on the polished wood of Drummond's chair.

Aemon grabbed his glass and walked to the seat beside Nelda, knocking the scratchling girl aside. Her hand slipped. The tureen crashed to the floor, splashing soup around Aemon's feet. Shards of ancient family pottery scattered across the flagstones.

Aemon shouted. He swung at the scratchling, but she ducked and sprinted from the room. The boy followed her, leaving the pitcher behind.

Tredan stood. "How dare you—"

"Look what she did—your sorry servant! Urchins!"

Tredan rushed from the room after the scratchlings.

Alrick reached beneath the table and retrieved a shard of the tureen. He climbed out of his chair, knelt at Aemon's feet, and collected the other pieces, creating a thatched pile on the table. Fray's black eyes shined back at him from beneath Nelda's chair.

"There's no need for that, little brother," Aemon said, staring down his nose at Alrick, who knelt in soup.

Alrick finished collecting the shards and stood. His soppy trousers clung to his knees, chilling him. "Mother would have wanted me to try and fix it. But I'll need all the pieces."

"Mending isn't a lord's work," Aemon said. "But maybe it's yours."

Alrick breathed. Tried to will his face to cool. "I've got a lot of mending to do. Might as well start with this."

"You're a mess. Is that why Father sent you away?"

"He sent me *to school.*" Alrick remembered the day he left. The mixture of fear and excitement at the adventure before him. His father's pride—that his son would learn to be a lord and return to the family seat to carry on their ancient line. But the line was split.

"Know why he sent me away?" Aemon ran a fingertip over the shattered edge of a pottery shard.

"No." Alrick smelled hot wine on his brother's breath. A scent that went much deeper than his dinner cup. Had he been drinking all afternoon?

"Because of you. Because your mother asked him to. And he listened like a trained pup."

Nelda laughed. Her black taffeta rustled. "It was because of the berries, Brother."

Tredan stepped back into the room. He carried a tray laden with bread and cheese and dry salted fish. Merewyn entered after him with a board weighted with a fatty roast.

"Finally, some service," Aemon said. He returned to his chair.

Alrick sat, his face still burning.

Merewyn plated the meal and they ate in silence—Aemon's eyelids sliding further shut as the meal progressed and the wine flowed. Nelda's veil hardly stirred as her fork disappeared under its hem.

Alrick could barely swallow. Grief and dry fish stuck in his throat, trapped like a strangled shout.

"Will you be touring the countryside much during your visit?" Tredan bore his eyes down on Aemon.

"Every inch," Aemon said.

"I suspect you'll be wanting an early start, then," Tredan smiled coolly.

"I'll take my time, Uncle. I have all the time in the world."

"We all have less than we think," Nelda breathed from behind her veil.

"I think I'll turn in early, just the same. Alrick? If you're finished, we can share a light back to our hall." Tredan slid his chair back, its heavy wood groaning across the slate floor.

"Thank you, Uncle. But I have some business to attend to before I retire."

Aemon laughed and stood, dragging his chair legs through the soup. "Coming, Nelda?"

"In a moment. I hear something."

"Suit yourself." Aemon took a candlestick and left—not to the eastern corridor, but up the stairs to Lord Drummond's chambers. As his light faded, Tredan bent to Alrick's ear.

"Step into my rooms before you go up."

Alrick nodded and began to lay the tureen shards out on the kitchen tray. Tredan squeezed his shoulder, took a candle, and left. The dimmed light made it harder to fit the pieces together, to see if any part was missing.

"Don't worry about it, snapdragon," Nelda whispered.

"What?" Nelda's words were ice water on Alrick's hot face.

"I always liked the willow set better, anyway."

"What are you talking about?"

She pulled back her wispy veil. The centers of her eyes stretched wide and black, her lips pale at the edges and stained a dark brown where they split into a manic smile. Her white hand shot out of a belled sleeve, the lace cuff dragging through and catching on the fragments of pottery. Her cold fingers closed over Alrick's and took the shard from his fingers. "I'm glad you're here. Sleep well, little one." Her voice did not seem to come from her lips, which had hardly moved as she spoke.

Alrick pulled his hand free and rushed from the room, his heart hammering in his ears, drowning out the chime of glass shifting and taffeta rustling, of quiet laughter, of Fray's nails tapping on the flagstones.

He hadn't brought a candle. He felt foolish for rushing away, but her hand was so cold. So fast. *Snapdragon.*

His eyes went wide in the darkness, searching for any scrap of light that might lead him to the west parlor and the stairs. He thought he saw a glow ahead—a bobbing candle. Perhaps a scratchling at evening work. He followed, stepping carefully over the uneven boards.

He swayed in time with the floor—like a sailor finding his sea legs. Soon he'd learn every current of this house.

The light disappeared around a corner and Alrick rushed to catch up. He turned and pain whipped across his face. The impact seemed to knock the floorboards straight.

He put a hand to his cheek and another in front of him. His palm met cool glass. A window.

As he blinked the wet away from his eyes, the light appeared again, outside—below, in the garden. It bobbed and whirled, blinking out and back again behind the wild overgrowth.

He remembered his mother's long basket, afternoons spent in the shade of her broad hat as she gathered stem after stem. The smell of green on her fingers as she squeezed his cheek, said *they are not as rosy as you, my little snapdragon.*

A small, cold hand slipped into his. His shout jumped back at him from the glass.

"This way, m'lord," the scratchling whispered.

Alrick counted his breaths in the darkness and allowed himself to be led though the tilting hall to the foot of the narrow staircase. The scratchling's eyes sparkled amber in the fading glow of embers in the parlor hearth.

"Thank you," Alrick said.

The scratchling curtsied and vanished back into the dark corridor.

Alrick climbed the stairs to Tredan's landing. Light and heat poured from the lab, and the sound of something thick boiling violently.

Tredan stepped out of the small side chamber. "Ah, Alrick," he said. His hands deftly disassembled a lead syringe. "I'm so sorry about that ugliness at dinner."

Alrick hadn't even thought of Aemon's outburst since he'd staggered from the room. He couldn't shake the memory of Nelda's stained lips, the dark hallway, the light bobbing in the garden. The light in the scratchling's eyes.

"I…wasn't expecting that." Alrick steadied himself against the doorframe. "Perhaps I should have been. But I'd thought—"

"That you'd lost a father and gained a brother."

"Yes. And a sister."

"I hope you have, Alrick. Grief does uncanny things, even to the sharpest wits."

"I think I'll sleep now, Uncle."

"I hope you will. Rest well, if you can."

Alrick nodded and turned back to the stairs. The ill scratchling whimpered behind him, and the sound followed him up till he passed the threshold into his quiet gabled room.

Uncanny things. Perhaps grief was his affliction as well.

He peeled away his soup-soaked clothes, now hardened like bullion-flavored plaster gauze. He pulled his nightshirt over his head and doused his hands and face with cold tea from the ewer before he climbed into bed.

The hearth crackled and the floor was warm from the furnace of Tredan's instruments below, but his sheets felt like coarse ice. He waited for them to suck the warmth from him, then give it back.

When he closed his eyes, he saw the brown line of Nelda's mouth. The gaping black of her pupils.

Snapdragon.

He forced the image away and held in his mind the sight of the ceiling of his dormitory at school. He had imagined the cracks in the plaster as iron tracks—his sleep a charging steam engine ready to bear him off to distant destinations.

Sleep came in a series of short falls. A drop into darkness—a sharp, cold resurfacing with barely a wheel of the stars. He ducked in and out of nightmares, the engine of his dreams unstoppable, its boiler bursting with coal before a heaving bellows. Only the icy light of morning froze that oven.

Alrick's eyes and throat felt rough, abraded with exhaustion and dust.

Memory fell on him in layers.

I'm at house Aldane.

Father.

Aemon.

Nelda's mouth.

Snapdragon.

He sat up. A scratchling stood in the doorway, a steaming pitcher in her hands.

He nodded and she entered, then another came behind her with a tray of tea. He could have cried in relief.

The scratchlings set down their charges and exited silently.

Alrick stretched his neck. It ached as if he'd ridden a mad horse over rough road all night. A hammering sounded in his ears. He wasn't sure at first if it was his skull throbbing—the blood pulsing in his temples—or the stomping of angry feet. As the tea worked and his head cleared, he realized the sound came from outside.

He pulled himself from bed and walked to the window, pressing his palm against the glass to melt a view through the sheet of frost that coated it.

Aemon and Nelda stood below in the garden. Nelda had abandoned her black taffeta for patched grey linen. She almost disappeared against the hoary grass.

Aemon lifted a heavy hammer above his head, his black coat tails flapping like crows' wings in the morning breeze. He brought the hammer down against the thick stone wall of the garden—Alrick's mother's garden, and Burgrune's before her. Stones fell. Chips of rock flew into the air and rained down to the weeds. He swung again. The wall slowly gave way.

Alrick ground his teeth, scouring the garden perimeter. The wall was grown over with ivy, dark stones peeking through the evergreen veil. A narrow path surrounded it—bright moss pulsing up through the flagstones. A canopy of overgrown trees screened the inside from view. Untrimmed branches met and mingled to fill the whole of the interior like a tank filled with slick algae.

Alrick couldn't locate an entrance. Aemon clearly wanted in.

He pulled again at the window sash, a shout rising in his throat, the word *stop* building in every muscle. His fingernails bent back against the dry wood. *Nails.* He ran his thumb over the dull iron circles pinning the window shut.

Outside, the hammer continued to swing, but the stone was slow to give way, the layers settled into each other over the years till they had calcified into one impermeable slab.

Alrick pulled fresh clothes from his trunk, dressed, and shook the creases from his jacket as he ran for the door.

He wasn't sure of the time. He hoped, as he made his way down the stairs, that it wasn't too late for breakfast. He'd need nourishment after confronting Aemon in the garden and talking the hammer out of his hands. *There must be a door. How hard had he even looked before he decided to destroy it?*

Tredan met him at the landing. He held something small out to him. Alrick took it—an iron key. Its teeth twisted slightly from generations of turning. "What's this?"

"That's the key to the garden."

"Mother's garden?" Together, they rushed through the corridor that connected their wing to the keep.

"It has always belonged to the lady of the house. Burgrune was more fond of it than your mother was. Perhaps because Burgrune planted things there that your mother could never stop from growing. They still come up every spring."

"Won't need this anymore, it looks like." Alrick squeezed the key in his palm, its teeth pressing against his bones.

Tredan smiled. "The stone wall was built up over an iron fence. As Aemon is about to discover."

Alrick smiled back, but already dreaded his brother's wrath. "I didn't see a door."

"It's at the north corner. Few who have sought an entrance have ever thought to check the corners. It almost doesn't even need a key." Tredan winked at Alrick.

"Have you been inside? Is everything dead?"

"I have—often. Not dead, no. Wild and thriving. Abandonment has suited it well—better than it has the house."

Alrick lifted his gaze as they entered the front hall, to the split beams and crumbling plaster. "Perhaps I should leave it, then."

"It'll be spring soon. I'll be needing some of the herbs and plants from it. I may ask to borrow that key back from time to time."

"Of course, Uncle."

The tone of hammering outside changed from chipping and skittering to clanging. Aemon's shouts came filtered, muted by the house walls.

The choc-choc of the hammer became the clop-clop of a horse's hooves.

Tredan diverted his path and veered toward the entryway. Alrick followed.

A carriage came to a stop in the stone drive in front of the house.

"Merry!" Tredan called over his shoulder into the house. Her round face appeared in a doorway. "Could you please have the children set refreshments in the parlor? Mister Legan has just arrived."

"Yessir," Merewyn said, and vanished into the kitchens.

"I hope you slept well, Alrick," Tredan said as they watched Lord Drummond's solicitor climb down the carriage steps. A reedy, wraithlike clerk stepped down behind him, clutching a writing box to his chest. Ink dripped from around the hinges.

"I suspect this will be uncomfortable—for some, if not for all of us."

"I'm afraid I didn't get much sleep at all, Uncle."

Tredan strode forward and grasped the short man's hand. "Mister Legan, good morning. This is Alrick Aldane, my late brother's son."

Mister Legan shook Alrick's hand. His palms were sticky with something oversweet he must have eaten on the road. His hairpiece, with rows of tatty grey curls, sat askew so that Alrick could see his spotted scalp. "It's good to meet you, my boy. Goodness, you're young for a lord. I thought you'd be quite a lot older."

"I'm seventeen," Alrick said. At times, that seemed old enough, but his confidence flagged under scrutiny.

Aemon and Nelda appeared, then, from around the side of the house. Aemon had abandoned his jacket. His shirt stuck to his perspiring arms and chest.

"And here are Aemon and Nelda, Lord Drummond's older children," Tredan said.

"Oh, I see!" Mister Legan said, finally releasing Alrick's hand and reaching for Aemon's. "You're the eldest son. My mistake." He turned back to Alrick. "I'm a second son, myself. A rotten business, but don't despair—do let me know if you'd like to study law!"

Alrick forced a small smile and wiped his palm on the inside of his pocket. "I hope that won't be necessary, sir."

"No, no—of course not. I'm sure your brother will take good care of you. Marry you off to money! Raise the family again!"

"Please allow me to take your case, sir," Tredan said, lifting the solicitor's tattered leather briefcase.

Nelda stood behind Aemon, hands clasped, head askew as if

listening to distant birdsong. Fray crossed the grey grass behind her, like a stretching shadow.

"Thank you for coming so quickly, Mister Legan," Aemon said.

"Of course, Aemon. Anything for Lord Drummond. I'm so sorry, my boy. A bad business, truly awful."

"Some good may come of it yet, Mister Legan."

"That's the spirit, lad. In life there is hope. Let's go see what expectations there are in this hope of yours, shall we?"

They filed inside. Alrick hung back. The main parlor now housed Father's body—laid out in a box, eyes stitched shut by the village doctor. He wondered if Tredan might lead them to the library, instead, or to his own cluttered parlor. The lady's parlor was likely just as dusty as Alrick's room.

The guilt of poor hospitality rattled Alrick's thoughts, but Tredan stalked ahead, confidently, into the parlor where Lord Drummond lay, as if his body would preside over this auspicious family meeting. Alrick followed them in.

Alrick cast his eyes to the floor—to the bushels of winter possets Merewyn had scattered to ease the scent of death. She had left the hearth cold, but even in the freezing room, the scent prevailed.

Tredan strode across the room to open a window.

Nelda crossed to Father's open box and stared down into it. Alrick thought he heard the click of her tongue, the whisper of her breath over her stained lips.

Even the cold air felt stifling. Alrick squeezed his eyes shut and felt the soft caress of a cold hand on his cheek. His eyes shot open.

Nelda still whispered into the casket.

A scratchling appeared at his side with a cup of tea and a dry scone. Had she touched him? He took the saucer from her and his stomach growled loudly.

Mister Legan turned to him, a handkerchief clutched to his nose, and chuckled. "Good lad, good lad—healthy appetite."

Alrick felt sick.

"Well, let's get started. Sooner started, sooner done, and we can get to a proper luncheon." Mister Legan gestured to his clerk, who perched in a crooked chair and placed his writing box on a narrow round table. He folded the lid back and set up his papers. Mister Legan retrieved the sealed will from his case. He ran his thumb over the dull wax. "My father put this seal here many years ago. It's my honor to break it now, for you." He bowed his head to them all, his wig slipping incrementally forward.

Tredan frowned and shuffled his feet, shooting an anxious glance to Alrick.

Alrick stared at the spots on the lawyer's scalp. The man was old, himself. How could his father have sealed Lord Drummond's will?

Mister Legan cleared his throat with a rattle of phlegm. "Witness all here the reading of the will and testament of Lord Drummond Aldane, fifth Earl of Gastwick, deceased on…Gracious, I am sorry—what day did he die?" He looked into the casket as if the answer could be divined in the pallor of Lord Drummond's sunken face.

"December eighth, eighteen-fifty-six," Nelda said. "At eleven-eleven in the evening."

Mister Legan looked at her in confusion.

"No, Sister," Aemon said, "That was Mother's date."

"So it was," she said. "He died, then, too."

"Mister Legan, he died yesterday. March fourteenth," Tredan said.

"Eighteen-seventy-three," Aemon clarified.

"Thank you," Mister Legan said. The clerk scratched furiously at his paper with his pen nib. "In attendance are his younger brother Tredan Aldane, his three children—Aemon, Nelda, and…I'm sorry, what was your name again, lad?"

"Alrick." He felt the rosebuds blossom in patches on his face. Something was not right. As his face grew hotter, the room felt even colder. He shivered.

"Alrick Aldane. There are no other surviving relatives?"

"No, sir," Tredan said. "There are distant relatives of his wives' families, but no surviving blood but us. None known."

"Then here before all with an interest in the estate and title of Lord Aldane, I shall read his statement of inheritance." He pulled a bent pewter blade from his case and used it to sever the wax seal on Drummond's will. Crumbs of red wax fell to the carpet, disappearing among the dry blossoms, into the filthy fibers. Alrick wanted to sweep them up. He wondered if the room would ever be warm enough again to soften the wax, or if it would stay hard forever, lost in the creases of this house. A broken seal.

Mister Legan placed a monocle against his eye. It magnified the watery iris as it bobbed along the lines of script. "I, Lord Drummond Aldane, et cetera, et cetera, sound of mind and body, et cetera, do hereby bequeath my title, lands, and fortune to my son Aemon Aldane, under the condition that he must provide for his sister in such a way as befits her station. Signed and sealed Lord Drummond Aldane, et cetera, et cetera."

Aemon's laugh boomed.

Alrick tasted plaster dust on his tongue from when he'd inhaled. Gasped, he supposed. But now there didn't seem to be enough air in the room.

Mister Legan was shaking Aemon's hand and "m'lord"-ing.

Tredan stood. "Mister Legan, I know—for certain—that there

has been a mistake. That will is an old one. Outdated. It makes no mention of Alrick—"

Mister Legan crossed the room and clapped Alrick on the back. His chair legs bucked on the uneven floor—the whole room seemed to pitch. "Oh, my boy, my lad. It was the same way with my father. And yours, too, I suspect, Tredan! Second sons! Bad business. But you're smart, like your uncle. Been to school, yes? Educated?"

"I-I haven't quite finished..." Alrick's thoughts spun. His father, himself, had told him he was to inherit house and title. Why did this man have the wrong paper?

"So young! So sad. But your brother will look after you. Educate! Learn a trade—come to me and learn the law—you're welcome anytime, my lad, anytime."

Alrick's mouth scraped against itself. Even his tongue felt cold. He went to take a drink of his tea and found that it had fallen, spilled down the side of his leg. A small hand appeared from under his chair and sopped at the mess with a filthy rag.

"Let us adjourn to lunch, then. This growing boy needs nourishment." Mister Legan and his clerk stuffed away their papers.

Alrick felt Tredan's hands on his shoulders. He was pulled from his chair and steered from the room. He glanced back at his father's casket.

Nelda had finally looked away from the body—at Aemon, who had joined her. "As befits my station? What is my station, Aemon?" She asked.

"Your station? You're a madwoman. You're lucky I love you." He kissed her forehead.

"You're lucky," she whispered. She turned away and fell into step behind Alrick and Tredan. Her pupils had shrunk to pinpricks and Alrick could see, now, that her eyes were cornflower blue—almost violet. They'd have been lovely if the whites of her eyes weren't so red.

Alrick felt the pressure of Tredan's hand on his back, and he remembered to walk—followed the half-skip tread of Mister Legan, the lumber of his slouching clerk, as they tracked Merewyn to the hall.

He heard the heavy footfalls of Aemon behind him, felt his heart leap ahead like a startled rabbit.

Second sons.

Even Merewyn was silent as she drew his chair out for him.

Aemon took Father's seat. No one objected.

A parade of scratchlings filed through the room depositing steaming platters along the sideboard. Small hens and roasted roots, piles of greens swimming in butter. Baked apples and dishes of tart stewed berries.

"A feast for the prodigal son!" Mister Legan toasted and lowered the red level of his glass by half. The scratchling boy filled it again before it touched the table.

"I have returned!" Aemon joined his toast.

Alrick could not lift his glass, or even his chin.

"Will you be travelling to your aunt's house? Bring your things to House Aldane?"

"I've already sent for them," Aemon said. "We brought most of what we own. But Nelda has her books there. And I may ask Aunt to send some of Mother's things. Bring her presence back to this house."

"Now that you're home again, I'm sure her spirit has returned with you," Mister Legan said.

"Oh, she never left this place," Nelda said. She lifted her red-tinged eyes to the light. Her hair fell back from her face, exposing the paleness of her complexion and the delicate lacework of blue veins beneath her skin. "She's been here, always."

Mister Legan's fork stuttered on its elevation to his face. He forced a smile. "Indeed. Well, who would ever want to leave this place, even in death?"

"No one," Aemon said. "Certainly not us. But we weren't given a choice. When the new young mistress wants you out, out you go—isn't that right, Brother?"

Alrick's face burned. "I was an infant then, Brother. I don't have any recollection of the circumstances."

"I remember the day," Tredan said. "Clear as crystal. But perhaps I'd best not speak of such things today." His grim face echoed the darkness weighing in Alrick's chest.

"You have always had an excellent mind, Uncle," Aemon said. "Nelda has a desire to take up Mother's old garden. I'd hoped we might call on your expertise in the matter."

"If you have time," Nelda interjected. "I know your work is important. I don't wish to distract you from your purpose."

Tredan's scowl relaxed. "Not at all, my dear. In fact, I was going to enquire as to whether you might have any interest in the garden. It would benefit my research immensely if someone were to tend it for me."

Nelda smiled. Darkness was trapped in the grooves between her teeth as if she had been drinking from an inkwell. "A benefit to your studies is a benefit to my own, uncle."

"Excellent. Consider it done. It won't be long before we can begin clearing out the winter dead."

"Speaking of studies," Mister Legan said, "Alrick, when do you intend to return to school?"

"I…hadn't thought to return. I had planned to stay here. Stay home."

Aemon scowled at him, his downturned mouth slick with melted hen fat. "I suppose I'll consider it. It's more than was offered to me, of course. And you ought to finish your education, if you've any hope of prospects. It's a very uncertain world." He picked sinew from his teeth with a broken wishbone.

"Alrick has expressed a keen interest in my lab," Tredan said. "And an aptitude for scientific study. I had hoped to take him on as an apprentice. I won't live forever, after all, and the Aldanes have many legacies to uphold."

"It's true, there has always been an alchemist at House Aldane; however the role has changed. I don't know what my father would have done without you, Uncle. Though I suspect he would have had better service." Aemon snapped his fingers for a scratchling to remove his bone-scattered dish. "But on those grounds, I see the value of Alrick learning your trade. I'd not want to upset the line of succession." He winked at Tredan. "Alrick may stay. So long as he devotes himself to his studies."

Alrick looked between Tredan and Aemon. Had Tredan abandoned hope of an appeal? Had he accepted this upheaval of Father's wishes so easily? When Aemon lowered his face to a fresh dish of food, Tredan shook his head once, gently, at Alrick.

A plan, then. He was permitted to stay. That was a victory—he could not search for a missing will from the confines of his school. He nodded back.

"I must note, indeed," Mister Legan said, "the service is a bit odd, isn't it? I've never seen the like." He stared into the pock-scarred face of the child who cleared his place.

"These," Aemon made a sweeping gesture at the row of scratchlings in attendance, "are Tredan's science experiments. Each presumed near death, and he saved them with the noxious concoctions developed in his lab. Why he then decided to keep them, I can't say. And why then to employ them is a mystery."

Tredan smiled, tight-lipped. "They're orphans. I didn't save them only to send them to their deaths in the workhouse. They're learning skills here. Merewyn trains them. They'll find good places in homes across the empire."

"And other houses will reap the benefits of our tolerance," Aemon added.

"Orphans," Nelda echoed. She reached a pale hand up to the rough cheek of a child. "We're orphans, too, now."

"Nonsense, Sister. We're adults. And Alrick soon will be. Our future does not rely on the generosity of others—we make our own way."

"For all of the last twenty-four hours," Tredan said. "When you write to your aunt for your belongings, please give her my best regards. I remember her fondly from her visits here. She always brought gifts for you children, and she wore the most alarming hats."

Aemon smiled as if his wine had aged to vinegar in his mouth. "I'll send regards."

"I will admit," Tredan said, "while the service and furnishings were more than adequate for me and my brother, they are a bit unconventional for a young lord."

"I'm relieved to hear you acknowledge it."

"I need to go to London for supplies for the lab, and for Alrick's studies. I would be more than happy to make enquiries and place orders for the household while I'm away."

"That would be most helpful, luv," Merewyn blurted from the serving board. "I'll have a list for you. And Master Alrick said he'd make a list as well."

Mister Legan began to chuckle.

Aemon sneered at Alrick.

"As my assistant, Alrick will accompany me to London. He'll need to meet my suppliers and become acquainted with their ways of doing business."

"Splendid! And you'll have to drop in and see me, too. Once he's spooned out your dragon's blood and powdered tiger's bone, perhaps he'll take an interest in law after all!" Mister Legan wheezed a laugh and downed more wine.

Tredan nodded. "We'll leave just after the funeral."

Alrick felt the shake of grief in his core again.

"While you're gone, we'll blast our way into that infernal garden," Aemon said. He rubbed at a raised blister on his palm.

Alrick's face blanched. "No need." He stood and walked around the table to Nelda. He pulled the key from his pocket and pressed it into her cold hand. "The door is at the north corner. Please stop damaging the wall."

Nelda curled long fingers around the key.

"It would have been yours, anyway. Either way. It was always meant for you." Alrick felt lighter without the cold iron in his pocket.

Nelda smiled. "Always."

"May I be excused?" Alrick asked. "I think I need a rest."

"Of course, dear boy," Mister Legan said. "Don't stand on our account. Rest, by all means. Egad, what a day, indeed."

"Yes, you may go," Aemon said. "Send an urchin if there's anything you require to make your room more...suitable. Since it appears you'll be staying."

Alrick nodded and turned away just as rage-filled vessels bloomed fuchsia across his face.

He made his way back to the bachelor's parlor—his parlor—a second son's—and up the stairs to his quarters. *His. Since it appeared he'd be staying.*

He buried his face in the thin pillow and screamed.

This was not the world he'd been promised.

He remembered Tredan's subtle shake of the head. But what could they do? How could they change the word of English law—the word of his own father set hard behind the family seal?

And what could they do, above all, from London?

More importantly, what might be done to his home while he was away? Would another hundred years pass at Aldane Manor in a few short days?

He heard the hammer again, but this time, he knew it was his own heart—pounding at the insides of his skull, chipping away at ancient walls.

CHAPTER FOUR

lrick took supper in his room and paced, wearing a track in the dust on the floor. He packed and repacked his case. He didn't know how long his uncle intended to be away, but he didn't want to leave the attic to find out. Every time he crossed the room, the distance felt shorter, the walls closer, until the lopsided bed seemed to take up the entire long room, pinning him to the knee-high wall.

Knee-high.

His father had called him knee-high once—had berated his mother for bearing such a small boy.

He'd been hurt, but his father had laughed. *"It makes no difference in these peaceful times. You'll never need to fight a battle for your land. It's yours—in your blood. All you'll need is the wits to keep it."*

He did need his wits. Needed them more than ever. His father had been wrong about the battle.

He'd asked his mother, after that exchange, to measure him almost daily. She'd marked his growth against the doorframe in her room. He remembered pressing his back up against the cold wood, holding his breath and hoping the air in his lungs would lift him an extra mark higher. He remembered the scratch of her pencil on the wall—feeling the vibration of it at the crown of his skull.

Her pencil marks—were they still there? *How much had he grown?*

He was holding his breath again—hoping, perhaps, that the buoyancy would carry him swiftly, silently over the tilting boards of the halls and into the lady's wing.

He made his way, eyes half-closed, feet following their muscle memory—the way to Mother. A route they would never forget.

The door to her parlor hung unlatched. He pushed against it and stepped inside.

White sheets still draped all the furniture, but a single chair by the fire—as if Nelda, herself, had doubted she might stay at House Aldane. There was nothing of hers, here, to show that she'd made herself at home yet.

Alrick plucked the matches from the hearth and lit a candle. He carried it to the chamber doorframe, pushed open the door so the space behind the panel was visible.

There were the marks. Silvery graphite—from knee-high up to nearly his shoulder. The rest of his progress unmarked. As if, when she died, he'd stopped growing. The marks measured her life—her motherhood—as much as they had his growth.

He caught a moan in his throat. Swallowed. His eyes burned, perhaps from the closeness of the candle. He turned away.

His face met a bone-mask face—ivory white, mouth black and gaping, eyes black and wide.

The thing wore Nelda's dress but did not have her voice.

"How you've grown, my snapdragon." She crouched. A pearl of white foam formed at her lips and fell to Alrick's shoes. Alrick saw the black, silken flash of Fray dart forward and a bright tongue lapped at the foam.

The moan freed itself from his throat and grew in a crescendo—a scream that set the figure in front of him shaking. He dropped the candle and it hissed at his feet. The creature's face was now the brightest thing in the room—black eyes beading red in the light reflected from the hearth's fading embers.

Alrick stumbled back, away from the gaping face, farther into his mother's old bedchamber. He fell onto the cold wood floor—somewhere near where his cradle had rocked—*crik crik crik*—he could hear it now in the falling of the creature's feet. His mind rocked with it.

"Alrick, hush. Stop, hush." Light flared again.

Nelda held a candle in the doorway. Her hair was tattered and full of leaves, eyes dilated—black, even with the candle by her face. Her chin was draped in foam, which spilled over her lips.

"What are you?" Alrick whispered. The question felt ridiculous even as he spoke it.

She smiled and dragged her sleeve across her chin, then ran her fingertips over the graphite on the doorframe. "I'm a doorway," she said, and licked her fingers. "The door of House Aldane."

She stepped closer to him, slowly. "I didn't mean to scare you. Didn't know you were here. I've been in the garden. My mother's garden. She left such things for me there. Delicious things that help me to see her. To hear her. Like your mother left for you…Thank you for the key." She reached out and ran a finger across his lips, smudged black graphite there that tasted like ash on his breath.

"Hush, hush," she said again. "There's nothing to fear. Our mothers are here—and always have been." Her face darkened. "Although…they aren't friends. But that doesn't mean we can't be, Alrick. Brother."

She helped him to his feet. He staggered. She pressed the candle into his hands. "You'll sleep better tonight, Brother."

A scratchling slid out from under the bed and grasped his other hand. She pulled him gently, leading him through the doorway and out of the room. His eyes were fixed upon Nelda's—her face as white as his was red—until her black eyes disappeared behind the door.

The next thing he knew, he was in bed. Sheets pulled tight. Snapping fire radiating warmth. His eyes slipped shut, and he felt his bed rock—back and forth like a cradle, like a ship tossed at sea, like a man lost on the twisting floors of his father's keep. *Crik crik crik*, he rocked and heard a song on the draft, and he slept.

A lrick woke to the hand of a scratchling on his cheek. The hand was hot and moist from the pitcher she carried. Another scratchling stood by the window, brushing the dust and wrinkles from his black jacket.

The funeral.

Sunlight poured through the window. He had slept late. He'd slept deeply, just like she promised.

He gasped and sat up, as if startled awake for the second time at his memory of the encounter with Nelda. He licked his lips, tasted faint graphite and something sour.

Alrick slipped out of bed, scrubbed his hands and face—scrubbed at his mouth—and wet and combed his hair. He applied a coarse brush to the pale film that had spattered across the toes of his shoes. He pulled on his clothes. The sleeves of his jacket did not quite reach his wrists.

How much you've grown…

Out the window, A row of carriages already lined the long drive. Father's tenants, friends, neighbors, peers. Aemon's peers. They had started without him. No one had come for him. He wondered if he had been slighted, or if they had forgotten him. Should he feel angry or hurt? He settled on both.

Alrick made his way down the stairs and through the plunging corridors to the keep hall. The dark suits in dim light made it look as if the air itself roiled in the room.

"Ah, Brother. There you are, finally. Gentlemen, this is my younger half-brother Alrick. Eleanor's son. He'll be staying here at Aldane with us, studying with Tredan."

"We're so sorry to hear of your father's passing, young man," one of the milling suits said.

"Thank you, sir," was all he could think to respond. Alrick didn't recognize any of their faces. If he had forgotten all of them in the six years he'd been away, it didn't feel right to judge them for forgetting him, also.

"It's difficult to lose a father at such a young age."

"Powerful man. Left a powerful big hole in the world."

"So glad you have your brother here."

They didn't seem to require a response, only to speak their script. He listened for the rustle of Nelda's black taffeta. He wanted to see her—alive and speaking with her own voice. Wanted to ask her if what he remembered from the previous night had actually happened. He could not spot her in the crowd.

"Aemon, where's Nelda?" He realized he'd interrupted one of his consolers. Likely someone important and powerful and determined to have his say of the proper platitudes.

"I'm sorry," Alrick said to the row of stunned spectacles. "I'm not myself today. Has anyone seen my sister?"

"Understandable, my dear boy. Only to be expected."

"She's sleeping," Aemon said. "Recovering. She had quite a spell last night."

"Oh dear—is she ill?" A man asked.

"No, my lords. My sister is a spiritualist. A medium. Father's death has, it seems, stirred up the spirits of the house."

A bemused chuckle circled the gathering, led by Aemon's tilted smile and raised brows.

Alrick shivered at the recollection of the warring voices in his sister's throat.

"We all grieve in our own way, I suppose."

"She'll need your guidance now more than ever, poor girl."

"No," Aemon said, "she needed me most fifteen years ago. Now, at least, we are at home and the future is at our feet."

"Hear, hear," the gentlemen said and lifted their glasses of brandy. "To the future."

Alrick took advantage of the moment and slipped away. He filtered through the crowd, dodging coat-tails and walking sticks. He met eyes with several scratchlings—their linen smocks stained black with boot polish as they marched like ghosts through the cheerful mourners.

Alrick made his way to the sideboard and claimed a glass of brandy of his own. Fray stood sentinel at the end of the table, his dark eyes tracking Alrick.

There, at the head of the room on a pair of plinths, was his father's coffin. The lid leaned against the wall behind it. It was surrounded by bushels of hot-house flowers, piled, reeking, to mask the scent intensifying in the box.

In the shadows beneath the coffin, between tall stalks of lilies, Alrick caught sight of a pale face. He thought it was a scratchling at first, till he saw the wild hair. The shocking blue eyes.

He walked over behind the coffin and crouched in the flowers.

"Nelda," he said, "everyone thinks you're still asleep."

"I think that's for the best."

"I wish I'd stayed in bed, myself."

"I'm glad you finally got some rest, Brother."

"I wasn't dreaming, then? What happened last night really happened."

"A little of both, Brother. I did see you. We spoke. We spoke to your mother and she spoke to you."

Alrick swallowed. The flowers were beginning to irritate his throat and eyes. A prickle spread through his body. The longer he spent up against the blooms, the less effective they were at their purpose.

"Aemon says that you're a spiritualist."

She laughed softly, so that the flowers bobbed on their long stems. "He should keep his mouth shut. Not long ago, such talk would get me hanged."

"There's something you said last night, you couldn't have known…"

"I don't always remember what the spirits say through me, Brother. I'm sorry if I can't explain it. Sometimes I can learn a voice— begin to understand—but this place…It's so loud."

"This hall was never meant for so many men with such important voices. There used to be tapestries, to dampen the echo—"

"Not them. Not the living. This house is full of spirits. So many of them are angry. So many are so young."

"Children?"

"The scratchlings. Some of them."

"What do you mean the scratchlings are spirits?" He remembered the hot, wet hand on his face that morning. It had felt real enough to him.

"Tredan can't save them all. He's only human. And my god, they all want their mothers. The howling!" She began to rock, to twist her hair.

Alrick took her hand in his. "Hush, hush. It's okay. Let's go find Aemon. Drown out the spirits with the old men talking about tenant yields."

He tried to pull her from the copse of flowers.

"I can't," she said, "I have to wait here."

"Why? Who are you waiting for?"

"For Father."

Alrick shivered.

"I'd know his voice. I want to hear it. I want to know what he has to say…"

Alrick stared into her eyes. The pupils were pinpricks again. Fly motes in periwinkles.

"Don't you wonder what he'd say about all this, Alrick?"

He nodded slowly.

"Tredan's going to help. He has Father's breath in a jar. His pneuma. He's going to brew me the tincture I need." She smiled and Alrick saw blisters in her mouth.

He backed out of the posies and took a long draw of his brandy.

"Alrick," she called from behind white roses, "please bring me some ribbon from London."

He nodded again, his eyes now level with the stitched lids of his father's. He could see black threads tucked into the loose skin. His father's lashes were the color of summer wheat, not black, but he supposed the doctor hadn't had gold thread at hand for the occasion. The lids strained against the stitches, draping back between each tether. He wondered if dead eyes were sightless, or if his father could see the room in small glimpses. See him standing there, staring into the darkness between those threads.

Alrick hurried away. As he melted into the crowd, Aemon stepped up to the coffin and all eyes followed him. He lifted his hands for silence and Alrick could see raised welts on them. Angry pustules swelling over his palms and knuckles. The same red marks crept under his sleeves and peeked out of his shirt collar.

"That'll be the Bryony," Tredan whispered over the commencement of Aemon's speech. His breath was heavy with brandy.

"The what?"

"The vine. Also called Lady's Seal. Burgrune planted it along her garden wall as extra security. Leave it to Aemon to throw himself against his own mother's poison."

Alrick nodded. "I'd be more worried about what Nelda is taking from it," he said.

"I am worried. That's why I offered to help her. At least I can measure her doses. Keep her safe—relatively. It's a wonder she's alive at all."

"I don't think she exists entirely in this world, Uncle."

"No. I don't think she does. Conveniently for us, the answers we seek happen to be in the world she frequents."

"She says she's waiting to hear Father."

"I don't think it'll be long. No doubt by the time we return from London, something will have stirred Drummond's spirit."

"How long will we be away?"

"Not long. I don't intend to be gone more than a few days. I can't leave Edyta that long."

"The new scratchling? How is she?"

"Not well. But she'll make it. Eventually, her strength will return."

"Nelda said a lot of them have died..."

Tredan tensed. "I do what I can."

"What you do is a miracle, Uncle."

Tredan smiled down at him. "I'm glad you think so. Because I'm going to need your help."

"I'm happy to help."

"Good. You can start by telling Nelda I don't wish to hear the voices of dead scratchlings."

"I don't think she can control it, Uncle. I don't think she knows what she says."

He nodded, pursed his lips. "There is much about her talent that I've yet to understand. Much I wish to learn. Until I do, I can't assume that any of the voices she speaks with aren't her own."

"You don't believe her?"

"As her uncle, yes. As a scientist, I cannot. Neither can you."

Alrick thought again of her pale face, dark mouth, of the voice tearing from her throat.

Snapdragon.

Alrick nodded. Aemon was still speaking—regaling his fellow lords with tales of Father's wisdom. Alrick found himself drawn to the stories. There was much he had never heard—the same man, but a different lifetime. Stories that predated Alrick and his mother's brief reign as Lady Aldane. It dawned on him what a short span of his father's life he'd seen. Only the years between his birth and his leaving for school. Did he even know the man? No wonder Aemon bristled with resentment.

He felt the knot tighten in his throat again. And as the speech closed and the casket was lifted and carried from the hall, Alrick felt at once cold with grief and hot with anger at the unfairness of the world.

He followed the sea of black suits from the hall, across the swaying boards—the heads of local lords bobbing in unison like flotsam on the waves.

They exited House Aldane under the coldest sun Alrick had

ever known, and interred his father in frigid earth, in a plot reserved only for the lords and ladies of the house. *Will I rest here? Will I be cast down the lane to the churchyard, like my mother?* Burgrune's grave already occupied the space at his father's side. Eleanor had been taken to the family crypt in the village churchyard.

He shook hands that felt like embers against his palm. Felt those embers grow and sting across his face. He watched them fill their carriages, pull away, the clap-clap of horses' hooves like the throbbing beat of his pulse behind his eyes, the hammer in his head, the soft footsteps of wraithlike children through his home—some of them in this world, some serving his parents in the next.

The hearth fire roared at Alrick's return and the room filled with heat so completely that cold steam rose from his clothes as he settled into the chair. The hiss of flames sounded like voices, like the whispers Nelda heard in every corner of their home.

Their home.

I'm waiting for Father.

He hadn't seen her in the flowers when they'd lifted the coffin. She must have moved or hidden herself more deeply in the blooms.

Heavy footfalls sounded on the stairs—continued past where they would have stopped at Tredan's landing.

Alrick turned to the doorway. Tredan stood, hat in one hand, coat in the other. "Are you ready to go?"

"Yes. Let me fetch my case and I'll be right down."

"I'm sorry if the journey feels too sudden," Tredan said. He spun his hat in his hands. "But it's for the best."

"I'm sure it is, Uncle. It's been a long time since I've seen London. I'm sure the diversion will be good for me."

"I think it will. Merry said you'd have a list of things for the household?"

Alrick's eyes darted to his desk. "I'm afraid I didn't get to it, Uncle. I felt, in the end, that I might not be well suited to the task."

"I think you're perfectly suited. Perhaps a short list of things that might make this room more comfortable for the duration of your brief internment here." He forced a smile.

"You really think it will be brief?"

"I intend it."

Alrick smiled. "I won't need much, then."

"We can discuss it on the road. I'll see you downstairs." Tredan bowed out of the room and his heavy steps receded.

Alrick pulled his case from the wardrobe. He slipped the incomplete list from his desk and dropped it in the flames. It curled away into ash.

"Could you put out this fire for me? No need to waste the fuel," he whispered.

A cold draft pressed his elbow and a scratchling appeared in his periphery and began tending the hearth.

"Thank you," he whispered.

The scratchling glanced up from his task and Alrick saw his eyes were clouded white. A small smile played across the boy's pale lips.

Nelda and Aemon waited in the hall to see them off.

"Don't be bringing any more disease into this house, Uncle," Aemon said. "No more of those urchins."

"I'm afraid I have already taken on some engagements that must be kept. But I shall take on no further engagements at present. I have other studies to see to."

Aemon's lip curled. "Yes. You have many duties."

Nelda reached out and grasped Alrick's hand. Hers were hot and dry. He wanted to bury his fingers in her palms and warm them.

"Red ribbon, Brother, if you can find it."

Alrick nodded. He squeezed her hands and smiled in a way he hoped was comforting.

Outside, scratchlings swarmed the carriage, tying down Tredan's cases. Tredan and Alrick climbed inside, and Tredan called out to the driver. The carriage lurched ahead. The scratchlings slipped off its sides and filed back into the house.

Alrick stared up at the receding façade of his home. The Norman keep resembled the ruined follies that decorated secret gardens and novel plates. The Georgian wings to either side seemed to keep the center from falling to pieces, but even they had seen better days. Crumbling lintels and lopsided entablatures gave the whole a weary expression. *I could build, like my grandfather. Lift the place up again and make it my own, leave my mark.* But first, he'd need to claim it back from Aemon.

The carriage swayed and rattled down the long drive and out onto the rocky chalk road that cut through the Aldane lands. The sun hung low in the sky.

"We'll drive through the night and reach London in the morning," Tredan said. "Rest if you can. We have appointments all day tomorrow."

"Where will we go?"

"The university. The apothecary. The hospital. The workhouse. And Mister Legan's office."

"We're really going to see Mister Legan?

"Yes, we are."

"Why?"

"Because, Alrick, I think you have found a sudden, profound interest in law."

"I haven't, Uncle. I want to study with you."

"And you shall. But your interest in law may be greater than you know. And your need more immediate."

"What can Mister Legan do for me? His hands are tied."

"I don't know. And I won't know until I figure out exactly what he's done for your brother. And what your brother did for him."

CHAPTER FIVE

Alrick thought they were rushing toward a morning storm, until the wind hit his face and he smelled the coal dust. And another scent, the perfume of sewer and fever. Rats.

"London daybreak," Tredan said. "The smell is worse at noon."

The outskirts of the city rattled past the carriage windows. They slowed to a stop in front of a narrow inn in a row of white buildings. Tredan climbed out and spoke to the driver.

"Have a rest, George. We'll make our own way about our errands. You've done more than enough driving for today."

George tipped his hat and set off in search of the stable.

"And we don't need any extra eyes," Tredan said.

The innkeeper saw them to their rooms and a porter brought their cases.

"I hope you're up for a busy day, Alrick."

Alrick felt fogged and ill, like the city around him. In the carriage, his sleep had not been sound. He'd dreamt of running through the tilting halls of House Aldane as his family heirlooms crashed to the floor all around him and cut his feet. He'd woken more with every shatter, each time curled into a tighter and tighter knot around his own knees. He'd finally given up on sleep and observed the stars instead.

"We'll have a cup of tea before we head out. I can see you're exhausted."

Alrick couldn't even remember if he had answered his uncle's question.

The tea tasted of industry, as if the sky itself steeped flavor into the brew. But it gave him strength to keep up with his uncle's long strides as they made their way down stone streets through narrow tunnels of sloping, overhung buildings where the gutters ran full and slow.

Alrick was torn between watching his step and feasting his eyes on the sights of the city. There were clothes on lines collecting soot as they dried, chimneys burping, hawkers calling out wares, from buttons to bridges. Alrick strained his ears for anyone peddling ribbons.

Tredan tugged on Alrick's sleeve and they stepped over the gutter into a narrow doorway with a carved white lily on the lintel.

Inside, the air coated him in a layer of balm. Alrick breathed deeply. Camphor and myrrh. Mint and fresh earth. The man behind the counter largely resembled the roots that filled the jars lining the shelf behind him. Even his hair had grown like wiry dendrites, his mouth a lumpy fold.

"Master Aldane," his mouth unfolded and approximated a smile. "So good to see you, sir. I have your order just here." He pulled a rough-weave bag from behind the counter. It jingled and clinked with small jars and vials.

Tredan nodded to Alrick and he stepped forward to take the bag. "This is my nephew, Alrick Aldane. He'll be my pupil and apprentice. He may occasionally fetch my parcels for me in the future."

"Of course, Master. Pleased to make your acquaintance, lad."

Alrick shook a hand gloved in dirt and wart. The man looked to Tredan after eyeing Alrick from under a crusted brow. "But weren't he yer brother's heir?" The gnarled hand slipped away back under the counter.

"I'm Lord Drummond's second son," Alrick said.

"Yeah, but I thought—"

"So did I," Tredan said. "So did we all."

"Indeed." The tendril brows lifted and sparkling eyes shone between the folds of his lids. Alrick thought he might have seen earth crumble from the creases.

Alrick wondered why this shopkeeper knew so much about his life, if his uncle was in the habit of gossiping about family business.

"In the meantime, there is much to learn." Tredan bowed and the root man returned the gesture. Alrick attempted it but was afraid to upset the heavy bag slung over his back.

They deposited Tredan's vials back at the inn, then hired a hansom for a ride to the university.

The inside of the school was as cramped and crowded as Alrick imagined the scholars' minds must be, and perhaps as dusty. Tredan followed a clerk and Alrick followed Tredan as they made their way up narrow stairways and down plank halls, gathering a growing stack of texts that Alrick balanced from navel to chin.

The smell of the books reminded him of his library at school—of dust and ink and glue, of late nights and promises of secret power. He ran his fingers over the embossed titles, trying to divine the words with his fingertips. He had no luck, but the texture of the linen binding soothed him.

When both their chins rested on towers of books, they dropped them into the hansom. "The hospital is just here. Driver, please pull up close to the entrance in about twenty minutes." Tredan brushed the dust of the school from his jacket.

He handed Alrick the thick handkerchief he'd been holding on the stairs and pulled another from his coat. "Tie this across your nose and mouth. Don't touch anything, and don't breathe any vapors coming off the patients."

Alrick felt a tremble begin at the base of his spine. He did his best to ignore it. "How can I help if I'm not to touch anything?"

"You're here to learn. Observe, watch. Look for signs of strength in the patients, evidence of a will to live. That's as much an ingredient in their cure as anything I can brew for them."

Tredan hammered on the thick wood door bound in bands of iron. A small hatch opened. "Master Aldane—back so soon? Did the last 'un not make it?"

"Edyta is doing well. But our family has grown over the past week, and our household requires more assistance."

"Fever's bad in here this season, Tredan. Might find nowt but yer own doom in here today."

"You say that every time, Emmett."

"One of these times, I'll be right," Emmett said. "Only you'll be too far gone to know it."

The hatch swung shut and the scrape of broad locks sounded from the other side. The door swung open on groaning hinges, though Alrick could not be sure that the sound had come from the door and not the corridors stretching off in every direction. Groaning echoed from everywhere, save for one corridor, which was silent.

Emmett closed the door behind them and handed Tredan the wide ring of keys.

"You're not escorting us?" Tredan slipped the ring over his wrist.

"Above my pay to open the doors today, m'lords."

"Is it really that bad now, Emmett?"

"Aye, sir, and then some."

"But who is seeing to them? Who is caring for the patients if no one will go in?" Alrick felt his own hot breath recycle into his mouth beneath the thick handkerchief.

"God," Emmett said, as he tied his cloth over his face and retreated to his post by the door. "Though it doesn't look like He cares overmuch."

Alrick could see Tredan's rage in the crease of his brows. He wondered if the admonitions building in his uncle's mouth would blow his handkerchief clean off his face. But instead of raging, Tredan turned and made his way deeper into the long, dark corridor. He chose the silent hall first.

"Alrick."

"Yes, Uncle."

"I may require the use of your hands, after all. Some of what you see today may bother you. Perhaps for the rest of your life. However, I would encourage you not to look away. Take it in. Witness the suffering of others. Then do something about it. The only way to keep your wits, to keep your heart from breaking, is to always be doing something to help."

"Yes, sir." Anxiety clutched at Alrick's heart. It was difficult to breathe under the cloth.

Tredan grabbed a trolley from a nearby alcove and led Alrick through a set of heavy doors. The room beyond was cold, dark, and open. Shelves lined the walls. Four narrow tables stretched across the space with large blocks of ice stacked beneath them. Narrow rivulets of water trailed from the ice to a corroded drain in the floor. Still, shroud-draped figures lay atop the tables. In the corner, more sheet-wrapped forms lay stacked like kindling.

"This is the morgue, Alrick, where the dead are examined."

Alrick felt as though he were walking through tar as he forced himself to walk into the room. The closer he came to the shrouded tables, the more foul the air became. His eyes watered, soaking the rim of the cloth across his cheeks.

"Read the labels on the jars. If you find any that contain brains or eyes of lunatics or opium addicts, please put them on the trolley."

Alrick looked over the crooked, stained, and peeling labels that only half-concealed the nightmares bathing in dark liquid. Livers and kidneys. Hearts, teeth. He found one that contained "the remaining eye of an hallucinator" and he placed it on the cart. By the time he reached the corner, he had three jars of eyes and two brains. He had to step around the pile of bodies to reach the other shelves. He squeezed his eyes shut.

Take it in.

He opened his eyes. The bodies looked almost liquid in the way they slid over one another, the curve of limp legs, the stretched arc of a neck weighed down with its heavy burden. The sheets sank into the bodies' caverns—the eyes, the mouths. Clinging. Squeezing. The smell here was strong enough to choke him.

His handkerchief felt too tight. He feared it might suffocate him, but feared the open air even more.

He stepped over the spill of corpses and resumed his search. Tredan had busied himself at a table. Wet sounds filled Alrick's imagination with alarming dread.

As Alrick completed his circuit of the room, Tredan placed his own findings on the trolley. His hands shone red and wet with quickly drying clots stuck in the folds of his knuckles. He walked to the basin and washed, turning the water the color of summer roses.

"Thank you, Alrick. Now we'll go select a charge. Remember, we're looking for a survivor. Someone with the fire to beat death."

They wheeled the trolley back to the front of the building and turned down another hall, this one better lit and echoing with the shrieks and moans of those whose faces pressed against the thick, bubbled glass of the small windows.

Tredan walked from window to window, peering inside. Alrick followed, taking his turn to look. The patients inside seemed to be either raging delirious, shaking with fever, or dead. They rocked on the floor, tore at their hair, wiped blood from their lips, or stared, sweating. None looked likely to live.

Scratches covered the walls of the dormitories. Paint peeled away and flaked onto the squalid floors. In one room, a small boy sat rhythmically devouring the slivers of pigment, his eyes lost in another world. Six dilapidated beds filled each room, but Alrick counted ten or more patients per chamber.

"Tredan. Is this fever or madness?" His heart wrenched for the people trapped in the small, filthy rooms. He'd thought his school dormitory was cramped and often resented having to share space with so many peers, but this…This was the nightmare version of his world.

"It likely began as fever. Or maybe hysteria. Any little thing, really, if there's no one out there to care for them. And how long could you stay sane in here?"

Alrick could smell the rooms through the doors. Smell it all through the handkerchief. Even when he breathed through his nose, he could taste it. Pungent ammonia, feces, and rot—as if the miasma of London all stemmed from these rooms. Tredan must have sensed the growing intolerableness, too. He handed Alrick a sachet from his pocket. There was still blood under his uncle's fingernails.

"Hold this to your nose. It will help keep the vapors at bay."

The sachet smelled strongly of mint and clove, ginger and anise. Alrick breathed it in, crushed the linen to his nose and lips.

"Why would anyone come here for help if all they get is madness and death?"

Tredan continued down the hall, his hands moving in his pockets. "None of them are here by choice, Alrick. This is where society puts them, where their families sent them when they can't or won't care for them any longer."

"I thought hospitals were supposed to heal people, not make them worse."

"If we study hard enough, if we mix the right medicines and offer the right care, maybe we can make that a truth, Alrick."

They turned into another long hall and went from window to window.

"I don't see how anyone could survive this." The knot in Alrick's stomach felt larger than his whole body. His mind had already begun forming a protective skin around his thoughts.

Take it in.

"You'd be surprised, Alrick. The human spirit is stronger than you can imagine. Some fight off death with one foot on the other side."

And some never stop fighting, from any side.

Alrick pulled the sachet away from his face and walked to another window.

In this room, several were clearly dead. The body of a woman lay on the floor near the door, between two broken beds. Another patient had sat, bare naked, on the corpse's back and ripped out handfuls of her hair and shoved them into her mouth. In the far corner sat another young woman, bald, her nose ringed in blood.

Her dark eyes were wide with exhaustion. She sat with her back in the corner, draped in a soiled sheet. She'd torn away a steel spindle from the headboard of a bed and clutched it like a sword as she stared at the patient that tore at the other. Her eyes darted to Alrick's, then back to the naked woman.

"Tredan. Here."

Alrick stepped to the side so Tredan could look.

"Well spotted. A survivor in every sense." He pulled the ring of keys from his wrist. "This is going to be a bit ugly. I'm sorry. If the doorman had escorted us as he is supposed to do, I'd have you wait in the hall, but—"

"I'm here to help, Uncle."

"Right. Thank you. That one," he nodded to the naked woman who had begun to peel and eat strips of the dead woman's scalp, "may become violent toward us when the door is open. I'm going to give you the keys. When you open the door, I'm going to run in and detain her. I need you to escort our charge from the room as quickly as possible. She may be afraid of you. She may lash out. I don't know how lucid she is or what they've given her. Be kind, but drag her from the room if you must. We don't want to be in there any longer than necessary."

Alrick nodded. The keys jangled a confession of his nerves. "Which key is it, Uncle?"

"Not the largest, but close. Not brass, iron."

Alrick narrowed his selection to the one that most suited the description. He slid it into the keyhole. "Are you ready?" He wasn't, himself. He wished he could pull down the walls of this building. Take it apart brick by brick and let the clean air in. Not pull one chosen survivor from the wreckage of humanity. He wanted to free them all, cure them all, and burn the ruins of this travesty.

Tredan heaved a sigh, his handkerchief like a sail across his chin, and nodded.

Alrick turned the key. The lock groaned.

Bodies slammed into every door along the corridor, faces wild and tattered pressing against the thick glass. Doors all around them banged and strained at the hinges.

Inside their chosen room, the naked woman continued to eat at the dead. The survivor's eyes shot back and forth between the door and the woman as if measuring one threat against the other.

Alrick pushed at the door and the screaming hinges sounded like the gates of hell itself. Tredan slipped into the room and crept up behind the woman. She did not seem to notice. Alrick stepped in after him.

The smell inside the room burned his throat, his eyes, made his chest feel as if he held a wildfire in his lungs. The tacky filth of the floor grabbed at his feet, and as he pulled each step away, a new wave of scent set his eyes to watering.

He held his gaze to the young woman in the corner, trying to communicate with a glance his intent to help. She had begun to shake.

He didn't notice the bone on the floor, its grained ivory blending in with the dirty tiles. The delicate thing crunched under his toes.

The naked woman's head snapped up and her yellowed eyes pinned Alrick in place. Her muscles tensed like a cat's.

Tredan was on her then. He leapt at her back and pinned her arms to her sides. She bucked and screamed, thrashing with an intensity incongruent with her wasted frame. Her scream echoed in the corner, where the young woman had dropped the spindle sword and covered her face with her hands. Three of her fingers were missing. The jagged edges of the wound had swollen with dark tissue.

"Hurry, Alrick!" Tredan shouted over the shrieking woman.

Alrick rushed to the young woman's side. "Come, we're going to take you out of here."

Her hands remained plastered to her face, her mouth agape.

He reached for her. She lashed out and struck him, the remaining nails of her hand raking the side of his face. He caught her wrists. Her skin was hot and pungent, and as he squeezed, pus dribbled from the sleeve of torn flesh that ballooned around her broken finger bones.

"Come with me. Run, now!" He wondered if he could even carry her if he needed to. She wasn't as young as the scratchlings. She must be nearer Alrick's own age.

Do something about it.

He reached down and scooped an arm behind her knees and another around her back. He lifted her from the dirty floor and staggered toward the doorway.

Tredan had wrestled the cannibal woman to the ground and pressed a knee into her back. Her arms wheeled madly, reaching for him as he tried to catch her flailing wrists.

Alrick half-dragged, half-carried the young woman through the door. She had stopped fighting him and hung limp in his grip.

"Tredan, come," he shouted back into the hellish room.

Tredan sprung off from the woman and sprinted for the door.

Alrick pulled the door shut just as the madwoman's black teeth slammed into the glass. He leaned, holding the door closed as he fumbled for the key, slipped it into place, and engaged the lock, then slumped against the corridor wall and slid to the floor. "What happened to her?"

"The wrong kind of help."

"And we're supposed to be the right kind?" He crawled to the unconscious woman he'd laid on the corridor floor. Tredan joined him and knelt over her. His uncle listened to her heart and breathing, examined the infection in her hand.

"She's going to need a lot more than strong will to survive this putrefaction," he said.

"What does she need? What can we do to help her?"

The only way to keep your wits. Keep your heart from breaking. Do something about it.

"She needs us, Alrick. Our medicine, the lab." Tredan stood and hefted the young woman into his arms and carried her toward the hospital entrance. Alrick hurried to follow.

"She needs surgery now, but we can't do it in this place. They've let the pestilence win, here. We'll take her to the inn."

Alrick couldn't think how the innkeeper would tolerate their room becoming a surgery. He lifted the crate of specimen jars from the trolley.

"Just one m'lord? It'll take you forever to save the world at that rate." Emmett had poked his head out from his closet by the front door.

"Shut up, Emmett," Tredan spat.

"I told you it was bad, m'lord. 'Abandon all hope' I says, and you walk straight through, bold as brass."

"Open the door, Emmett, or shall I hand her to you while I do it myself?"

Emmett grabbed the keys from Alrick and busied himself at the locks, swinging the door wide and shooing them through. The door slammed shut behind them and the locks ground back into place.

"Goodbye, m'lord!" Emmett called through the narrow hatch in the door. "I'd hate to think I'd miss the chance to say it, should this be the last we meet!"

Tredan ignored him. "When we arrive, Alrick, I want you to go straight to the innkeeper. Say that I have injured my back and I require a kettle, firewood, a hot bath, and as many towels as they can spare. Carry as much as you can yourself and keep the porter in the hall."

"Yes, Uncle. But won't they hear her? When you…when you cut her?"

"No, she'll be asleep, Alrick. She won't feel any pain."

Alrick nodded. He'd learned more that afternoon with Tredan than he had in his entire last year at school. And his uncle was right, it would bother him, possibly forever. But he felt hope, too, that he did indeed have a future, a purpose—a title to replace the one he had lost. The alchemist of House Aldane may very well suit him better than lord.

They loaded their charge and their cases of jars into the hansom. The driver, alarmed at the addition to their party, made swift progress through the streets back to the inn where he was more than happy to speed away.

Alrick hurried to the counter where the innkeeper busied herself pouring ales for gentlemen engaged in a heated game of dice.

"What is it, lad. Quick, I'm busy."

"Pardon, ma'am, but my uncle's hurt his back. He requests a kettle, firewood, bath, and towels." Alrick felt the lie sour on his tongue. Or it might have been the smell of the hospital wafting from his clothes.

"Master Tredan's hurt, is he?"

"Yes, ma'am."

"Like last time?"

Alrick wasn't prepared for such a leading question. "I'm afraid I wasn't here last time. I don't know."

"Tell Master Aldane I'll leave the goods in the hall outside the door. And there's an extra fee for cleaning up a room that looks like a butchery, and another for the laundry."

Alrick paled. He wondered what the innkeeper must think of his uncle, if she knew he was trying to help someone or if she thought he was some sort of perverted murderer.

"Thank you, ma'am. May I take the kettle now?"

"That bad, eh?"

"I'm afraid it's urgent."

The innkeeper disappeared beside the hearth and returned with a large iron kettle. She shook her head and glared at Alrick as he hurried up the stairs.

Tredan had been preparing. He'd dragged the desk to the center of the room and opened the shutters so that bright afternoon light arched across the table, floor, and walls. The fire roared.

The young woman lay on the desk, still wrapped in the foul sheet. Alrick placed the kettle on the fire.

"Alrick, bring my bag of medicines from the apothecary, please." Tredan pulled a wrapped leather parcel from his bag. Alrick dragged the heavy sack from the wardrobe.

"Bring me feverfew, arsenic, and opium."

Alrick took the jars and vials from the bag and lined them up on the mantle, inspecting the spider scrawl that stitched across each label. He brought the ingredients to Tredan.

Tredan set a brass bowl on the bed. Put on these gloves." He handed a stained pair of lambskin gloves to Alrick. "And put a pinch of each in this dish. A small pinch. We can always add more. Too much is deadly."

Alrick blanched.

"Add water from the kettle to the bowl—just a bit. Do not breathe the steam."

Alrick pulled the gloves onto his shaking hands.

The clang of the washbasin and the thump of towels sounded outside the door. "Thank you," Tredan called through the closed door.

"I'm charging you for the towels this time, Tredan!" the innkeeper shouted as she receded down the hall.

"Fine, fine," Tredan whispered.

Alrick's fingers hovered over the opening of the vial labeled arsenic

"Hurry, lad, if she wakes up, this will get ugly."

Alrick plunged his fingers into fine powder and drew out a pinch. He added it to the bowl, then added a pinch of the seeds from another jar, and a splash of hot water.

"Add just enough water to soak this rag," Tredan said, handing him a coarse cloth. "Leave the gloves on. Let it steep a bit, then lay it across her mouth and nose."

Alrick did as he was told while Tredan dragged the basin and towels into the room.

Alrick laid the hot rag over the woman's face. Her eyebrows twitched and her head rocked, eyelids fluttering like she was trying to escape from beneath them, but soon she stilled. The tension melted from her neck and shoulders. For a moment, Alrick feared he'd killed her, but the rhythmic rise and fall of her chest reassured him that he had done his job.

"She won't feel this? Any of it?"

"No. She won't. Nor will she have any memory of it. Perhaps no memory of the last four hours, which would be a blessing." Tredan pulled the black leather roll closer and unbuckled it. It relaxed open to reveal an array of surgical tools. Tredan pulled them from the kit and laid them out on the bed. Scalpels and tweezers, syringes, a bone saw.

Bile rose in Alrick's throat. Tredan handed him a leather strap and buckle.

"Fasten that around her arm just below the elbow, as tight as you can. We must squeeze the blood vessels closed."

Alrick wound the strap as he was told. The limb was twig-thin and pale, covered in bruises of every shade and degree. He pulled the leather taut, watching the woman's face for any sign that he might have hurt her. Her eyes remained still. Peaceful. All but dead.

"Excellent. Alrick, you're doing well."

"Thank you, sir."

"While I work, heat more water. Fill the basin. Prepare another dish of the herb mixture in case she wakes." Tredan picked up a dainty scalpel.

Alrick was relieved to turn away, but his eyes drifted back, as if drawn by magnets to the fine movements of his uncle's hands.

Tredan cut into the flesh of the woman's arm. Blood spurted across the floor then slowed to a trickle as he cut deeper and deeper, working his way around the limb's circumference, exposing pale tendons, red meat, and finally the bright bone at the center of it all. When he'd cleaned a section of bone, he put down the small blade and picked up the saw.

Alrick poured water into the basin and filled the kettle again. The pitcher was empty. He'd have to visit the pump in the kitchen.

He heard the scrape of steel teeth against bone, a grating drag, again and again. He lost count of the strokes, but they finally ceased.

"A towel, please."

Alrick handed him one. Tredan slid it under the young woman's arm and wrapped it around the broken, delicate hand and slender wrist that he then set aside.

"Hot water."

Alrick handed him the kettle, and his uncle poured scalding water over the wound.

The woman moaned.

Alrick dashed for the brass bowl. He soaked and replaced the medicine rag. Her moans muffled, then ceased.

Tredan put a plate on a rod into the fire. He cleaned out the skin just below the tourniquet and pulled it closed over the wound, then dribbled a clear liquid over it that hissed and foamed. He threaded a needle with black cord and began to sew the skin shut, enclosing the tattered end of her forearm in folds of skin. When the stitches were in place, he pulled the rod from the fire and lightly dragged it across the seams where blood still oozed.

Tredan pulled an empty jar from his case. "Alrick, please put the young lady's hand in here."

His fingers numb and clumsy, Alrick fumbled with the lid of the jar. He'd been feeling faint, but thought he'd kept his composure well.

"Alrick?"

Tredan took the jar from him and twisted it open. Alrick lifted the woman's hand from the towel, but it slipped away and landed back in the folds of cloth. His fingers tingled, as though he had wrapped belts around his own limbs.

"Alrick, were you wearing gloves when you reapplied her medicine?"

Alrick's heart sank. "Sir, I forgot."

"Go—now. Wash your hands at the pump with scouring soap. Don't touch your face. Bring back more water, if you can manage."

Alrick clutched the kettle and pitcher to his chest and raced for the kitchen. He stormed past the innkeeper who shook her head and cursed under her breath. Alrick set the pitcher and kettle on the floor and scrubbed his hands with coarse pine soap, rubbing it into the creases of his knuckles and digging under his fingernails. The tingling continued farther up his wrists and he worried about his ability to fill the containers and bring them back.

A scullery maid entered and started at the sight of him in her kitchen.

"Miss, could you help me? I'm having trouble. I've hurt myself and I need these containers filled with water and brought to my room."

"T'yer room? This isn't that sort of establishment." She smirked at him. "I'll call the porter for you." She disappeared from the kitchen.

Alrick lifted the kettle. He could hold it if he balanced it between two hands, but then he couldn't fill it. *Idiot. What a stupid, obvious mistake.* Alrick's anxiety soared as he thought of Tredan and the young woman waiting for the fresh water they needed.

The porter entered, a cloth tucked into his shirt and a bit of carrot in his beard. A scowl on his face. He nodded to Alrick.

"So, you've done hurt yerself as well, then? Or is my story slipping."

"I'm afraid I injured myself while trying to help my uncle," Alrick said.

The man stepped around him, filled the kettle and pitcher, and gestured for Alrick to walk ahead. Alrick led the way back to the hall outside their room and reached for the containers, hoping his hands would hold.

"Thank you, sir."

"You don't want help in?"

"I'm fine from here, thank you for your assistance. I'm sorry to have interrupted your dinner."

The porter sucked at his teeth. "Yer uncle's secrets are becoming unpopular with the locals, lad. People taken. Bloody messes. Disappearing kids." He tugged at his beard and Alrick caught the scent of beef broth. He didn't know how much longer he could hold onto the heavy containers in his tingling hands.

"My uncle is a healer. A doctor. He's trying to help."

"That's what all witches say, boy."

Alrick paled. The tingling in his hands reached his face. Then the rosebuds came, the heat and the rage.

"I won't stand for those accusations, sir."

"Calm yerself, lad. I just want to know if I have a need to call the constable."

"No!"

The door to their room creaked open. Tredan stood in the doorway in a nightshirt. He clutched at his back. "What's this commotion? Alrick, have you brought water for my bath?"

The porter kicked the door the rest of the way open. Alrick gasped.

The room was back in order. Towels lay draped across the floor with the tub sitting atop them. There was no sign of the young woman. Tredan's tools, jars, and packets had been hidden away.

The porter's eyes swept the room. He scowled at Alrick, then at Tredan, nodded, and stalked away.

Tredan helped Alrick with the water. They placed the kettle on the fire to heat. Tredan lifted the pile of clothes from off the bed and tucked them all into his trunk.

"Where is the young woman?" Alrick asked.

"Here." Tredan lifted the last of the clothes and pulled back the sheet. Her pale face was peaceful in the firelight. Tredan had washed the filth from what was left of her hair.

"We must pack our things now, Alrick. It's too soon to move her or I'd leave at once. As it is, we'll leave before dawn. We'll call on Mister Legan on our way out of town."

"I never unpacked my case, sir. It's all there."

Tredan paused in his packing and looked at Alrick. "No, I suppose you never had the chance, did you?"

Alrick shook his head. The frenzy of the day was wearing off and the last several days came crashing down on him, one after another.

"You did very well today. Exceedingly well, considering the challenges that arose. You're going to make an excellent apprentice." Tredan smiled.

"But—" Alrick held up his tingling hands. They looked paler than normal.

"Your hands? Oh, everyone does that. Consider it a rite of passage." Tredan laughed. "But you won't be much help packing. Keep an eye on the water for me and let me know when it boils. Rest yourself. Keep those hands warm."

Alrick settled into a chair by the fire and held his hands to the flickering heat. It soothed the pinpricks and brought a healthy shade back to his skin. He stared into the fire and timed his breathing with the respirations of the young woman. He hoped that the medicine he had mixed would help her forget that day. And the uncounted days she'd been locked in that room.

Of course, they had yet to even hear this woman speak. Might not she be just as mad, herself? If not when she entered that room, then certainly now…Alrick didn't think he could blame her if her wits had fled. If her mind was the only part of her that could escape that hospital room, then he hoped it was far, far away. Someplace warm and clean.

Alrick wondered if she would be happy at House Aldane. *How will we convince Aemon to keep a servant with only one hand? And if she's mad as well?*

Alrick's breathing had quickened and fallen out of pace. *I won't let him send her back there.*

Tredan came up behind his chair and squeezed his shoulder, pressed a small steaming cup into his hands. "Drink this."

Alrick looked into the cup. A few inches of hot water rippled inside, small dark granules floating in it. It smelled like summer flowers. "What's it for?"

"It's only lavender and chamomile. To help you relax and get to sleep. Tomorrow is important, and it will be difficult, no doubt."

Alrick sipped the floral water. He felt no dramatic effect, but his eyes did grow heavy in the warmth. He felt a blanket draw across his knees as he sank further into the chair.

The hospital still haunted him. He didn't want to help only one person at a time. He wanted to get them all out.

When I'm lord, I will build my own hospital. A real one, for healing people, not for shutting them out of the way.

But he was up against the same limits as his uncle.

What could a second son do?

When I'm lord…Maybe I can hold both titles, lord and alchemist.

CHAPTER SIX

lrick woke to the sound of glass breaking, of Tredan cursing and of George Bellows apologizing and shifting a heavy bag of samples in his arms.

The fire had died down to a low pile of glowing embers. A chill crept up through Alrick's feet. He shivered under the thin blanket and reached to pull it closer, then yelped. His skin burned. The numbness had gone, replaced by a raw red that oozed clear liquid.

"You've a sensitivity to that, I see," Tredan said. "It's an uncommon effect, but I have a treatment for it. Unfortunately, I won't be able to mix it till we're home."

Home.

"Are we leaving now?"

"The inn, yes. London, not yet. I still plan on stopping by Mister Legan's office."

Alrick lifted himself stiffly from the chair and wrapped the blanket around his shoulders. He stoked the fire; his raw knuckles felt as though he'd shoved them into the embers. He supposed it was better to have both of his hands in pain than to be missing one altogether.

He cast his gaze back over the room, but even as the fire grew and the light stretched, the young woman was nowhere to be seen.

"Is she…did she—"

"She's in the coach," Tredan said. "We felt it best to keep her out of sight."

Alrick dropped the blanket to the chair. "What can I do? How can I help?"

"Follow George to the coach and wait there. Keep an eye on things while we finish loading the cases."

Alrick followed Mister Bellows from the room, stepping over a small mound of broken glass in which nested a single cloudy eye, and around a tub full of bloody towels.

The London smog seemed to have become particulate ice overnight and Alrick shuddered against the cold as he climbed into the frigid chamber of the coach. His coat was there on the bench beside the slouched and sleeping young woman. He picked it up and took a seat beside her, then draped his coat across her shoulders and over her lap.

She was wrapped in a clean sheet—one of the inn's, no doubt. But Alrick couldn't imagine it did much to keep her warm.

As the sun rose, light billowed brown through the icy haze. Tredan and George finished fastening the cases to the coach as a lamp's glow bloomed in the small kitchen window of the inn.

"I left our payment on the desk, plus a reasonable overage. I don't think I'll be back to stay here. I dislike their talk of witches," Tredan said as he settled onto the bench across from Alrick.

The carriage pulled away into the empty lane just as the innkeeper appeared on the step gesturing curses with a coal scoop.

"To Crookes Street, to see Mister Legan, please, George," Tredan called up to their driver.

"Will he be in so early?" Alrick asked.

"Probably not. We'll be waiting for him when he arrives."

Alrick took in the condition of his clothes. There was some evidence of their encounter in the hospital, the surgery, sleeping in the chair by a sooty fire. "I certainly don't look like a young lord. Not even a second son," he said, brushing at a stain on his knee.

"You look a bit like a young doctor," Tredan said, and smiled. "We'll say we had trouble on the road. Appearance makes no difference—the law is the law."

"He seemed quite certain the law was settled."

"Yes, but he is employed by our family, as was his father—who was the one who would have inscribed that old will. He must, therefore, investigate our concerns. It makes no difference who is Lord Aldane as long as Lord Aldane pays his bill. He should have no preference one way or another whether you or Aemon holds the title."

Alrick nodded and continued to work at the stains on his clothes.

They pulled up to the lawyer's office just as the sky reached full morning. They had not been parked long when Mister Legan's clerk arrived and unlocked the door. The round form of Mister Legan soon followed.

"Go on, Alrick," Tredan said.

They met Mister Legan right at his door. He jumped and flattened a hand to his heart. "Good gracious! Master Tredan, Master Alrick! I did not expect to see you so soon after our meeting."

"Alrick has thought of some questions he would like to ask you about the study of law."

Mister Legan laughed. "Tired already of your uncle's frog's eyes and fish lips, are you, my boy? Come inside, come in—we'll have tea and words." He held the door for them and they stepped into the modestly furnished parlor.

"Eames, could you please set some tea? Our business begins bright and early today." Mister Legan's clerk finished setting the fire and slouched from the room. "Is there anything else I can get for you? Travel must have been rough." Mister Legan's eyes wandered over Alrick's disheveled suit.

"No, thank you. We thought we'd just stop in to ease Alrick's curiosity before we see to some errands for the house," Tredan said.

"And I'm so glad that you did. Tell, me Alrick, what can I do to assuage your curiosity? Are you thinking of pursuing the gavel?"

"No, sir." Alrick hadn't thought he'd be the one doing the talking. "It's just that…many have come forward with the belief that my father had a more recent will than the one read and enacted the other day."

Tredan gave Alrick a small nod.

"Oh dear," Mister Legan said. "Many, you say?"

"Friends of my brother. Our more distant relatives. Several at the funeral were very surprised to hear of Aemon's succession," Tredan said. "I, myself, witnessed a more recent will, and often heard my brother declare Alrick to be his heir. We wondered if perhaps some other version of his wishes might exist somewhere. And we've come to entrust you with the task of finding out, as is your duty to the law and to our family."

Mister Legan was silent and apparently in shock as Eames returned and served the tea.

Alrick had to exercise an excess of manners to not devour the scones on the plate. He realized he'd forgotten to eat dinner the previous evening.

"That is quite shocking news. A most alarming declaration. And as the guardian of Lord Drummond's legacy, there should be no surprises for me. My father left impeccable records, and according to them, he has never once filed an amendment to his will." Mister Legan punctuated his insistence by shoving a scone into his mouth.

Tredan watched him chew in silence.

"Could you look into the matter, please?" Alrick asked.

"I'm afraid I can't," the lawyer said around a mouthful of pastry. Alrick lowered his scone.

"Why not?" Tredan asked.

"I was contracted by the family for Lord Drummond's arrangements. I'm afraid my employ with the Aldane family ends there. Unless your nephew, Aemon, wishes to continue with our office, which of course I would be delighted to—"

"So you're saying, sir, that you don't work for us." Tredan's face flushed and Alrick felt his own following suit.

"I'm afraid that's correct." Mister Legan struggled to swallow the dry scone and hurriedly sipped his tea.

"But what of your offer to Alrick? If he should need anything?"

"My offer was out of friendship. Charity, if you will. Out of sympathy for my client and his orphaned son."

"I see," Tredan said.

"I'd still be happy to educate the boy. Take him on as apprentice. Don't we all know what a cold world this is for second sons. Perhaps I can impart some knowledge upon the lad that he can use in his quest…But if you ask me, it is a hopeless one."

"Well," Tredan said, "I suppose it is simply a matter of finding out who Lord Drummond's real lawyer was. I don't think we'll require any further assistance from your office. I suppose we must at least thank you for your candid response."

Mister Legan's teacup rattled against the saucer. His face had paled behind his whiskers. "At your service, sirs. Unofficially."

Alrick chewed his scone. It weighed on his tongue like the stones of House Aldane.

A commotion grew outside the office.

"Please excuse me," Tredan said. He set down his cup and walked briskly from the parlor.

Mister Legan stood.

Alrick understood what his duty must be. "Mister Legan?"

The lawyer, concern writ deeply across his face, turned to Alrick. "Yes, my boy?"

"When you last spoke with my father, did he mention me at all?"

"Of course not. You weren't even born yet, my boy." He moved closer to the door. Shouting sounded outside.

"So, it must have been at least seventeen years since you spoke?"

Mister Legan finally focused on Alrick. "I know what you're getting at, lad, but it's no use. Yes, it's been close to twenty years since your father visited this office and my father took down his wishes. Lord Drummond was always loath to leave home—and why shouldn't he be, with a handsome young wife and new son to keep him busy? But I stayed informed of events." He turned his attention back to the growing altercation in the street and moved into the entrance hall.

Alrick followed him, trying to divert his attention. "And how did you stay informed without any word from my father?"

Mister Legan's jolly persona was slipping. "The Aldane family is much larger than what you keep under your roof. The ones he abandoned, for example."

"Aemon and Nelda?"

"Just so. And all his wife's family."

"How can you say he abandoned them when he left them everything?"

"Young man, I really must see to my—"

"You work for them, don't you? You always have." He had finally won Mister Legan's full attention.

"Young man, I don't think, after all, that you have the right sort of mind for law. You are all speculation."

"I agree, sir. I'm far better suited to science."

Mister Legan smiled sourly. "Thank you for your visit, Mister Aldane. May you prosper in your chosen venture."

Alrick bowed and offered a handshake, but Mister Legan, seeing the condition of Alrick's skin, grimaced and headed for the stairs that must lead to more private offices.

Alrick hurried outside. The commotion had quieted somewhat. Tredan was showing a sheaf of notarized papers to a scowling policeman.

The tails of George's coat were visible through the bent door of the carriage, from where came a string of shrieking gibberish. Alrick ran to the carriage door and pulled George out of the way. He climbed inside and was met with a rapid barrage of scratches to his face. He held up his hands to fend off the blows, but the nails against his raw skin made his head spin with pain. He dropped his hands and allowed his head and shoulder to take the blows.

"Please, miss, I won't hurt you. I'd like to explain." He forced his hands to remain at his sides, to show he meant no aggression, and he wondered if the blows to his face would ever stop. Finally, they did.

The woman collapsed back against the carriage seat, clutching with her one hand at the sheet that had fallen loose.

Alrick slowly retrieved his coat that had fallen to the carriage floor and handed it to her. She snatched it from him and covered as much of herself as she could.

"Miss, I'm sorry we frightened you. My uncle is a doctor. We're taking you somewhere we can make you well again."

Her eyes showed nothing but panic as she searched his face. He imagined he must look frightful. Exhausted and grieving, filthy, and now with welts rising across his face.

He reached, moving slowly, into the basket and handed her a flask of water. "You've been very ill. And the hospital, they weren't… They couldn't cure you. My uncle will help. He's done this before, many times."

She stared at the flask in her hand and began to weep. She moved her injured arm toward it and tapped the lid.

"Oh! I'm so sorry." Alrick reached forward to grasp the flask and remove the cork.

She lunged and bit his hand, lashing her hot tongue over the blood on his knuckles. He shouted, and she returned the scream in kind.

Tredan jumped into the coach and it lurched forward, gathering speed over the uneven cobbles in the old lane. The bent door rattled where it would no longer latch.

"Well. That was expensive," Tredan said.

Alrick clutched his bleeding hand.

The young woman chewed the cork out of the flask and spit it onto the carriage floor. She withdrew as far as she could on the narrow seat and noisily drained the flask.

Tredan pulled his small case from under the bench. He handed Alrick a rag and bandage, then poured an acrid liquid over a strip of cloth. "Hold your breath for a moment, Alrick."

Alrick pursed his lips.

Tredan waited till the woman was done drinking, then leaned forward and held the cloth to her nose and mouth. She struggled weakly for a moment before falling back against the window. Tredan straightened Alrick's coat over her. "It's good she woke long enough to drink something," he said.

Alrick nodded and dabbed at the cuts on his face.

"You tried to explain, I imagine. Did she seem to understand?"

"No, sir," Alrick said. "She was furious. What did you mean by 'expensive'?"

"Bribery, my dear boy. Another art you'll need to learn."

"But we've done nothing illegal, have we?"

"Of course not. Not illegal. My papers are in order. But it would have taken hours—maybe all day—for them to verify everything. I needed the officer to come to that conclusion more quickly."

If the law were in his hands, Alrick would have felt the need for further investigation. Nothing about their traveling party looked legal, even if it was.

"Bribery is an art I could perhaps learn from Aemon," Alrick said.

Tredan's eyebrows raised. "So you made the most of your time with Mister Legan?"

"I did. He hasn't seen or heard from Father in nearly twenty years—since just after Nelda's birth. He doesn't work for us because he works for Burgrune's family. I don't know their last name."

"It's Sibald. That makes sense. It's why his information was old, and why Aemon would have contacted him. Why he has no interest in helping—it would be unseating his client from a wealthy peerage."

"But who was Father's real lawyer, then? After I was born?"

"I don't know. I don't even know if he had one. He didn't care much for them."

The carriage slowed to a stop. Tredan looked out the window. They were in front of a row of small shops. People bustled up and down the street, breaking around their carriage like a river around a stone.

"Wait here," Tredan said. "I won't be long." He climbed from the coach and disappeared into the flow of people.

Alrick rested back against the seat and closed his eyes, felt his head begin to spin. Exhaustion gripped him. Grief, hunger, terror, and the rush of energy used to get through the last few days rendered him immobile. Sleep claimed him.

He woke to the jolt of the carriage leaving the cut stones of London streets and taking to the rutted roadways that would lead them home, and found that his coat had been draped over him. He looked to the young woman. A thick, down blanket had been tucked in around her.

The seat beside Tredan was crowded with parcels. Tredan flipped through a catalog of home fineries one of the shops had to offer. "Do you think Aemon will order the velvet seat for his privy?" Tredan asked.

Alrick wanted to laugh, but the cuts on his face and the throbbing in his temples prevented it.

"We have to stop him before he places an order here." Tredan reached into the pile of parcels and handed Alrick a flask of tea and a package of sandwiches.

Alrick tore into the package. The first sandwich was gone before he even identified its contents. Salty meat, slabs of crumbling cheese. He stared at the back pages of the catalog, at the ridiculous luxuries there. He wondered what Aemon would order—in what ways he would change their home to make it his own.

"Were they poor? When they lived with their aunt?"

"As I understand it, they had everything they needed. Your father wouldn't have had it otherwise, and I'd certainly have intervened, if necessary."

"Of course."

"But I imagine there was an awareness that none of it belonged to them. Most of all not the love of their father."

"It's hard to picture Father being so cold to his own children. Why banish children? I admit, it bothers me. I never thought of it, then, but now…" Alrick felt energy returning to his body, and with it, the anxiety of all his cares.

"It bothers me, too. It always has. But it was more your mother's doing. Her actions were out of fear, and seeing her afraid enraged your father. He was very much in love with her, and protective of both of you."

"But why was she afraid? Aemon and Nelda were only children."

"Yes, but cunning ones. They had their mother's wit. And Nelda had her garden. She harvested some of Burgrune's poison berries one day, and Aemon fed them to you. You nearly died. I almost couldn't save you. For a few hours, I thought you were already gone. Then you woke up." Tredan folded the catalog and tucked it into a band of twine around one of the packages. "Your mother was never the same after that. The terror of that night, I think, drove her a little bit mad. She had your father send the children away. She was convinced it was a purposeful attempt on your life. She thought she was protecting you."

"Was it?"

"Purposeful? None of us ever knew for certain. I don't think Nelda meant anything by it. She'd often eaten those berries herself, as had Burgrune. It's unlikely she gathered them with you in mind. As for Aemon, I can't say."

Alrick brushed crumbs of cheese from his coat. "I suppose we'll find out soon enough."

"How so?" Tredan opened his own packet of sandwiches.

"If he wanted me dead then, I doubt his mood has improved over the past fifteen years."

Tredan frowned. "He'd draw a lot of suspicion from his peers if he tried something like that now."

"He doesn't seem to care much what they think, anyway," Alrick said.

"No, but he very much wants to appear lordly. We'll have to frame any aggression against you as unbecoming."

"Nelda frightens me, but I don't think she means harm."

"She doesn't mean it, no—but it happens anyway. Her gifts are all curses. Be kind to her, yes, but cautious."

"Her gifts—do you mean the voices? The ghosts?"

Tredan nodded. "I'll be working with her. I may be able to brew something that can help, so she doesn't go digging in the garden on her own, the way her mother did. It's what killed her, in the end."

"Something from the garden killed her?"

"It may have been the foxglove, or the nightshade. I suppose it makes no difference. It's why Drummond put the stone wall around the iron one—to keep the children out. It didn't stop them, obviously."

Alrick sighed. The history of his house was heavier than he'd realized. He felt a new ache of sympathy, of affection, for his siblings. A renewed promise to work toward the unity of their family.

"Ah, and here—there's this." Tredan reached for another packet and handed it to Alrick.

Alrick peeled back a corner of the paper and saw a bright coil of red ribbon.

"Oh—thank you, uncle. I forgot the ribbon."

"Understandable."

"Still. It would not have been a good start to everything for me to have ignored such a simple request." Alrick rubbed his forehead and instantly regretted it. Both his hands and his face stung.

"It was the least I could do after all the help you've given me these last few days."

"I'm your assistant. It is my duty."

"You are an excellent assistant, Alrick. But you're also Lord

Aldane, whether Mister Legan declares it or not. And from what I've seen, you'll make an excellent leader, as well. Aemon will not. Your people deserve you. It's our duty to give them a leader that's worthy of them."

Alrick flushed and felt the cuts on his face burn anew.

"Get some sleep," Tredan said. "That fight begins tomorrow."

CHAPTER SEVEN

Every chimney of House Aldane eked a trickle of smoke into the fresh morning air.

"They must have every hearth in the house ablaze," Tredan said as the carriage pulled along the gravel drive. "They'll have seen us coming, I'm sure. When we stop, get out quickly and close the carriage door behind you. George will take the coach to the stables. The servants will unload it. You're to distract Aemon and Nelda with the parcels—the shopping, not the specimens, please, unless that works better—while Merry and I sneak the girl up to my lab."

Alrick bit his lip and nodded. He couldn't peel his eyes from the glowing warmth of the windows. Soon, tea and a bath. Rest, he hoped, though Tredan's talk of battles suggested otherwise. He wondered how long it would be before he could truly rest.

The carriage stopped and Alrick stumbled from his seat into the gravel. He lifted his eyes to the sight of Aemon's boots crossing toward him, followed by Nelda's bare feet and Fray's shaggy paws. Tredan helped Alrick steady himself.

"Welcome home, Brother. Uncle. I trust your trip was successful?"

"Indeed, Nephew." The carriage jumped forward and made its way toward the back of the house. "George and the children will bring the parcels to the hall."

Aemon's grin was fixed, rictus tight "Yes, I'm sure you're exhausted. Let's get into the warm."

They took their seats by the fire in the main parlor, where the furniture had been arranged back into place, as though a coffin hadn't dominated the room only days before. The whole length of the wide hearth had been filled with wood, as if they planned to roast a boar.

Alrick's neck ached from the jostle of the carriage, from the impact of the young woman's blows.

"We didn't want to impose too many selections on you. We chose a few necessities and brought this for you to see." Tredan handed Aemon the catalog. Its long descriptions and ink drawings of fine things instantly stained Aemon's fingertips as he flipped through it.

George entered with the first armful of parcels. He turned to Tredan. "Sir, Merry would like to know what you wish done with the case of vials."

"Ah, I'd better assist her with those. Please excuse me for a moment." Tredan slipped out of the room. Alrick recognized his cue and peeled himself out of the chair. He handed parcels to Aemon and Nelda while George went back for more.

Aemon mumbled about the adequacy of tableware. Nelda squealed over a packet of garden tools. They tore through paper and scattered it like leaves, and the more George brought, the more energy they seemed to have. There were linens and bolts of silk and taffeta, a silver tea service, fresh blankets. Aemon had a new walking stick with a carved ivory knob and Nelda had sheepskin slippers that she slid over her dusty feet. Even Fray had a new leather toy, which he dragged under the table and worried at, lovingly.

Alrick grew increasingly uncomfortable at the excess. It was like Christmas, he supposed. Like every Christmas they'd never had here in their home. He handed Nelda the final parcel—the coil of red ribbons. She smiled and stood and kissed him on the cheek. Her breath smelled bitter and earthen. "Thank you, brother," she said. His scratches tingled where her mouth had been.

"Thank our uncle. I'm afraid he's more skilled at selecting ribbons than I am."

"Nonsense," Tredan said as he reentered the room, his feet crashing through cast-off papers. "It was all Alrick's doing. Goodness, I've missed the show."

Nelda and Aemon both smiled—Aemon reluctantly, as if he couldn't help it.

"Well, I feel just like Father Christmas," Tredan said. "The bearer of gifts who's been all around the world in a single night."

"You both must be exhausted," Nelda said.

"I'm afraid we are. If you don't mind, I think we'll go and rest awhile before we join you for dinner." Tredan glanced around the room and snapped his fingers for a scratchling. Nothing stirred. He stepped toward the kitchen corridor and called, "Meg? Tom?" No one came.

Tredan's good nature melted. He turned to Aemon. "Where are they?"

Nelda's eyes lowered and Aemon's smile took on its more familiar, nasty cast.

"They wouldn't suffice, Uncle. Something had to be done."

"*Where are they?*"

"Manchester," Nelda blurted. Aemon struck her. Tredan lunged for Aemon, grabbed his hand, and twisted his arm behind his back.

Alrick rushed to Nelda and led her to a chair. She didn't cry. She didn't even touch the reddening side of her face.

Rosebud. Snapdragon.

"Where in Manchester?" Tredan asked as Aemon's knees sank toward the floor.

"The workhouses. Where orphans belong."

"Orphans like you?"

Aemon's knees hit the carpet and he coughed out a laugh. "No. I'm a lord." He slid free of Tredan's grip. He nodded toward Alrick. "Orphans like him, if you don't tread carefully, old man. He looks more like your urchins every day."

Alrick looked away from Nelda's still face to see Aemon's shaking finger pointed at him.

"We're tired. We're all tired after the last few days. Let's rest first, and address this issue later," Alrick said. He saw Tredan's shoulders relax.

Give them the leader they deserve.

Tredan backed away, then turned and headed into the dark hall toward his parlor.

"I'm going to bathe and rest a while," Alrick said. "Enjoy your things."

He followed the echo of Tredan's heavy footfalls, but as he passed the door to the lab, it was closed. He decided not to knock and continued up to his room.

His hearth was cold and dark, perhaps the only fire in the house not lit. He sighed, started a fire, stacked it high, and set the kettle on to heat water from the basin. He noticed, then, the small pile of parcels on his bed. He hadn't even considered that some of his uncle's purchases would be for him. He pulled the paper back carefully, folded it, and set it on his desk.

There was a down blanket lined in fleece. A set of new pens and bottles of ink. A stack of notepaper. Some goggles. New lambskin gloves. The largest parcel, which spanned nearly the width of his bed, made him sink to his knees on the dirty carpet. His own telescope. It had a spindle stand on which to mount it.

Energy renewed, Alrick set it up immediately, and he stared through the misaligned, blurry lenses, adjusting this knob and that, until the water for his bath had heated. He'd need to consult with Tredan about how to set it properly. It was difficult to resist going to him immediately, but they both needed their rest. And Tredan would be seeing to his new patient, also—and all without the aid of the scratchlings. *I'll do something about that, as well.*

Alrick filled the tub with each kettle full as it heated, the previous cooling as the next cooked so that the water was pleasantly warm by the time it was full. He scrubbed himself, grating away at the caked-on dust from the road, the grime from the hospital. There was blood in the seams of his fingernails and in his hair.

It seemed as though life with his uncle, though not always pleasant, might prove more interesting and adventurous than life as a lord. He knew as much about chemistry as he did about tenant farmers. But he had more to consider than his own wishes.

The leader they deserve.

Aemon's treatment of the scratchlings, and of Nelda, was a dark portent of what the people on Aldane lands could expect from their master if Aemon stayed lord. A brimstone temper and little justice.

The water in the tub dirtied beyond comfort long before Alrick considered himself clean, but the warmth had relaxed his tight muscles, and his exhaustion returned like weights tied to his extremities. He resolved to bathe again later, pulled on fresh nightclothes, and crawled into bed.

The daylight in the windows made no difference. He did not even remember pulling the blanket over himself.

He woke to a scream, to confusion at the late angle of light. To the sounds of panting and running feet on the stairs.

Merewyn's face appeared in the doorway. Something was wrong about the angles of it, the colors, but Alrick's sleep-heavy eyes were slow to adjust.

"Come quick, m'lord; your uncle needs you." And then she was gone again, her heavy breaths growing distant down the stairs.

Alrick struggled out of bed. He searched for his robe, his shoes. The scream sounded again, and he abandoned the search. The steps were ice against his feet, but he moved quickly. He ran into the lab to see Tredan struggling with the young woman from the hospital.

Alrick wasn't sure how to intervene without escalating the situation. Merewyn stood in the corner, her hands over her mouth. Alrick saw, then, why her appearance had struck him. Her eyes were surrounded with dark russet rings of bruises. A cut split one of her cheeks.

"Merry, what happened—"

"He leaned in to treat her and she was just lyin' there waiting…"

"I meant to you, Merry—" Alrick knew he'd have to resolve this situation with Tredan before he could finish speaking to Merry about her face.

He ran to Tredan's bag and found the bottle of sleeping spirits and the cloth. He held his breath and soaked the rag, then stumbled through Tredan's mess to the wrestling pair. He was astonished how, ill and injured as she was, the woman held her own against a man of Tredan's height. A survivor, indeed. Aemon had not put up nearly as much fight.

Alrick waited for an opening, then reached in and pressed the rag to the young woman's face. She weakened slowly, hand and bandaged arm still fluttering at her opponent. When she stilled, Tredan eased her to the floor, head pillowed on an old jacket. Tredan sat beside her and caught his breath.

"Thank you, Alrick." His face now resembled Alrick's, thatched with red scratches. Like Merry's.

"Did we do wrong in bringing her here?" Alrick asked.

"It'll be for the best, Alrick. It takes time."

"But Aemon will never let her stay. He wouldn't allow the others, and in her condition…"

"We aren't going to tell him she's from the hospital."

Alrick looked at the young woman's slumped figure. Her tattered hair, bloody fingernails, and missing hand. "I think he'll guess it, uncle."

"We'll keep her a secret till she's well. Then I'll tell Aemon that I have a distant relative who has recently suffered an injury and needs to convalesce in the countryside. We'll make her a guest, not a servant."

"How are we going to keep her a secret if she keeps screaming and scratching our faces?"

"I have medicines that will heal our faces quickly, and clay powder to hide the marks. Besides, Cassandra didn't do that to Merry." Tredan waived a hand toward the shaking housekeeper.

Merry sniffled into her sleeve.

"Merry…" Alrick stepped toward her, but she backed to the wall. "How did that happen? Who did that?" Alrick felt his stomach twisting.

"Aemon. I didn't like the way he was treating the little ones. I told him so."

Alrick's rosebud rage bloomed. Any hope he had harbored of peace between him and his brother vanished. He'd oust him. Replace him. And quickly—before he could strike out at anyone else. Before he could shift another brick on this land.

Alrick turned to storm from the room, to confront his brother, to throttle him if he must, but his face met the pale cheeks and wide eyes of Nelda. She stood in the doorway, staring at the girl on the floor. Merry hurried past them and vanished down the stairs.

"Pay her no mind," Tredan said, covering the young woman with a long white shirt. "What can I do for you, Niece?"

Nelda's all-black eyes lifted to Tredan's face as he stood and walked to her.

Alrick went to the young woman. Cassandra, Tredan had called her. Where had he learned her name? Alrick lifted her from the floor and carried her to the chamber off of Tredan's lab. There was no sign of Edyta. Had Aemon sent away the sick child, as well? He laid Cassandra on the cot and pulled the blanket over her before hurrying back to Tredan and Nelda.

"I just came to see if you were able to obtain the herbs you needed, Uncle," Nelda said. Her voice sounded distant, hollow, lost.

"I did," Tredan said. "And I need you to stop eating freely from the garden. It isn't safe. Especially this time of year. Some of those roots grow stronger when they've wintered."

"I've noticed." Nelda smiled her black-toothed smile. "I'll come to you, Uncle. I'll bring you what I find in the garden."

"Good. Now, what did you take this evening?"

"Winter cherries."

"And is it working?"

"I didn't take them to make it work. Tonight I ate them to make it stop." A pink line of spit trickled from the corner of her mouth.

Tredan clasped her shoulders and led her to a chair. "I can give you something for that. It will help you rest a while."

"Thank you, Uncle."

"Alrick, bring me the bag from the shop, please."

Alrick pulled the woven sack from the corner of the room where it had been dropped earlier.

"Get me chamomile and valerian. And the mortar and pestle."

Nelda's eyes traced his steps as Alrick sorted vials and packets and assembled the necessary ingredients for Tredan.

"That one looks like a gaggle of spider's legs," Nelda said. She'd followed him to the cabinet, lifted a jar and shook it in front of her face.

"Tastes about like them, too," Tredan said.

Nelda pulled a face and laughed.

Alrick prepared a powder under Tredan's instruction, and he heated some oil and beeswax in a pan over the fire. Nelda conversed quietly with the shadows by the hearth as they worked.

Alrick added the oil to the powder, mixed them, then poured the medicine into a sheet of small butter molds. When they had cooled, Tredan popped them out of the molds and tumbled them into a small glass bottle. They looked like little flowers under a bell jar.

Nelda had wandered to the far wall where she browsed Tredan's collection of blue bottles. She ran her fingers over the labels and paused at one.

"This has mother's name on it."

Tredan's face grew somber. "Yes."

"And the date—the day she died." Nelda's fingertip continued down the row of blue bottles. "And Father. This week."

"When you are tired or need a break—or when you're upset, let one of these melt under your tongue. It will absorb, slowly, and give you time to make yourself comfortable." Tredan held the bottle out for Nelda.

"When will we be ready for these, Uncle?" She traced her fingers over the blue bottles, the fading labels of the ones up high covered in dust. "The Aldane pneuma."

"I don't know. Not yet. I have an idea, for something…Someday. You'll be able to help me, when the time comes, when our work together begins to yield results. Then, we'll be ready for these."

"But what—"

"Don't worry about them." Tredan pressed the bottle of wax pills into her hand. "Keep these someplace cool, not near the fire, or they'll melt. Take one now and get some rest."

She gripped the bottle, offered a small dark smile, and whisked from the room.

Tredan dropped into a chair. "Thank you for your assistance, Alrick. With this, and earlier."

"Uncle, she saw Cassandra."

"She'll have forgotten her by morning." Tredan scraped a thin sheet of wax from the bottom of the pan and stored the flakes in another jar.

"Those pills will make her forget things?" Concern tightened in Alrick's chest.

"Not on their own. Not if she keeps her promise to stop eating from Burgrune's garden. In combination with what she has already taken this evening, there will be an amnesiac effect, yes."

Alrick nodded. His mind was lost in a fog of the grey morality of his uncle's actions. "Thank you, Uncle."

"For what?"

"For the gifts. The tools. Especially the telescope."

Tredan's weary smile returned. "Oh—thought you'd like that. We'll get it tuned later so you can begin stargazing."

"Have you eaten, Uncle? I'm afraid I slept though dinner."

"You did. And I'm not hungry, thank you, but if you'll be in the kitchens, could you bring me back an extra kettle and a bottle of brandy?

"Yes, Uncle. I'll be back soon."

"Thank you, Alrick."

Alrick took a candle from the table by Tredan's door. The sun had fallen low enough that the corridors would be dark, now. He reached the bottom of the stairs and walked, still barefoot, through the sloping corridors to the keep. He made his way across the wide hall to the kitchen stairs. Alrick remembered, as a child, following behind Merry's wide skirt, hoping to discover a tray of sweets left unattended on the kitchen work table. He hoped for much the same, now.

He entered the back stairs through the door by the sideboard. Everything grew darker as he descended. Even the candle grew dim as if protesting the stifling confines of the lower house.

The kitchen fire still smoldered, but the glow in the heart of the wood made the rest of the room seem even darker. The floor felt warm and sandy against the bottom of his feet, the old stone heated by the ovens and coated in stray flour.

The very bricks of the walls smelled of bread. Alrick's stomach growled.

He traced his candle over the long table till he found a loaf tucked under a cloth. He ripped a piece free and chewed as he made his way to the pantry.

There was a clatter behind him. He spun around, but the candle guttered and its glow didn't reach far enough to reveal the source of the noise. He stilled and waited. Perhaps it had been a mouse. A falling spoon. No other sound came, so he turned back to the pantry. He filled a pocket of his nightshirt with dried apple and a wedge of cheese.

Footfalls scraped behind him.

He turned again, more slowly this time, and walked back to the center of the room. He couldn't see anyone.

A plate had appeared on the table. It had ham and greens on it, and beside it was the kettle and brandy he needed for Tredan.

Alrick's heart hammered, but he smiled. "Is this for me?" He did not expect an answer, and none came. He put the bottle in his pocket, slipped the kettle handle over his wrist, and lifted the plate.

"Of course he couldn't find you all. You're much too clever. I'm glad. Thank you."

He thought he saw, for a moment, the bead of an eye flash in the glow of embers.

Alrick hurried from the kitchen and climbed the narrow servants' stairs to the hall. The candle flame bloomed into full light when he stepped into the open space. It played over the curving sweep of the floor like moonlight on the heather.

"Brother."

Alrick jumped. A piece of his greens slopped from his plate to the floor.

Aemon sat at the head of the table, feet resting beside an empty bottle.

"I didn't see you, Aemon."

"No, but I saw you. Sneaking down to the kitchens?"

"Yes. I apologize for missing dinner. I was more exhausted than I thought."

"No matter. You seem to know your way around the kitchen, in any case. Though you're not very good at carrying service." He pointed to the mess at Alrick's feet. "Perhaps you'll get better with practice." He pounded the table. "Merewyn!"

Light grew in the passageway as Merry came hurrying.

"See what a mess Alrick has made? Clean it at once. And have him watch you. I want him to learn how it's done."

Alrick set his things on the table and bent to the mess.

"I said watch, Alrick. And learn."

Merry gently pressed his arm and Alrick stood aside. "Just let me do it, m'lord, it's better this way." She pulled a rag from her apron.

"What did you just call him?" Aemon stood unsteadily from his chair.

"Apologies, m'lord," Merry curtsied to Aemon. "I was only teasin' him. Called him that since he was a baby, every time he made me break my back. Like now." She whipped her rag toward Alrick.

Alrick saw what she was doing. He hoped Aemon couldn't.

"Watch yourself, woman," Aemon said. "The new servants arrive tomorrow. Younger, stronger, and less insolent than you."

Alrick stood by, hands itching, as Merry scrubbed at the floor. He had to focus on not bending to help. He knew that it would end badly for both of them if he did. But out of the side of his eye, he watched Aemon. His face was red like Alrick's rosebud rages, but more from drink than from temper. So, he was more cruel when he drank. Alrick wondered what herbs or mixtures Tredan had that might counter the effect. Perhaps something that would make him sleepy or sloppy instead. He shook his head. Tredan might not approve of such an application of medicine. But Alrick didn't dismiss the thought altogether. Perhaps he was adopting his uncle's grey morals after all. Where was the line where medicine became a poison? Or a poison a medicine? He imagined the line might shift, like the floor of the hall seemed to do, and he stood so still he shook.

Merry had finished wiping the floor clean. Alrick bent to help her stand.

"I don't know what to do with you, Brother. You stoop to

servants? Should I allow you to serve, then? Or teach you to be a gentleman—if that's even possible." Aemon stumbled toward Alrick. His boots were undone and caked with leaves. "Or should I send you off to finish school? Or to an orphanage? An asylum? The workhouse?"

Alrick dug his nails into his palms, his rash stinging in sweat. "I'm happy to stay and learn from our uncle, Brother. His studies are a legacy in our family. I would like to carry that torch for our generation. To be of service to you and our sister in that way."

"You'd be *happy*. You would *like*. Count your blessings, Alrick!" He turned to stumble from the hall, pitching and keeling over the floor to the stairs leading to the lord's chambers. "Count them down, down, down," he said as he ascended.

"Your brother is a brute," Merry whispered.

"And a bully and worse," Alrick agreed. "I'm going to do something about it, Merry. It may take time. I may need some help."

"You have my help, m'lord. Always. But you've not got much time." She limped across the floor to the kitchen stairs and her small quarters.

Alrick picked up his things and made his way back to Tredan's lab. Tredan stood bent over his bubbling vials, goggles obscuring his face.

"Shall I put this kettle on for you, Uncle?"

"First go eat—upstairs. You should never have food in here."

Alrick looked at his open plate. "Is it dangerous?"

Tredan cocked his head. The goggles had sent his auburn hair at odd angles. "You might contaminate a sample. But also, yes, quite dangerous."

"I'll be back in a moment." Alrick ascended to his room. His fire had been built up to a warm blaze. His bed was made with his new blanket, the pitcher full of hot tea. He smiled. He wondered if Tredan knew—if he should tell him, or if it was better to keep it as secret as possible. Tredan's genuine rage at the expulsion of the scratchlings might be the only thing saving the others from discovery. He decided the secret did not belong to him. He would allow the children to make themselves known at their own choosing.

He ate his food quickly and drank from his pitcher of tea. He was beginning to like the aroma of bergamot on his hands after washing. Like a gentleman's rose water.

He hurried back to the lab and put the kettles on for Tredan, as many as he could find amid the clutter. Pots of water bubbled in the coals.

"Aemon was down in the hall," Alrick said.

"What was he doing there at this time of night?"

"Drinking. Bullying Merry."

Tredan uttered a curse that sounded like the hissing of his pipes.

"He's more cruel when he drinks. Is there an herb to treat that?"

"Not directly, that I know of. Nothing save putting him into a stupor can alter the frame of such a mind."

"He was nearly there on his own."

"Good. Then there will be few interruptions this evening. I take it you had a nice, long rest?"

"Yes, Uncle."

"Good. You're going to need it."

CHAPTER EIGHT

Alrick peeled the filthy gloves from his hands and laid them in a basin of steaming water. The goggles followed. It took everything he had to not crawl into the basin himself—to scrub the damp filth of the lab out of his pores.

Maybe just my aching feet.

Alrick had marveled at how much Tredan, decades his elder, had moved spryly about the lab for hours, while his own body ached and stiffened. He supposed that the last six years spent at a desk had not suited him well. Alrick had no gift for athletics, and Tredan's lab was not far shy of sport.

In the end, for all their work, they had a quart vial of a thick elixir, slightly sticky and tinged with lavender. It smelled both green and sour.

It was for Nelda.

"It will encourage her visions," Tredan had said, "In small doses. A large dose is fatal. She will need to be closely watched when she tries it, and an antidote administered immediately if concerning symptoms present."

Alrick had sealed the vial carefully with warm beeswax and set it on the shelf. The experiment would take place the following evening. Tonight, actually, since the clock had passed midnight.

After the elixir had been brewed, Alrick dissected the eye of a madman. The only madness he found within had been a kernel of his own. But he had placed the lens on a slide, as instructed, and delivered it to Tredan. There was no way, of course, to work with eyes and not feel as though they were watching. Judging.

He rinsed the congealed jelly from his gloves, hung them up to dry, and hooked his goggles next to them. He cleaned himself as best he could and went to Tredan to say goodnight. Soft voices came from the room beside the lab.

"...difficult to understand why you're here, but you're healing well. When you're better, everything will make sense."

He heard the young woman whimper. Alrick peered around the door. She clutched her severed wrist and cried. Tredan held a cloth to her brow, then slipped it slowly down her face to wipe her tears, and she faded back to sleep.

Tredan motioned Alrick forward. "I think she has exhausted her rage. She is more aware, now, of what has happened. Soon, I hope, will come some form of acceptance."

"You said her name is Cassandra?"

"Yes—Cassie. She is sixteen, just a year younger than you. I will have to think of a place for her to have come from. Our family line has dwindled so much, our options are few."

"Perhaps she could be someone from my mother's side?"

"I think that will have to be the case, though I don't know how that would sway Aemon and Nelda to allow her to stay."

"Perhaps say that her mother has cast her out after a disfiguring fever. Perhaps they will have sympathy for her? They will have no trouble believing ill of my mother's family."

"That is true enough. We can try. If it doesn't work, we might at least find her a place on a tenant farm."

Alrick doubted a farm would suit her needs. But he would find her a place and she would live. He wished he could have saved more that day.

Do something about it.

His rage at Aemon bloomed afresh. To have cast out those who had so recently been saved…When Aemon was gone, they could return to work. To the cause. No healing could occur with Aemon in power—he was a hot infection keeping the wound open.

Alrick would be the medicine. If necessary, the scalpel.

Nelda paced, agitated, as Tredan and Alrick spooned small doses onto squares of wax paper spread across her dressing table. Alrick squeezed his lips shut against the bitter fumes that clung to his tongue when he leaned over the work.

"Start with one. It's potent, but I don't know your tolerance. It could be quite high, given the time you spend in that garden." Tredan tapped the disc of hardening syrup to test its firmness. "If you require a second dose, you may take one thirty minutes after the first. No sooner. You need to see if there are any adverse effects before taking more. A third dose may yet be taken, but no more than that. Alrick, when these have hardened, please place the remaining doses in this bottle." His fingernail rang against the glass bottle next to the milky lavender pools of his concoction.

Nelda's pacing path became irregular, erratic. She advanced on them and retreated, Fray spinning around her feet.

Tredan turned his attention from his elixir to her. "Are you sure you're in the right frame of mind for this? You seem unwell."

Nelda panted, almost laughed. "I've had nothing today. No herbs, no food, no water. I wanted my mind hungry. My body hungry."

Tredan nodded. "That will likely accelerate the metabolizing of the solution. Your reaction may be stronger under those circumstances."

"I know. That's why I did it."

"Of course. Yes. If there are ill effects, we will give you this—" Tredan held up two vials, then handed them to Alrick. "Ipecac followed by charcoal. You will purge the majority of the solution, and the charcoal will absorb more. You'll still be ill, but not beyond our treatment."

Alrick held the bottle of ipecac and ran his thumb over the foiled label. "What would the ill effects be? It all sounds unpleasant, to me."

"Tremors or seizures. Heart palpitations. Hot, dry skin, or excessive perspiration. You'll know the danger when you see it. There won't be any doubt, should you witness it."

Alrick nodded. He couldn't help now but to question his career choice. What if she died? Or another patient did? At some point one of them would. What then?

"Is it ready?" Nelda's hands shook as she reached toward the wax paper.

Tredan tapped a lavender tablet. "Yes, they're ready. You may take the first dose."

She grabbed a square of paper from the table and popped it in her mouth. The paper scraped against her teeth as she chewed the toffee-like elixir from it. She spit the wad of chewed paper at Tredan's feet.

Nelda closed her eyes and began whispering too faintly for Alrick to hear her. A minute passed.

"I don't feel anything," she said.

"Remember it can take as long as thirty minutes to take effect." Tredan's eyes never left her face.

"Then you didn't brew it strong enough." She resumed her anxious pacing.

"I brewed it safely."

"It's much faster straight from the plant."

"Yes, and much more dangerous."

"I know what I'm doing!" She rounded on Tredan and Alrick saw that her eyes had indeed begun to dilate.

"Even experts can misjudge these plants, Nelda. They are unpredictable. We can't have you taking unnecessary risks."

"So, you are also the expert on what is necessary?" She moved closer to Tredan till her face nearly pressed against his.

Alrick tensed. This was not the quiet sister who had begged him for ribbons. This was Burgrune's daughter.

Tredan straightened his shoulders, lifting himself to full height and away from her gaze. "Yes. I earned that by growing extremely old, which you will never do if you continue to ingest uncertain doses of toxic plants."

She sneered and her resemblance to Aemon was briefly clear.

"Don't worry," Tredan said, "It will work. Have patience."

She wrung her hands till the joints popped and cracked like the fire in the hearth.

Alrick set the vials of ipecac and charcoal on the dressing table and tugged at the damp collar of his shirt. The fire wasn't necessary. Nelda's room was hot; her windows shut tight against the cool spring night, the curtains drawn, plush carpets cushioning his feet away from the cold, ancient boards. These carpets were not threadbare scraps like those in the rest of the house. These had seen less use over the years. And none at all in over a decade.

His eyes traced the patterns in the weave. The heat made it hard to breathe.

Alrick stared at the angles of the room, searching for something familiar—some friendly intersection. He had spent much of his first few years in these quarters. His mother had refused to use a nursery and had kept him close. His bedroom had been the small chamber that Burgrune had used for a dressing room.

In the smoking firelight, with his sister beginning to quietly rave, everything felt strange. Even the angle where the ceiling met the wall seemed to pinch and stretch as if they stood somehow in the throat of the house, sliding down its gullet.

A clatter and shouting sounded from the hall. Merewyn's scream rang deep as a brass bell.

"Tredan!" Merewyn called.

Tredan unfastened his watch from his waistcoat and pressed it into Alrick's hand. "Watch her," he said, and ran for the door.

Nelda stopped her pacing at the sound of the scream. She stood in place and stared at Alrick. Her hair had come undone from its plait and rose around her in a tangled aura. One eye had gone full black.

"Alrick, I know my business well enough to know I'm going to need all three doses."

"I know," Alrick said. "I agree. But we're going to pace them, as Tredan instructed."

"Why are you in charge of me, little one?"

"I'm not. Never. I'm in charge of that stuff." He nodded to the buttons of medicine crystalizing on the paper.

Nelda smiled. The spaces between her teeth had taken on the purple shade of Tredan's elixir.

The shouting retreated from the hall and faded back toward the far wing of the house. Toward Tredan's wing, and the lab.

Alrick's heart hammered. If Aemon had found Cassie…The hot room felt suddenly cold as he considered the consequences of a brawl in the lab. He reached up and undid the knot in his tie, pulling it away from his damp throat.

"Is it time yet?"

Alrick blinked the nightmare from his eyes. The clock face seemed to twist around frozen hands. The air between his face and its face felt as thick as cold soup. "I…I think we're close."

Nelda's smile widened. "May I have another tablet of your medicine, Master Alrick?"

Alrick nodded and blinked the fog from his eyes to note the time again, to pace the next dose.

Nelda reached to the dresser.

Paper rustled, crumpled. And again.

Alrick spun, but Nelda already had both discs of elixir pressed between her grinning teeth. She did not pause to let them melt, but ground them up, swallowed, paper and all. She laughed.

"Here they come," she said. The black of her eyes widened.

Darkness blanketed them. Alrick thought the fire had gone out or that the room had filled with smoke. The air was thick against his face. Breathing became even more difficult as Alrick's heart raced.

Nelda breathed in rough gasps. Alrick fumbled in the dark for the antidote, afraid Nelda was in growing distress. His hands played over the effects on the dressing table, searching for the familiar foiled bottles.

A woman's voice pressed against his ear, low and rasped.

"What is he doing here with you?"

"Mama." Nelda's voice sounded far away.

"Get him out. Out. OUT."

"No, Mama. He's helping me hear you."

"A push into the hearth."

Alrick felt pressure against his shoulders and ice flooded his body, made his hair raise and his teeth chatter.

"Mama, forget about the boy. He's only a servant here, now."

"He is a threat."

Alrick swept his hands out into the room and found Nelda's face in the darkness. He ran his fingers over her features, searching for signs of poisoning, of distress.

Her face twisted and relaxed in alternating rhythms. Lines creased skin that had been smooth and her mouth opened unnaturally wide as she shrieked, *"OUT, OUT, OUT."*

"You should see the pretty ribbon Alrick brought me from London, Mama."

"He brought you a satin noose."

"Aemon has fine clothes again, just like you used to make."

The drapes rustled.

A small trickle of blood fell from Nelda's lips. Something in the darkness swept it from her chin.

"Red ribbons, red ribbons," she growled. Her throat sounded hard, full of stones and old nails. "Are you caring for the children here, Mama?"

"Everywhere. Vermin."

Nelda giggled. "That's what Aemon calls them. I think they're nice."

"Nice when I'm hungry. Nice with wine. I remember wine. I remember children."

"Mama, I can't see you."

The general darkness of the room twitched.

Alrick flinched. Hot pain filled his hand, and he realized he'd broken the vial of ipecac. The bitter oil coated his palm and stung in the cut. Sweat wrung from him. He shivered.

"There you are, Mama."

The voice Alrick thought was Nelda's had grown younger, babyish.

"Mama."

"Mama. Mama."

Was it more than one voice?

Here they come.

"Vermin, vermin."

"Get out, out. Out."

Pressure returned to his shoulders, like hands on his back. His feet slid over the plush carpet. Terror gripped him, freezing his thoughts.

"Alrick!" The hands vanished. The darkness contracted, condensed over Nelda's face.

"She's here, too."

"Bitch. Usurper."

The gravel voice spoke over itself, word overlapping word as Nelda's lips moved impossibly fast. More blood spilled down her chin and neck.

"She has it, Alrick. It's in her hands, Snapdragon."

Nelda's head whipped back with a snap and the shadow over her face poured into her mouth. It bulged in her throat as it writhed its way down her body. Fray sat back on his haunches and howled.

Alrick shook his head and wrung the cold sweat from his eyes. He stumbled and dropped the watch. It rolled toward the bed, where a small, white hand shot out and grabbed it. He knelt to pick it up and saw a scratchling's face beneath the curtain. The fire flared and a dozen black eyes reflected back from under the bed. Small, freezing fingers slipped the watch back into his hand.

The door rattled.

"Alrick!" This time it was Tredan's voice. The door shook harder. It sounded like the manor walls might come crashing down.

Alrick stumbled toward the door. Somewhere, through the fog in his mind, he knew he needed the door open.

"Open it and we'll measure you," a sweet voice lifted from Nelda's upturned throat. *"Measured and found wanting,"* the gravelly voice replied.

A rasping sounded in the lock, and then a rattle, and then Tredan burst in. He grabbed Alrick by the collar and threw him out into the parlor. Fray startled from the rug and bolted into the bedchamber.

Alrick gasped. It felt like the first breath of air he'd ever had. His throat and lungs spasmed, tugging for more air. It both burned and soothed his throat, like peppermint. He looked back into the room. Nelda stood with her head back, mouth open wider than a mouth should be. The darkness still twisted inside her, the skin of her neck stretching and bunching with its manipulations. Fray circled her feet. He whined and nipped at Nelda's ankles.

Tredan pulled another vial from his pocket and popped the wax from its top.

"Brother, brother, the celibate alchemist," the gravel voice crooned. *"Tom cat chasing vermin through the door."*

Tredan poured the clear liquid into the gaping cauldron of Nelda's mouth.

Many voices gargled and groaned. Nelda's hands fell to her sides. Tredan caught her as she buckled. He carried her to a couch and laid her down.

Tredan ran to the hearth and examined the fire. "God damn it!" He slammed his hand against the bricks of the mantel.

Alrick stumbled into a chair and let himself fall against its cushions. He wanted to help. To fix where he had failed. He brought his palm to his nose and sniffed. He ran his tongue across his wound and pulled at the fine glass splinters with his teeth. He tasted of copper and licorice.

"Alrick, stop," Tredan forced his hand away from his mouth "You've had enough for one night."

"Enough? What?"

"She put herbs in the fire. Things from the garden—to augment the dosage."

"She took it all."

"Of course she did. You couldn't have stopped her. Especially not after she drugged you. I shouldn't have left you alone."

Alrick felt cold hollows where his angry rosebuds should be.

"Did it work, at least?" Tredan asked. "Was the experiment some form of success?"

Nelda mumbled in her sleep on the sofa. But she sounded like herself.

"Her voice…She was speaking, but with too many voices."

"More than one?"

"They're still here." Alrick could still see the relics of the dark shadow when he blinked.

"The voices?" Tredan held Nelda's wrist. He leaned his ear close to her.

"Everyone who's died. The little ones. The mothers. *Mama.*" Alrick trembled. "Does no one ever leave here?"

Tredan turned back to Alrick and leaned toward his face, peering into his eyes. He frowned in curiosity. "You see them, too? Excellent."

Alrick leaned forward and vomited onto the carpet.

Tredan laid Nelda's wrist across her chest and tended to Alrick. "I'm afraid you'll have to sleep this drug off, Alrick. I have nothing for you to take." Tredan brought him the ewer from the bureau and Alrick drank deeply from it, washing the taste of sick from his tongue and teeth.

"Head to bed. Drink lots of water. I'll stay and see to Nelda."

"I'm sorry, Uncle," Alrick croaked.

"No need to apologize. We're both off the map, here. Sleep. I'll take care of the mess."

"The little ones will get it."

"Go sleep, Alrick. We'll examine this evening's events in tomorrow's daylight."

For once, the planks of the hall seemed straight and even and it was Alrick who twisted and pitched across them. He stumbled up the stairs to the landing and remembered the screams. The commotion. His vision of the lab in ruins.

He stepped inside Tredan's quarters, half expecting to see Aemon dead on the floor.

Instead, he saw Cassie. She sat up in a chair, sipping from a steaming cup that shook in her single hand. Alrick stumbled to a stop. He didn't want to frighten her.

"Are you feeling better?" The light from the fire played over the rows of sparkling vials and bottles, adding to his disorientation.

Her lips twisted and Alrick flinched, ready for a barrage of screams.

Instead, there came a small voice, raw and out of practice. "Yes."

Alrick nodded. It made his head spin. "Good. Let us know if we can do anything for you. We're here to help."

"Thank you." Her hand brought the cup to her lips and she sipped, a small stream of tea running over the edge at the sides of her mouth. She didn't seem to notice.

"Good night," Alrick said.

The girl nodded, more a spasm than a gesture.

Alrick finished the ascent to his room. His fire was bright and warm. His tea fresh. A hot brick had been placed inside the sheets at the foot of the bed.

"I suppose without a whole house to serve, you've decided to spoil me," he whispered.

He walked to the wardrobe and changed into his nightclothes. When he turned back to the bed, the sheets were drawn back. Alrick hesitated. One—at least one—was here in the room.

"Are you well?" he whispered to the seemingly empty space. "Do you need anything?"

There was no answer. "You're not a servant here. In fact, now that my brother dismissed you all…" Alrick thought for a moment, that he saw the bedclothes rustle. "To me, you are a refugee. My uncle brought you here and we have a duty to you. So, really, let me know if you need anything."

A small white face smeared with ash flashed from under the bed and then vanished.

Alrick crouched and peered underneath but saw nothing there.

"Was that you, earlier, in Nelda's room? Were you there, or are there more of you here?"

No response came. No child appeared.

Alrick extinguished the candles and crawled into the warm bed. The hot brick had baked scent from the linens—Merewyn's soap, the sun from the line, dust, the faint smell of tea from Alrick's own skin.

He settled back into that comfort. His vertigo rocked the bed beneath him. Rocked him right to sleep.

He dreamed of his mother. She chased him down halls that twisted and flipped and spun. She screamed at him to take his medicine, to take the antidote, and she waved a fistful of broken glass. Blood poured from her hand, dripped down her elbow, and ran in a trail down the front of her ivory lace dress. He outran her to his room and hid under the bed among a writhing pile of scratchlings. They squeezed against him, legs hooking his arms, around his neck, the bristle of their cropped hair scrubbing him with soot. One slid its small hand into his mouth and grasped his tongue.

Alrick woke, gagging.

Tredan stood over him, his hand inside Alrick's mouth, pulling his tongue forward as he dropped a sour brown solution into his throat.

"I'm sorry, Alrick. I didn't think this would wake you. I'm actually relieved." He poured in the rest of the medicine and released Alrick's tongue.

Alrick sat up. His head felt heavy, swollen, and it ached fiercely. He reached for his pitcher of tea to wash away the taste of the medicine.

"Am I ill?" he asked.

"Drugged. It took me a while to figure out what Nelda put into that fire. I had to know before I could select the proper counter for it. You'll be okay. There are some unpleasant aftereffects, but nothing permanent."

Alrick nodded and wished he hadn't. "How's Nelda?"

"Better off than you. She has quite the tolerance for toxins."

"How is Cassie?"

"Still sedated. I'll keep her out till that wound heals more. Perhaps if she's not waking up to intense pain, she'll be more rational."

Alrick blinked to clear his bleary eyes. "But she was up last night I saw her drinking tea in the chair."

Tredan laughed "I don't think you should trust anything you thought you saw last night. You inhaled an hour's worth of powerful hallucinogens. I'm surprised you even made it to your own bed."

Alrick rubbed soot-colored crust from his eyes. "I could use a bath, Tredan. A real one. Could I borrow the kettles?"

"Of course. I'll send Merry up with the tub and I'll fill the kettles myself."

"Thank you, Uncle."

Tredan left and Alrick relieved himself in the chamber pot. He went to the lab to help with the kettles, but they were already gone, as was Tredan. He must have taken them to the kitchen pump.

Alrick peeked in at Cassandra. She slept as she always had, but Alrick could see the faint stains of tea on the front of her robe. He walked out to the chair where he'd seen her sitting, and there were signs of the spilled tea there, too. Of course any chair might have tea on it, especially in Tredan's messy quarters. And the tea on her robe might have been spilled by Merry spooning it into Cassie's half-conscious mouth.

Alrick wondered if Cassie had been in that hospital for long, and what her care had been before then. Perhaps she had a tolerance for sedatives like Nelda's for toxins. Perhaps his eyes had not lied.

And he could not help but wonder how much of his dream was true, too.

CHAPTER NINE

A small contingent of farmers' daughters lined the front hall. Alrick, Nelda, Tredan, and Aemon stood by as Merry introduced them.

Anne and Martha, a cook and scullery, and Susan and Elizabeth as chamber maids.

"I suppose they'll do, Merry," Aemon said. "Undertrained. But so long as they understand their duties and know that I mean to restore this house to the elegance that it has lacked in the last few decades."

"They understand their duties, sir, and they're fit for it." Merry anxiously brushed a speck of lint from Anne's apron and put it in her pocket.

"And when will the others arrive?" Aemon walked past the girls, studying them impassively.

"Tomorrow, sir. A footman and a butler."

"Excellent. Ladies, your first task will be to ready your own chambers. I don't know in what condition you'll find them. The previous occupants were half savage. When that is done, kitchen maids can begin in the kitchens. Chamber maids, please begin polishing the house, starting with this dusty hall."

They bobbed awkward curtsies in unison.

Alrick hoped the scratchlings really had vacated the rooms—that they'd found somewhere secret and comfortable to sleep.

The maids filed from the room, Merry trailing after them, whispering instructions.

"Farmers' daughters." Aemon shook his head. "Still. Better than feral children. We'll see the fair running of this place soon, Uncle, you'll see."

Tredan nodded a half bow, clearly unwilling to engage with Aemon's prodding. Alrick searched his face for signs of rage, or any indication that he knew the children still remained. He showed nothing.

"If the butler is arriving tomorrow, so will the furnishings we ordered. He was to oversee the shipment."

Nelda made a mew of excitement. "Did you tell him to bring my ribbon?"

Aemon frowned at her. "No. I did not instruct our butler to purchase more ribbon for you. That's a job for a ladies' maid. Or Alrick, apparently. It would be degrading for a butler."

"You brought me ribbon once, for my birthday, when we were younger. Do you remember? Auntie gave you a coin at the market. You spent the whole thing on a ribbon for me."

Aemon squirmed and sneered. "I can't even fathom what you do with all that ribbon, sister."

She laughed with a sound like a penny rattling in a glass bottle and Alrick wondered how the same throat had produced the menacing growls he'd heard the other night.

His head still ached. His eyes still stuck fast with soot upon waking, as if he could never wash the ash of her herbs from his eyes. He had not returned to Nelda's room since, and Tredan had promised that all future studies would be conducted in his parlor, not hers.

"Why not in the lab?" Alrick had asked.

"You'll see," was all Tredan said.

And he would, soon. They were to conduct another study that night, after the new help was dismissed for the evening.

A sconce fell from the wall beside Alrick, the stone it had been set into crumbling away behind it like sand. Plaster cracked from the hole like a spider's web.

"Place is falling apart. We'll need a builder in next." Aemon kicked at the pile of debris. "Merry!"

She appeared, huffing, at the foot of the stairs.

"Send one of the girls to begin work on this room now. It needs immediate attention."

"But m'lord, the girls' chambers—"

"There are still four of you to work up there. Do you see this dirt pile here?" He began striding toward her.

"Yes, m'lord." She shot back up the stairs before he reached her. Aemon followed her.

Alrick moved after him—to stop whatever it was that was about to occur. Nelda's cold hands fell on his shoulders.

"Let me," she said, and moved up the stairs to the sound of shouting that had already begun overhead.

"I'll be amazed if those young ladies even need their chambers tonight. I'd be on the road home," Tredan said.

"I doubt they've much choice," Alrick said.

"True enough. Their fathers are likely debtors to our land. I wonder if the girls will even be paid, or if they're indentured."

Alrick's teeth ached from clenching them. He'd been waking to the sound of his jaw grinding, the noise working its way into his nightmares. Like crumbling stone.

The house really did seem to be falling apart around him. Plaster collapsed. Beams splintered. Stone flags snapped underfoot. The board floors seemed more twisted than ever. There was so much to fix. And the sooner he had the authority to fix it, the better.

The shouting faded upstairs.

"Do you know where my father kept his papers? Reports on the land, the farms. Deeds."

"In his desk, I'm sure," Tredan said. "In his rooms. It wasn't something he talked about much."

Alrick watched the stairs as a frightened maid hurried down, followed by Nelda, who led Aemon by the hand.

"I need to get into that room," Alrick whispered.

Alrick's hands smelled strongly of tea, ink stains still tracing the creases of his skin where bergamot had not been enough to wash them clean.

He folded the letters and addressed them as Merry had instructed. He hoped at least one of the shops remained open. It had been over a decade since House Aldane had placed an order. If all three responded, there would be an abundance of ribbon and lace.

Alrick carried the letters down through the chaos of the hall to the back kitchen door. He slipped them into the mail basket, turned, and started at the sight of the kitchen maids. "I'm sorry to interrupt," he said.

They curtsied silently.

"I forgot there would be anyone here." He looked across the main table. There were doughs and vegetables in the works. A plucked bird hung over the fire. "This all looks very fine," he said. It smelled better than fine. "Thank you."

"Sir," they both said, bobbing curtsies again.

"I'll try to do better to stay out of the way." He slipped back upstairs into the noisy hall.

George had been brought in to assist in the hall. He stood atop a ladder, hammering a long chain to a beam. Other such chains hung around the room, supporting iron rings full of white candles that lit the room like daylight. The heat from those dozens of small flames and the ceaseless industry of the new servants warmed the room so that Alrick's wool jacket began to itch against his perspiration. He took it off and hung it over the back of his father's chair. Aemon's chair.

"George?" he called up the ladder.

"Aye, lad?" The man's voice was strained with the effort of his work.

"How can I help?"

"Can you fetch another ring and candles from the box there? This one's about ready."

The rings that held the candles were heavy. Alrick slung one over his shoulder and grabbed a fistful of white candles from a crate nearby. They'd go through the whole crate in a day if Aemon insisted on lighting the room like this all the time.

He and George fastened the ring to the chain and filled it with candles. George walked to a bracket on the wall and hoisted the whole apparatus till it was level with the others.

One of the new maids—Elizabeth, Alrick recalled—tugged at the oak sideboard. The old wood creaked against the flagstone floor, but barely moved. Alrick hurried over to help.

Elizabeth skittered nervously away from him.

"Here," he said, "Let's push together." *I'm not like my brother,* was what he wanted to say.

She tentatively returned to his side. They leaned into the ancient wood and shoved it just enough out of the way so that she could clean behind it—a place Alrick didn't think had ever seen rag nor water before. Their work in this room bordered on archaeology.

"Sir," Elizabeth said, shaking him from his reverie. She rose from behind the sideboard and, turning to him, she blushed.

"Yes, miss?" He wasn't sure how to address her. He would have to ask Tredan before Aemon caught him in another breach of etiquette.

She held her hand out to him. "I found this behind there."

He held out his hand and she dropped something small, cold, and heavy into his palm.

The candles all flared at once. Hot wax dribbled onto them like viscous rain. The maids shrieked and buried their faces in their arms. The heat in the room grew and the wax that held the family's baubles upright on the tilted tables melted into water and vases slid and crashed to the flagstones.

Elizabeth screamed and backed toward the doorway to the kitchens. George crossed himself. Merry came running from the east wing just as Aemon's boots appeared on the stairs. Both of them froze when they saw the mess of wilted candles and shattered ceramics.

Hot tallow ran in narrow streams between the flags, gluing shards of broken pottery in small razor mounds.

The room began to cool and the wax slowed, clouded, grew opaque.

George cleared his throat and picked at the globs of wax in his beard, the powdered plaster on his hands turning the wiry dark hair white. "There was a kind of sudden…heat, m'lord. The candles just—and everything fell…" He gestured toward the chandeliers above, where curling wicks still glowed at the tips. The new candles had diminished down to small nubs that looked like worn teeth.

Merry grabbed a broom from the corner and began sweeping shards from the sticky wax pools.

Aemon's chest heaved. The cords of his neck stood out, straining. His eyes settled on Alrick's.

"These were my father's things!" he roared.

Alrick spun the small object in his hand. It had cooled as he held it, as the room had done. As if it had been warmer hidden behind the old oak, and now chilled as it was held close.

"Don't mind these things, sir," Merry said, her voice a quivering, attempted calm. "These bits belonged to Miss Eleanor. I don't know that your father cared overmuch for them." She glanced quickly at Alrick.

He knew she was lying. These things predated his mother. But would Aemon remember them? Had he been the type of child who would have noticed his mother's baubles?

Aemon stalked across the room. He knocked into Merry, sending her sprawling into a pile of shards. She yelped, and the other maid, Susan, hurried to her as Aemon continued his advance on Alrick.

Elizabeth stepped back behind the sideboard as Aemon neared.

Alrick slid his hand into his pocket and dropped the small found object there. He felt the weight of it—the cold of it—against his thigh.

"What the hell are you doing in here, brother?" Aemon's face was close. His breath smelled like bread and honey, but no wine. No spirits. Perhaps there was hope that he might be reasoned with.

"George needed some assistance. I thought I might make myself useful." He held his brother's gaze.

"Did you do all this?" Aemon gestured at the mess.

"I don't understand. I don't know how a hundred candles can suddenly melt, brother. I've never seen anything like it."

"I have," Nelda's voice sing-songed from the entrance to her wing. "Don't touch the wax," she said. She skipped barefoot over the debris to George's ladder and climbed.

Aemon's rage—once hot and clear—had cooled and clouded into confusion, like the wax across the floor.

Nelda spun atop the ladder, which rocked on the uneven floor as she moved. Alrick hurried over to steady it.

She took in the whole scene below, muttering to herself. "Lost things found, found things lost. Things stuck that don't belong. Things that do are missing."

Aemon shook his head. "Come down from there, Nelda. You'll hurt yourself." He crossed to the ladder, reached past Alrick, and helped guide Nelda back down to the floor.

"It's a note," she said, dropping to the floor and running her fingers over the trails of wax. "From Mama."

Aemon pulled her to her feet. "You were meant to be resting before dinner."

"I needed to read Mama's message."

"To bed, sister." He walked her to the entrance to the ladies' wing. "Alrick, see that all of this is cleaned up before dinner."

"Don't!" Nelda shouted. She twisted away from Aemon's grip. "Mama will be mad."

"She always was," Aemon said. "Alrick, do it yourself. I intend to have a proper dinner in my own hall tonight." He disappeared down the hall, dragging a struggling Nelda behind him.

Alrick took a deep breath and let it out slowly. "Merry, are you alright?" He could see red on her apron.

"If you'll excuse me, m'lord, I need seeing to." She sounded more annoyed than injured.

"Yes, of course. Go tend to yourself, and rest awhile. We'll take care of this." Alrick nodded to George and George returned the nod.

Elizabeth came out from behind the sideboard. "I'll help."

"Thank you. George, could you fetch a small spade? It will clear the wax faster than a broom. Elizabeth, please boil some water so we can scrub up the rest. And bring some dry rags. Susan, could you help Merry, please? I need to go tell Tredan what's happened. I'll meet you all back here in a few minutes."

The maids curtsied and scattered to their tasks. George headed for the door, out to the grounds shed where the tools were kept.

Yes, just leave the room empty for a bit.

He backed out of the hall and into the corridor to his wing. As he entered the parlor at the base of the stairs, he whispered, "Could you help, friends?"

He heard a rustling.

Many hands make light work.

He pulled the cold object from his pocket.

It was a brass ring. The inside of the band had worn smooth, an old inscription rubbed illegible. The top formed a broad disc set with a black stone. A lady's mourning ring. Beneath the disc was a small knot of brass. He rubbed his thumb over it and the disc sprung open, revealing a hollow inside. Under the top lid was set a portrait, badly corroded, of someone in a dark suit. Inside the bottom hollow, a small pile of silver powder residue, blackened at the edges. A bitter scent rising from it made his eyes water.

Alrick snapped the ring shut and slipped it back into his pocket.

Had it belonged to Burgrune? Perhaps the man in the photo was his father. It was too worn to see. And what was the powder? It didn't smell like snuff. He needed Tredan.

His uncle was in the lab, bent over elixirs, concentrating the doses for Nelda's next conversation with the spirits of House Aldane.

"I can't talk now, Alrick. There's a reaction in progress that can't be paused. I need my full concentration to follow it through—I'm sorry."

Alrick nodded. "Before dinner, if you have a chance, then, Uncle. There are things you should know before you see Aemon again."

"I'm intrigued," Tredan said.

"I'd stay and help you, but I have to clean the hall. There was a small accident. A strange one."

"I don't care to lose my apprentice to servitude, Alrick."

"I'm sorry. It's a long story. I'll tell you when you're not working."

"Come when you're done in the hall. Assuming this incident will require considerable time?"

"I'll be back in a few hours."

"Perfect."

Alrick went to his room, first, and slipped the heavy ring into the small drawer of his desk and locked it. He didn't put it past Aemon to search his pockets. Not that his room was much safer.

Alrick felt another rush of anxiety.

This is my house. He can't rule me here.

Invisible hands had done much to progress the work of the hall. Alrick set to what remained before the others returned. If they were surprised at how much had been accomplished in their absence, they kept it to themselves. Maybe they, too, had noticed small tasks completed when no one was looking.

They set to work, silently, as if waiting for an angry spirit to strike out. They cleared the room and finished the scrubbing. The candlewax had added a nice polish to the old flagstones, and they shone with a dark richness Alrick hadn't seen before.

The crate of candles had all melted into one cohesive blob. George fetched a new crate from the storeroom. They refilled the fixtures, but lit only the ones above the main table. By the time they were finished, it was the only light left. The sun had set, and the smell of cooking rose from the kitchens.

"Thank you all for your help," Alrick said.

George and Elizabeth nodded.

Alrick hoped the hidden scratchlings heard him, too.

They parted ways. Alrick went to find Tredan and to clean himself up for dinner. He wasn't sure if he had more clean clothes, and he regretted not adding a few shirts for himself to his clothier's order.

Tredan met him on the stairs. "Ah, I was just looking for you. I regret putting you off earlier. My apologies. I suspect I will regret it even more before our conversation is over."

"Hello, Uncle. I was just coming to see if you were free to talk. And to clean myself up. I'm a bit of a mess."

"Please—come use my washstand. I've just filled it with hot water. You can tell me everything as you wash."

Alrick nodded and followed Tredan into his room. He removed his soiled shirt and told Tredan of the strange ring, the sudden flare of intense heat that had filled the room, the melted candles, the broken housewares—of Nelda's strange interpretation and Aemon's rage. Of the new maids' fear.

"It sounds like I missed an exciting afternoon," Tredan said.

"I wish I had." Alrick pulled another sliver of pottery shard from his palm.

"I'm assuming Aemon doesn't know the value of the pots that were in the hall." Tredan looked pained. "Or else I'd have no doubt heard the commotion as he murdered you all."

"Merry told him they were my mother's tasteless trinkets. I thought I remembered them being already very old when I was old enough to understand that I shouldn't touch them."

"Yes, very old. Some much older than House Aldane itself. Such a pity. If it was an angry spirit, as Nelda claims, it must have been very angry indeed.

"When she spoke that other night—as herself but also as her mother—she was enraged."

"I suspect we'll hear more of that tonight. Worse, perhaps, given the day's events. I'm glad we'll be meeting here instead of in her rooms."

"Do you think the ring is hers? Burgrune's?"

"I suspect so. Likely it had been her mother's. I would guess it's her father in the picture. They both passed away during her time here."

Alrick nodded. Water dripped from his wet hair down his brow. "I should give it to Nelda, then," he said.

"I agree. But first, would you let me investigate the substance inside?"

"I was going to suggest it."

"Excellent. Bring it with you tonight. It may prove useful. I'll take a closer look at it tomorrow."

"Thank you, Uncle. And thank you for the hot water." Alrick picked up his shirt and excused himself to get dressed for dinner.

His room was warm and tidy. A fresh suit of clothes lay folded over the back of his preferred chair.

"Thank you, friends. For everything today."

He dressed and prepped himself into as neat an appearance as he could manage, opting to leave the ring locked in the desk until it was time to begin Nelda's ritual.

He remembered, then, the beautiful things he had seen cooking when he'd interrupted the new staff at work. Some of his dread lifted. He may have to deal with Aemon's abuse, but at least he'd face it on a full stomach.

He bent down toward the underside of the bed. "There's bound to be some commotion at dinner tonight. Keep a weather eye out, and steal yourselves a hot meal when the chance comes. I'll take the blame, if anyone notices."

He needed only the glow ahead to navigate the dark corridor to the hall. The rings of candles cast down beams of light that bounced off the wax-polished floors. Crystal and silver glittered across white linen spread over the table.

Alrick took his seat across from Nelda. Aemon and Tredan hadn't yet arrived.

Nelda was dressed in her black taffeta again. He heard its rustle as she kicked her feet under the table, and the clatter of Fray's teeth as he nipped at her slippers.

"I hope you're feeling well, sister." Alrick could see she'd deprived herself again—starved her body of nourishment and stimulus so that Tredan's medicine would have maximum effect.

"I will be soon enough, Brother." She smiled—not the dyed horror of a berry-chewer, but like any nice young lady might. Her blue eyes were clear and bright. One would have to know her to see the glint of madness there.

Alrick supposed the madness could be passion, or even anxious glee, to the casual observer. A vivacious young lady, and not, as she called herself, a doorway to the dead. He did his best to return the smile.

Aemon arrived then, looking very pleased with himself, with the setting he had orchestrated in the hall. "This is so much better," he said, taking his seat. "Almost proper. We'll get there soon." He lifted his glass and grimaced to find it empty.

As if she sensed the coming storm, Merewyn hurried up the stairs from the kitchen. She held two bottles of wine. Martha and Anne followed with a tray of bread and cheese and a steaming tureen of soup—the very one Alrick had glued back together with painful precision. He could hardly see his repairs, though a small drip did appear in one side.

The maids laid the course on the sideboard while Merry poured the wine.

Aemon emptied his glass before she had finished circling the table.

Alrick's mouth watered as the soup came 'round. He was so hungry, he realized he'd been unaware of the conversation that had begun.

"Alrick?"

"I'm sorry?" he shook his head and cast his eyes around the table, his cheeks beginning to bloom. He realized he'd been asked a question, but he didn't know by whom. He searched the faces at the table.

Aemon sneered. "I asked how you enjoyed getting to know our new staff today."

"Oh. Very much," he said. "They're all quite industrious. I think they'll do well." No one was eating, and he wondered if it would be rude for him to begin. His stomach growled. He realized too late that Aemon had been trying to bait him. He decided to continue— to fill the awkward silence. "You know, George is quite skilled as a carpenter. He might be of use on some of the projects you had planned, Brother."

Aemon chuckled and drained his second glassful. "You completely destroyed this room."

"No, that was Mama," Nelda said.

"It was a mess," Aemon said, waving his glass. Merry refilled it. Alrick noticed she was filling his glass from a different decanter than the one she used for the rest of them.

Alrick's eyes darted from Merry to the wine, to Tredan. He stared pointedly at his uncle. Was there something in the wine? Or had Aemon demanded a finer vintage for himself? Alrick felt both were equally possible.

"Sorry about the mess, Brother. As I said, I can't explain it. But all that wax on the floor seemed to be just what these old flags needed." Alrick toyed with his spoon.

Aemon stared at him. Alrick decided to start on his soup, that eating couldn't make the awkward silence any worse. He tore off a piece of bread and began to chew.

Nelda giggled.

Tredan cleared his throat. "I'm looking forward to meeting more new staff tomorrow, and seeing the things you bought for the house. Tell us, what did you order? What does Saint Butler bring us on his sleigh?" Tredan took a spoonful of soup.

"Things that belong in a lord's house," Aemon said. "Carpets, tapestries, new chairs to replace those that are too worn. Fresh linens. Preserves to restock the pantries till we can get the garden going again."

Tredan nodded as Aemon spoke. "All wise purchases, nephew."

"But no ribbon," Nelda murmured.

"I said things for a lord's house," Aemon growled back.

"It's a ladies' house, too," she said. Wax dripped from the iron rings above to the linen on the table, into the soup and wine.

Aemon glanced up at the fixtures. "I suppose it is, in a way. Perhaps I should take a wife. Let her see to the running of the house." He turned his gaze to his sister's startled expression. "If I let you run the house, there would be bows tied round the beams and none of us would be permitted shoes."

Nelda shrugged rather than rise to his jab. "So take one," she said.

"We'll see what Mama thinks of her." She stared at him over the rim of her glass. The cut crystal caught light that failed to brighten the dark circles under her eyes. A blob of molten wax landed on her glass and she licked it clean.

Alrick emptied his plate. With the distracting edge of his hunger assuaged, the tension at the table settled into his gut.

Susan cleared the plates and Elizabeth brought fresh ones, clean and dust-free, and soon filled them with steaming goose and piles of vegetables in hot butter. It was delicious, but anxiety tightened Alrick's throat and made it difficult to swallow.

"Tell me, nephew, where you found our new butler," Tredan asked.

"He worked for one of my mother's friends," Aemon said. "She passed away, and he's been looking for a new post."

Alrick and Tredan shared a quick look. This butler would no doubt be Aemon's eyes below stairs. *He's not to be trusted. And he'll be everywhere.*

Alrick thought of Merry—of her working under the authority of one of Aemon's creatures. The best he could hope for was that he might underestimate her, as Aemon had. *Merry may very well stay a few leaps ahead of them both.*

"And what time is he due to arrive?" Tredan scraped wax from his goose and took a bite.

"Well, I told him to hurry, naturally. So, early, I expect. I have the highest expectations of him."

It occurred to Alrick that this new butler may be Aemon's creature now, but if he had any self-respect, perhaps he could be turned. Could a man like Aemon command unconditional loyalty? Alrick didn't think so.

"Well, I shall try to be ready to receive him bright and early," Tredan said, smiling around a mouthful of his dinner.

"I think I shall sleep in," Nelda said.

"You pout like a child," Aemon said. He reached across the table and pulled a leg from the goose.

"I'm finished. I have things to do." Nelda stood.

"Tying bows?"

"No. I have no more ribbon." She walked from the room, black taffeta studded with white wax, like the stars in the night sky that Alrick had been watching through his telescope. Fray followed her, his claws clacking against the polished flags.

"You'll miss dessert!" Aemon called after her.

Her plate was nearly untouched. Alrick suspected the temptations of elixirs exceeded that of food for Nelda.

Aemon turned his attention to Alrick. "And how do your studies go, Brother?"

"I'm making progress," Alrick said.

"Is that true, Uncle? You're not coddling the boy with false encouragement?"

"Alrick is an excellent pupil. He's obedient, ambitious, thirsty for knowledge. I think he'll make an excellent scientist."

"Ah, good. Well, let me know if he slacks at all. I have it on good authority that he'd make an excellent house maid."

Alrick lost count of the fills of Aemon's glass, but Merry poured the last of the dregs from his special decanter.

As Susan and Elizabeth cleared the course and brought out dessert, Alrick saw her slip away to the kitchen with the empty pitcher. She returned just as Tredan remarked on the quality of the pudding.

"It is good," Aemon agreed. "I'm sure it's been some time since you've eaten properly, Uncle. No more fixings tossed together by a pack of enslaved children.

Merry and Elizabeth exchanged worried glances and hurried about their tasks.

They finished their meal in silence, Aemon continuing to empty glass after glass until his head began to dip closer to the table.

Tredan nodded to Merry.

Merry whistled and George appeared from the service hall. He and Tredan lifted Aemon from his chair. Aemon's head bobbed back limply. Hot wax spattered his face, but he didn't flinch. They carried him up the stairs to the lord's chambers.

Alrick stood, unsure what role to take in this scheme. Merry patted his shoulder.

"He'll sleep well tonight. Be ready to meet our new arrivals in the morning, m'lord. I don't know if your brother will be up to it."

Alrick put his hand over hers and felt the bandages that circled the cuts from the broken pottery Aemon had pushed her into.

"Please be careful, Merry. If he knew…"

Merry smiled and took his plate. Alrick gathered the rest and followed her to the kitchens.

Alrick pulled the ring from the desk. It had gathered dust as if it had been sitting for years and not hours. He blew the dust clear and placed the ring in his pocket. He wouldn't have to worry about Aemon searching his pockets tonight.

His meal felt like a ball of lead settled in his middle. He sipped tea from his pitcher, hoping for calm, for fortification.

Alrick made his way downstairs to the parlor.

Tredan was there, leaning against the mantle. He looked paused in reflection, but Alrick suspected he was guarding the fire from toxic additions.

Nelda had not yet arrived. Her doses already sat, ready, in a line on top of the mantel.

Alrick pulled the ring from his pocket and held it out to Tredan. "Do you want to take this now?"

"No, Alrick. I think it's best you hold onto it until our visitors have left."

"Visitors? I thought only Nelda was coming?"

"Nelda, and whatever spirits she brings with her. The ones who follow her and whisper in her ear."

Alrick settled into one of the chairs by the fire. He pulled a book out from behind the cushion at his back and placed it on the table. "Do you think it's real? What she hears? What she says?"

Tredan ran his fingers over his creased brow. His fingertips were stained lavender.

"Her mother was the same way. She used the garden too, and to the same purpose. The herbs would enhance the effects, if used properly. It's one of the reasons I learned my trade—your father begged me. I did my best. In the end…" He pushed a square of medicine-coated paper across the dark slate of the mantel top. "I think I failed."

"Failed?"

"She died from poison. She took it herself, but I provided it. I warned her not to take it with anything else, but she didn't listen. Or she forgot. Sometimes her mind was so hazy, I don't think she knew what day it was, or what she had already taken. Or perhaps she wanted to push herself further, to test the limits of her ability. She believed that the closer she was to death, the clearer she could hear the dead."

Alrick twisted the mourning ring in his pocket. *Closer to death.* "Is that what you're testing?"

"It's part of it. It's why I limit and time the doses. I never did discover if the power Burgrune claimed to have was true. If she really did speak with the dead, or if it was madness—either natural madness or madness born of substance abuse. And now Nelda…She has either inherited or learned the same."

"Now Nelda…" Alrick felt a reluctant shift toward anger. His face heated. "My sister is your experiment? Not to protect her so much as to clear your guilt about what happened to her mother?" The thought of Tredan—or him—handing Nelda a dose that might kill her set his hands shaking.

"She agreed to the study, Alrick. She knows. She's a part of it—as much a student as you are. She wants to know what science can do for mysticism. How our disparate studies can combine to…reach new realms. We all seek the same answers."

Alrick stood and walked to his uncle's side, examined the drops of purple resin on the paper. "And you're being more careful this time?"

"Of course!"

"But you can't control the garden. You let me give her the key."

"She and I had a talk, after last time. About what she did to you, and to herself. She understands better, now."

"And you trust her? She trusts you?" Alrick held his uncle's gaze in the firelight.

"What choice do we have? I brewed an antidote this time. Not just an expectorant. It will reverse some of the effect, instead of just minimizing it." He pointed to the small bottles on the mantel.

Nelda strode through the arch from the corridor. She had traded her taffeta for a dun-colored linen shift and pinafore. Her hair was wild, barely secured by a scrap of frayed ribbon. She looked like one of the scratchlings, her pupils barely pinpricks sunk in the center of radiating irises.

"I'm not knocking tables or turning cards, Brother. You saw for yourself."

I do see for myself. Why can I see them, too? Alrick wondered how long she had listened from the corridor. "I can't know what I saw. You drugged me."

"All the better for you to see." She smiled.

Tredan cleared his throat and rubbed the oak smoke from his eyes. "Shall we get started?"

"Yes," Nelda said, her urgency clear.

Tredan handed her the first dose and pulled the watch from his waistcoat pocket.

Nelda slipped the dose carefully from the paper this time, prying and scraping it away with her teeth. Her eyes fixed, unblinking.

Alrick watched as her pupils expanded, stretching wide into black pools that swallowed her irises like hungry stains. Her dark gaze shifted from Alrick to Tredan and back.

Tredan pulled a pen and notebook from his jacket pocket. "What do you hear, Niece?"

"I hear choking. Coughing. Crying."

"What words, Nelda?"

She opened her mouth and a sound like drowning poured out.

The watch ticked. Nelda choked. Alrick eyed the antidote on the mantel.

"Uncle…"

"That's not her. She's okay." Tredan's eyes were as fixed open as Nelda's as he watched her intently, the muscles in his face tense as Alrick hadn't seen them since the hospital.

"Mama," Nelda rasped. A line of blood leaked from the corner of her mouth.

"Tredan," Alrick walked to the mantel and grasped the vial of antidote.

Tredan pressed a hand to his shoulder. "No. Not yet."

Nelda gargled and cleared her throat. "There aren't any words. No clear thoughts. Just dying. Trying to breathe." She reached out a hand and waggled her fingers.

Tredan made a note of the time in his book and placed the next dose into her open hand. She shoved this one into her mouth and chewed, paper and all.

Alrick watched her pale throat work the paper down. Her long fingers twisted in front of her. Her pupils expanded again, blackness overtaking the veined sclera.

"How now, Niece?"

"I heard you." Her voice was gravel again. Stone on stone. Ash on porcelain.

"You're okay?" Alrick asked.

Nelda's blackening eyes snapped to him. "Dead. Dead. Dead."

"Do you need help? Do you need the antidote?" Alrick held the vial out, saw where the curve of the bottle matched the cut curve in his palm. Where the safety broke before. Where it failed. He'd failed. I won't repeat Tredan's mistake.

"Too late. Much too late," she growled. "You were born too late for any of this." Her mouth stretched wide. A sound bubbled out. A choke? A cough?

Alrick's face felt cold under a sheen of sweat.

"Shh, let her speak," Tredan said. The fingers wrapped around his watch clenched white.

Alrick felt sharp heat against his leg. He realized he was standing too close to the fire. The brass ring in his pocket had become a brand. He stepped away from the hearth, toward a torn chair.

"Are you going to kill my only daughter, Tredan?"

Tredan paled. "No."

"You'd give her anything. Feed her anything, to hear my voice again."

The hinge of Tredan's watch cover bent back in his grip. "No."

"I'm here. Is this where you want me? Is now when you beg for forgiveness, as if I haven't heard you, every time?"

"There was nothing I could have done to stop you, Bea."

"So how will you stop my girl?"

"You know I can't."

Nelda's mouth grew wider, eyes blacker.

"She could stop herself, if she wished," Tredan said. He picked up the third dose and held it out.

Nelda grabbed it and dropped it whole into the wide chasm of her throat.

"Can you hear him yet?" Tredan asked.

The gravel voice answered. *"I know what you're trying to do."*

"Brother. Drummond. Are you there?"

Nelda's eyes had clouded fully black and she seemed to rise from the floor, growing taller, or floating up from the dingy carpet. Alrick slid from the chair and stood, stepping back as Nelda's long hair lifted about her as if she floated in water. Alrick stared up at her, then down to her toes that dangled beneath the hem of her dress, inches above the rug. His heart hammered, sweat slicking his face.

"You won't find it." The candles on the mantel melted into clear pools. *"It isn't yours to find."*

The ring in Alrick's pocket had grown hotter, even far from the fire. He pulled it out, felt its impression seared into his fingertips. He held it up to the light. "Is this yours?"

He felt the focus of those dark eyes twist to him.

The shriek that followed seemed to come from the walls themselves.

"Mine!" it called.

"Yours," Alrick nodded, and held it out.

Nelda grabbed it just as it flared poker-red and she closed her hand around it. Steam escaped between her fingers and the smell of burnt flesh filled the room.

Tredan reached for her hand. "Nelda, no—" He pried her fingers open, but the ring stuck fast to her palm. The smoke drifting from her fist turned green.

"What's in that ring, Burgrune? What's the silver powder? Tell me! For Nelda's sake…"

"*Father!*" she growled. "*All our fathers!*"

Her black eyes blanched white, pupil and iris gone.

Alrick leapt forward with the vial and poured the antidote over her tongue. The oil pooled with the blood collected in her mouth.

Nelda's hand shot up and gripped his throat. The hot ring pressed against his neck, burning, driving into his windpipe.

He stared into Nelda's eyes, into the veined whiteness that pulsed with the rhythm of his own heartbeat. Her vice grip held him close, his lungs spasming for air.

A crescent of pupil appeared from beneath her purple eyelids, then more, as her eyes rolled back into place. The blackness began to contract. A glimpse of blue appeared.

"*It's all mine. You can't take from the dead. We leave it where we will,*" she whispered into Alrick's face.

Her breath chilled his hot cheeks. His head spun as his vision began to cloud. He felt Tredan's hands prying at the fingers around his throat, but they didn't move. Alrick's face tingled, numbed.

Tredan pulled a second vial from his pocket and thrust it between Nelda's teeth. He forced her chin upward and the vial drained.

Her grip relaxed. Her hand fell away as her knees sank to the carpet. The ring fell to the floor between them. Alrick joined her on the floor, gasping.

Nelda's eyelids fluttered, and she opened them, irises clear and blue again. She braced herself against a stack of books.

Tredan knelt at Alrick's side and picked up the ring. "Merry! Cold water, please!" He shouted up the stairs.

Merry stumbled down the stairs with Tredan's pitcher. Tredan took it from her and poured what felt like ice over his neck, then he turned and poured the rest over Nelda's hand. Alrick hoped the hiss he heard came from the hearth and not from his flesh. But he felt nothing. He supposed he would, later.

Alrick remembered, once, grasping the handle of a lamp that had burned too low. How the metal had sunk into him. How his mother had held ice wrapped in silk to the burn, telling him he'd be okay.

"You'll be okay," Nelda whispered. *"Things like this heal, snapdragon,"* she said.

He felt ice on his throat again.

Nelda gagged.

Alrick sat up and leaned toward her. "I'm okay, Uncle. See to Nelda."

She gagged again. Her throat made a sound like one of Tredan's boiling beakers.

"I don't think she's fully herself yet," Tredan said.

"What's happening to her?" Alrick crawled over to his sister and propped her up, away from the unstable stack of books.

"Mama," she whispered.

"She's…" Tredan pressed a hand to her cheek, her forehead. He held a hand in front of her mouth.

"Mama it hurts. I can't breathe, it hurts."

Tredan's face paled. "Edyta?"

"Take me back to Mama."

"What is happening, Tredan?"

Tredan's shaking hands gripped Nelda's. He took a bandage from his coat and pressed it against her burned palm. "She's hearing a scratchling," he said. He laid her hands in her lap and gently touched her eyelids. "Edyta, I'm so sorry. I tried. I tried."

Alrick climbed shakily to his feet and backed away from the couch. He picked up Tredan's notebook from the mantel and took notes. Names. What it was she said. He couldn't note the time. Tredan had dropped his watch too close to the fire. The hands spun around the face like a wheel down a hill.

Nelda's pleas became mumbling, became whispers in a choir of small voices.

Tredan's shakes became tremors.

And Alrick's pain finally bloomed.

CHAPTER TEN

Alrick groaned. Tredan stood and turned to him. He grabbed the pen and notebook from Alrick's hands, flipped to a new page, and scrawled something across the paper.

"Go to the lab. Make a paste of aloe, dry peppermint, and willow and put it right on the burn. And check on Cassie for me. I'll see to your sister." He tore away the sheet of paper and handed it to Alrick.

It hurt to lift his arm. A recipe. Ratios and mixing instructions.

"Thank you, Uncle," Alrick said. He glanced at Nelda—eyes sunken, lips flecked with blood that stood out against pale skin. Her hair splayed around her in a tangled nest over the dusty stack of books beside her.

"She's okay?"

"She is. She's not ill. This is…the ghost of an illness. This is Edyta haunting me. Nelda is simply the conduit. It will stop when the dose wears off."

"But we gave her the antidote. Twice. Shouldn't that have stopped it?"

"I would have thought so. I don't know. I'm not certain where the effects of medicine end and Nelda's natural ability begins. How much of this could she do without any herbs at all? It's possible she's simply more vulnerable in her exhaustion. I'll study her over the next few hours. Let's hope we discover the answers to your questions."

Alrick nodded, winced at the motion, and folded the paper in his hands. "So, Edyta is dead?"

"That appears to be the case." Tredan's voice shook as much as his hands did. "Go see to your injury, Alrick. The longer you wait, the worse it will get. An infection there could be very dangerous."

"Yes, Uncle."

Alrick felt the tight skin of the burn pull and stretch and sting with every movement of his head. He mounted the stairs, careful to hold himself as still as possible. He turned into Tredan's rooms.

He started, and immediately regretted it as pain shot through his neck and face.

Cassie sat in the chair again, messily sipping tea, staring at him. She didn't respond to his startled jump, or the yelp of pain that followed.

"Cassandra," Alrick said. He breathed and let his heart settle. "I knew I had seen you up. Tredan didn't believe me. Are you well?"

"You're not," she said. Her voice was small, broken.

"I've had a small accident. If you'll excuse me for a moment, I need to mix something for this." He bowed. The skin on his neck pulled and he flinched again. Cassie nodded.

Alrick entered the lab and crossed to Tredan's shelves and pulled down the ingredients necessary for his medicine. The mixture didn't require heat—just a mortar and pestle, a bowl, and a jar to store the medicine.

It was difficult to focus through his pain. He looked at the list of measurements and added an extra pinch of willow. A splash of poppy. He took a sip of quinine.

When the mixture was finished, he carried it to Tredan's chamber and used his mirror to coat the wound. He could see the crisp impression of Burgrune's ring. The shape of the bronze indelibly laid into his flesh like the brand on a cow. Or a slave.

"I've got one of those."

Alrick jumped again, less painfully this time, now that the medicine had begun to work.

"Cassie, you probably shouldn't be in this room—"

She lifted the hem of her shift.

Alrick's face heated—the hot blood beneath his skin causing his pain to return afresh.

Cassie lifted her skirt to her thigh, exposing a pink, puckered circle around the shape of a number four, or perhaps an A.

Alrick squeezed his eyes shut. "I…I'm sorry to hear that, Cassie. That must have hurt."

"It did," she said.

He heard the soft rustle of the fabric fall back into place and he opened his eyes. She was standing close, her eyes searching the skin of his neck.

"You're going to have a mark. Forever, like me. So everyone will always know who you belong to."

The chill that followed the flush of his skin was almost a relief. "I don't belong to anyone," Alrick said.

Cassie raised her eyebrows. "Lucky, then." She stared at the mark again, and at the bowl of paste in his hands. "If mother knew I was going to belong to witches, she'd have killed me. To keep me safe, she'd say."

"Oh. Cassie, we're not witches. Tredan is more like a doctor. A scientist."

Her eyes travelled over Alrick's shoulder and scanned the wall behind him. He glanced over his shoulder, out the chamber door to the lab and its shelf full of blue bottles. *Pneuma*. The last breaths of dead Aldanes.

"I hear what you do. I know what you are." Her eyes met his again.

Alrick swallowed. The skin of his throat protested.

"It's okay," Cassie said. "Mama would have killed me anyway. Eventually. You saw."

Alrick's throat tightened. "The woman in the room. The one Tredan fought? That was your mother?"

Cassie nodded.

"Oh, Cassie. I'm so sorry. We didn't know. What can we do? Should we go back for her? Can we help her?"

"Help her kill me?"

"No! Of course not, I mean get her out of that hospital."

"How long have I been here?" Her expression hadn't changed. She didn't seem upset, despite Alrick's shock at the things she said.

"A week. Ten days or thereabouts," Alrick said.

"She's already dead, then. They'll have killed her. She killed that other girl in the room. They won't have let her live, after that."

Alrick's legs felt weak, but he turned and led Cassie out of Tredan's chamber and back to the sitting room.

"I'm sorry, Cassie. If we had known…"

"There was nothing you could have done."

"We could have brought her here."

"No." She shook her head.

Alrick rubbed his eyes. They were beginning to itch and burn. "Did we do wrong to bring you here? Do you wish we had left you there?"

Cassie looked down, examining her bandaged wrist. "I don't know yet."

He met her gaze, trying to blink the dryness from his eyes. "If there's anything we can do, that I can do, please tell me. I am at your service."

"Where are the others? The ones I hear—the children from the hospital."

Alrick swallowed again, past the lump in his throat, the burn, the pain. "My brother sent them away. It was against our wishes. He doesn't approve of my uncle's work."

"And this is the extent to which I'm to trust you? You are at my service, and the next thing you say is a lie."

"Cassie—"

She stood. He grasped her shoulders and whispered in her ear. "I'm trying to protect them. If my brother finds them, the ones that are still here, I don't know what he'll do. People would be hurt."

"Does he know about me?"

"No." He shook his head, the skin of his neck pulling back and forth, the medicine stinging where the skin split. "He can't know; he can never find out, or he'll send you away, too."

"How do you plan to deceive him? Your fancy house is not a very large house."

"We were going to wait till you were well. Healed. And invent a story for you. That you're a distant relative of my mother's family, come to stay, to convalesce in the countryside."

Cassie ran her hand over the tattered remains of her shorn hair. She slipped a finger in her mouth, poking at the places where teeth should have been.

"We would say that you've been very ill. That you need country air."

"And? Dress me in satin and ribbons? What about when I don't know how to speak or dance or eat properly? Your story won't hold. Your brother is a lord. He'll be able to tell that I'm just another street urchin."

"He wasn't raised a lord. We'll teach you what you need to know. We have time."

"Time while I lie locked in that cupboard of a room."

Alrick sighed. "It isn't locked. Tell Tredan you're awake, that you're well. You can trust him. He's helped many in your situation."

"Has he? Where are they now?"

Alrick's mouth opened, but he couldn't speak. He didn't have an answer. Not one she'd like.

Mama. Edyta's spectral voice was haunting more than just Tredan.

"Cassie, I don't know if we've done right by you, bringing you here, at least right now. But you're alive, and I don't think you would be if you'd stayed in London. Things here are in turmoil, yes, but I'm going to set them right."

"Yes, I heard. I hear your uncle speak. Plan things. He talks when he writes, you know. And sometimes he talks to me. Tells me things he can't tell anyone else—anyone awake. Good luck with your plans, Alrick."

Cassie crawled back onto her cot, pulled the quilt up to her shoulder, and turned away from him. "You might just kill us all, but I'm on borrowed time, anyway. I'd be dead by now. It's true."

Alrick saw her pale hand creep up and pick at the plaster of the wall, breaking away crumbs of it. Just another part of the house weakened, another piece falling apart.

Sleep was impossible. Every angle of his head on the pillow, every shift of his shoulders, set the burn ablaze in pain. He reached for the jar of medicine at his side table. His fingertips brushed it and it rolled away.

The frustrated tension in his jaw set new pain free. He climbed out of bed and reached to the floor for the jar, the dim glow of embers hardly enough to see by. He heard the hollow sound of the jar rolling farther. He reached for it, brushed the cool glass, and felt it twitch away from him.

As he stretched, a cold finger trailed over his cheek, down his neck toward the burn.

He flinched away and spun. The room looked empty. Silent. Not even the softest breath sounded within his hearing.

"Who's there?" His whisper croaked harsh and half-formed.

The glass jar struck him in the back of the head. The force knocked his teeth together and narrowed his vision to a single speck of glowing ember that burned white hot like a brand through his skull.

A deep laugh echoed through the darkness, and his bedroom door blew open, banging into the wall and cracking the plaster there. A rush of cold air fed the starved embers and a red glow bloomed in the room.

Alrick reached a shaking hand to the throbbing knot forming on the back of his head. Pain dizzied him. He rubbed his eyes. The room remained empty. He stumbled to a chair and sat.

Small, cold fingers grasped his hand and pressed the jar into his palm.

Alrick trembled, almost too much to open the jar. He scooped more medicine onto his finger and applied it, clumsily, painfully, to the burn.

It helped, but not much. Not enough for sleep, not after what had happened. Not with the lump on his head, not with something—someone—in his room that he couldn't' see.

That was no scratchling. Who else is hidden here?

Alrick stood and touched a candle wick to the hearth embers and let light fill the room. He searched every corner, but there was no one—not even the flash of an eye or the swish of an apron.

He stepped out onto the stairs and made his way to Tredan's chambers, crossed the quiet sitting room, and entered the lab. It was dark inside, the perpetual flames turned low for the night, the elixirs above them bubbling softly.

Alrick could hear the deep sound of Tredan's even breathing coming from the bedchamber. He helped himself to the lab stores, a dash of coca tonic and a bit of willow tea to relax the pain in his neck and dampen the intensity of his nightmares.

Delusions. Hallucinations.

Hauntings.

Alrick supposed this was a form of science. If the happenings continued after he was sedated, an outside force must be at work. If they stopped when his mind stopped, perhaps that was the source of his problems. It wouldn't be proof. But it would be data.

He swallowed the bitter tonic he had invented and returned to the stairs. Whispers sounded from below—from the dark sitting room at the base of the staircase.

Alrick pinched out his candle and crept closer, listening.

He couldn't make out the words, but there were at least two voices—which might mean nothing if Nelda had decided to sleep the night in their chair.

Alrick could already feel the effects of the tonic on his wits—like his thoughts were bubbles floating to the top of cold honey. He knew he should hurry to bed. Rest while the medicine worked. But he felt his feet drawn, step by step toward the hiss of whispers in the dark.

It was as if he could hear only the esses—a whistle impossible to stifle—and the soft staccato burst of tees.

Perhaps it is only the fire.

"No," one of the voices became more forceful.

Alrick stepped lower until he was just out of sight of the room.

"*You must,*" said the deeper voice. Alrick knew it, then, as the graveled throat of dead Burgrune. "*I need my strength.*"

"Mother, I am your hands now. I am your strength."

Alrick edged to the side, keeping within the shadow of the stairs, to where he could glimpse into the room.

It was Aemon. He looked disheveled and unsteady on his feet. Whatever Merry and Tredan had given him, it had worn off in the night.

Nelda sat upright on the chair, her head thrown back, throat bulging. Her hair was slick and limp with perspiration. Her arms hung at her sides, palms up, wrists smeared in blood. The hot ring hadn't left a mark on her skin. Burgrune's voice ripped from her throat as if it scoured those membranes raw on its way out.

"*There is more to do than you can do alone.*"

Nelda convulsed. Her throat swelled and contracted and smoke rose in a black ribbon from between her lips. The darkness collected at the corners of the ceiling, beyond the reach of the dying fire.

Nelda slumped back against the chair.

Aemon stood. He scooped Nelda into his arms.

Alrick slunk back further out of sight as Aemon carried her into the corridor.

The room grew darker in their wake, or perhaps his vision dimmed, clouded with the fog of his medicine.

Alrick retreated backward up the stairs, convinced that if he turned away, those shadows collected in the corners of the room would overtake him.

He stumbled into his bedroom, his candle clutched, melted

against his hot fingers, but he did not make it to his bed before the tonic took him.

His legs gave. He scooted as close to the fire as he could—the thin carpet fibers rough against his cheek, dust thick in his throat as he let sleep take him.

Pain woke him again—this time the pain of trying to pull away from the carpet, where the fluids oozing from his burn had fused to the filthy fibers.

He shrieked as he pushed himself off the floor, leaving a tissue-fine sheet of skin behind. He panted through the pain as the cold morning air kissed the exposed rawness of his skin.

Feet tapped up the stairs and across the floor behind him.

"Can I help you, sir?"

It was Elizabeth, carrying a breakfast tray.

Alrick still panted, supporting himself on his elbows. The coverlet from his bed had been pulled across him. He composed his breath before speaking.

"Could you please bring me the jar from the bedside table?"

"Of course, sir." She set the tray down on the desk and brought him his jar of medicine. A fine web of hairline cracks had spread across the thick glass.

He struggled upright, felt a hand under his elbow, lifting him, guiding him to the chair.

"Are you all right, sir? Would you like me to fetch Master Tredan?"

"No, thank you, Elizabeth. I'll sort myself out and go to him later."

"Can I get you anything else, sir?"

"Is my sister up yet?"

"Well, yes." She wrung her hands.

"What's wrong?"

"She's up in the attics, sir. She's been up there for hours, looking for something. We offered to help, but she said…"

Alrick rubbed crumbs of dust from his eyes. "She said her mother is helping her, didn't she?"

"Yes, sir. Is she okay? Should I send Tredan to her?"

"No need. Thank you, Elizabeth. I'll go myself."

She curtsied and exited.

Alrick flinched at the steam rising from the breakfast tray, just as the smoke had risen from Nelda's mouth last night. The smell of the food turned his stomach.

"You can have that," he whispered to the room. "I'm not hungry."

He staggered to the wash basin and cleaned the dust from his face, gently scraped it out of his wound, teeth squeaking together as he clenched his jaw. He spread more medicine over the cleaned burn. It stung where the skin had broken.

He wiped the greasy mixture from his fingers and headed downstairs. Tredan's door was closed. He supposed his uncle needed to keep Cassie out of sight of the new servants.

There were several attics in House Aldane. Alrick's chambers, the ones above the lord's chambers, and the ones above the east wing. Alrick assumed Elizabeth had meant the east wing attics, as those were above the lady's chambers. Nelda's chambers. Alrick didn't know what they were used for. They would have originally housed servants, but so few servants remained at House Aldane that most of them kept to the larger attics above the central keep, or in the chambers down near the kitchens.

Alrick caught himself timidly sniffing the air as he approached Nelda's quarters. If she was burning herbs again, he didn't dare enter.

The lady's wing was far more opulent than his and Tredan's bachelor rooms. Each lady of House Aldane had, in turn, improved upon them since their original build. The layout now reflected his late mother's tastes, but Nelda's touch could finally be seen in the small details of the room. Ribbons. Bushels of dried flowers. There was no scent of smoke. No crackle of fire, even. The parlor hearth was dark. No light came from the bedchamber—its fire was also out, the heavy curtains drawn across the windows. A dragging clamor sounded from overhead.

Alrick climbed the staircase.

"Nelda?"

He heard muttering and the crash of a trunk lid slamming shut.

Alrick entered the attic, twin of his own room, but this one full of trunks and crates, and even more dust than the rest of the house combined.

Nelda's face appeared over the edge of a box that sat near the doorway. There were dark circles under her eyes. Her face was smudged with dust and her hair hung in bramble knots. Fray's head also emerged, from behind another row of cases.

"Nelda, it's almost time to assemble for the butler's arrival."

"I don't care much," she said, and her face disappeared.

Alrick stepped farther into the room. "He's bringing things for the house. That should be nice—making the place feel like home again."

She tossed her head back and cackled. Moths stirred from the crates.

Alrick peered over the box behind which she sat. She was nested in a pile of crumpled linen, dusty furs, chipped teacups, and bushels of colorful feathers.

"What's all this?" he asked.

Nelda drew a pale ribbon from the back of an old nightdress and snipped it free with a pair of tiny brass scissors. "Mother's things."

"Oh. I had no idea they were still here." He ran his hand over the patchy, balding velvet of an old chair. "We could use them, if you like. Dust them off. Do you want me to carry things down for you?"

"Your mother's things, too," she said, and handed him a handkerchief.

It was edged in fine tatted lace and embroidered with his mother's initials.

"Oh." Alrick ran his fingers over the threads. He wondered if his mother had stitched these letters, or if it had been done by a devoted housemaid. He slipped the square into his pocket. He exhaled and watched the dust in the air dance in front of him. "What can I do for you, sister? We really do need to go downstairs."

"I'm looking for mother's hair," she said. "She needs it. Aemon needs it."

Alrick pursed his lips. He slid his hands into his pockets, gripped the delicate handkerchief. He resigned himself to disturbing Tredan.

"Nelda!" Aemon's voice boomed from below.

She stood, and ribbons and feathers spilled from her lap into the heap at her feet. She crawled over the crates and trunks and slipped down the stairs.

Alrick heard Aemon's scolding tone and the sound of the big copper tub hitting the floor. He ran his fingers over the brim of a hat he desperately wanted to recognize, but didn't.

Alrick left the room of artifacts and went down the stairs. Susan was pulling a comb through Nelda's tangled hair as Elizabeth began to fill the tub from a row of steaming kettles over a fresh fire.

Aemon had already gone—probably to fetch him and Tredan and issue a similar scolding.

Alrick imagined he did not look much better than his sister, as far as decorum went. And he found that he, also, didn't care much.

He walked out into the hall. Tredan and Aemon were there, and Martha and Anne. Merewyn entered, carrying a tea tray, and George entered through the terrace door.

"Nelda will be late," Aemon said. His face twisted into a sour expression. "Elizabeth and Susan are seeing to her, so they will also be late."

"Is she all right?" Tredan asked.

"No, Uncle—she's her usual self. Do you have a cure for that in your bottles?"

Tredan swallowed and Alrick was sure he was holding back a terse reply. "I do, Nephew. Unfortunately, the ceasing of one's usual self is rarely advised."

Aemon sniffed. "Well, keep it handy. I may become desperate."

Tredan flinched and shot Aemon a look saturated with anger, laced with worry.

Aemon led them in procession to the front of the house, where the convoy of carriages had begun to arrive.

"There hasn't been this much traffic on Aldane Road since the day of your naming," Tredan said, squeezing Alrick's shoulder.

"Except for the funerals," Aemon added.

"Those are always exceptional," said Tredan.

Rain had rendered the roads muddy, so the carriages moved slowly, and they watched as their new footman leapt out and pushed the wheels free more than once.

By the time the carriages stopped in front of the house, the footman was messier than Alrick, and Nelda stepped, clean and dressed, to his side.

The butler was an older gentleman—trim and tidy—with lines in his face that mapped a life of dissatisfaction. The footman was close to Alrick's age and appeared to feel just as out of place.

The butler approached Aemon and bowed. Aemon smiled.

"This is Mister Skillson," Aemon said.

The footman followed in the butler's example, and Aemon introduced him as "Shepherdson."

Introductions were brief, and the staff set to unloading the three heavily laden carriages of their supplies. Basket after basket went down to the kitchens.

Alrick helped lower a large piece of furniture and carried it to the hall. He and George propped long rolled tapestries across their shoulders and hauled them in.

"I have some mail to deliver as well," the head driver said, approaching Tredan. He handed him a letter and then pulled out a stack of wide, white boxes for Alrick.

"What on earth is all that?" Aemon asked.

It took a moment for Alrick to remember his order from the clothier. "Oh! I nearly forgot." He searched for a lie. "Just some basic linens. Nothing of consequence."

Nelda wandered away to examine a chaise lounge that had been set in the gravel that was clearly meant for her parlor.

Tredan paled, the letter crimped in his tense fingers. His other hand tugged absently at his beard.

"What's the matter, Uncle?" Alrick set his packages down and hurried to Tredan's side.

"Bad news?" Aemon asked. "Another sick urchin in London?"

Tredan ignored him.

"Matthew and Katherine are dead," he said. "A fever. Their daughter has only barely lived." He looked up pleadingly at Aemon. "I'm being asked if she can come here, so I can oversee her recovery."

"Who are they? Were they? Is this another orphan you've collected?"

Tredan shook his head. "Matthew was Alrick's mother's favorite cousin. He spent a lot of time here, years ago. His daughter, Cassandra, and Alrick were playmates as babies."

Alrick felt the warmth of realization pass over his face and hoped his expression didn't belie the story Tredan had gone to such lengths to concoct. He was relieved to think that no one was truly dead—that there were no new orphans in the family. The plan must be in place. Cassandra must have finally spoken to Tredan. That would have been why the door had been closed.

Tredan approached Aemon. "I know what you think of her family, Aemon—and I don't blame you, not one bit—"

"No. I won't have any more of her blood in this house," Aemon said. He turned away, back to the arrival of his new things.

"They're only related by marriage. Her other relations have turned her away. That poor girl. Please, Aemon. She was a lovely, sweet child. She's younger than Alrick. She could be Nelda's companion. Perhaps she'd have a calming influence on her."

Aemon paced in the dirt, avoiding Tredan's gaze, watching the last of the crates come down off the carriage and disappear into the house.

Tredan stayed on his heels. "It's only for a while. Until she's better. I'm sure there are other places she could go, then—other places she'd likely wish to be. She could take rooms at a resort, once she's well and ages into her inheritance."

Nelda had crawled onto the chaise and fallen asleep in her gown. Aemon stopped and stood over her.

"Cassie could do some good here, I think. Nelda could use a friend. A caretaker," Tredan pressed.

Aemon turned from his sleeping sister to Tredan. "The minute she shows any sign of her family's ways, she's gone," he said, and stalked into the house after his new furnishings.

Tredan smiled at Alrick, and Alrick smiled nervously back. Was it too soon to bring Cassie out of the lab? She'd seemed nervous, talking to Alrick, about what would be expected of her to uphold such an elaborate lie. She was right about all the training she'd need in order to convince them all of this dubious backstory. Did she even want to stay?

"What are all those?" Tredan nodded to the pile of boxes Alrick had set on the ground.

"Fabrics and ribbons. I ordered them for Nelda."

"That was kind of you."

"I think I'll set some aside for Cassie. She'll need them."

"A good plan. I hadn't thought of that. Yes, we'll need those and a number of other things. I better talk to Merry."

"I know where we can find much of what we need," Alrick said.

"Do you?" Tredan asked. He half smiled, a look of surprise crossing his face.

"I was just with Nelda in the attic above her room. It's full of our mothers' clothes—things that could be made over new, so they're not recognized."

Tredan nodded. "I'll send Merry after them. She'll know what to take and what not to. And she can make them over for Cassie."

Alrick lifted the stack of boxes, surprised at the weight of all that cloth. "When Merry looks, could you ask her to look out for something for Nelda?"

"Of course. What was it she was looking for?"

"Well, I'm not entirely sure. She said she was looking for her mother's hair."

Tredan pulled at his beard again. "What an odd request. Perhaps her mother had a wig? Or hat? A fur? I'll pass the word along. Merry may know what it means."

"Thank you."

"Now, let's get inside so I can take a look at your neck. How is it healing?"

Alrick realized he hadn't felt much pain since the new application of medicine. His head hurt worse. The cold fear of the night before sent a shiver up his back. "It's feeling better this morning. Last night was difficult."

"Yes, I saw you'd come for a tonic. I hope it helped?"

Alrick blushed with guilt over raiding the lab stores. "I did sleep, at least."

"Sleep can be better than any medicine in a bottle," Tredan said.

They walked into the house and to their parlor. Alrick unpacked his boxes and set aside a few of the simpler cloths for Cassie's wardrobe. Aemon might take it as an afront if she was dressed as well as, or better than, Nelda. He repackaged the nicest pieces, as well as several spools of brightly colored ribbons, and rang for Elizabeth.

"Could you please deliver these to my sister?" he asked her.

"You don't want to take them yourself?" Tredan asked.

"No," Alrick said. "She should enjoy them in peace. Or hate them. I don't know—I've never bought cloth before."

Elizabeth grinned over the stack of boxes. "I'll let you know how you've done, sir," she said, and laughed quietly as she left.

Tredan opened his kit on the parlor table and applied fresh medicine and a clean bandage to Alrick's burn. He pulled one of his own cravats from the back of a chair and wrapped it around Alrick's neck to hide the dressing. "You look sharp in that. Which is good. I'm afraid you're going to have a scar."

"That's what Cassie said."

Tredan paused in his fidgeting. "I'm sorry I didn't believe you before, when you said she was awake. She told me she'd spoken to you. Twice."

"You had no cause to believe me, with the state I was in that night. I didn't fully believe myself."

"Still. You are my apprentice and my partner. I won't discount your word so easily again."

Alrick smiled. "Why did she do it?"

"Pretend to be asleep?"

Alrick nodded.

"Survival, I suppose. She didn't know us, or why she was brought here. She lay quietly and listened, got to know us through our private conversations. It's telling, Alrick, that she came to trust you first. That means something."

"She could have escaped, anytime."

"To where? The fields and forests? No. She did what she had to do. I don't fault her for it."

"Did the medicine never work for her? It was meant to help her to not feel pain…"

"I'm afraid she was likely in a great deal of pain, Alrick. The herbs we gave her for the surgery would have worked, regardless, but the simpler mixtures we've given her since seem to have had very little effect. They won't have done much to ease her suffering. Her tolerance for the medicine is too high. As is, apparently, her tolerance for pain. She acquired such tolerances throughout her life, it seems."

Alrick's eyes stung and his face heated. She'd lain there, for two weeks, in pain, because she was afraid of them. All while knowing her mother was far away, dying. He bent his head and felt his neck sting again. *A small wound. Almost nothing, truly.*

"Did she say what it was that caused her to be hospitalized?"

"No," Tredan said. "But physically, she's healthy. It may have been something psychological. Some form of defiance that a doctor deemed hysteria, in order to remove the burden from some incapable parents."

Alrick looked up. Tredan didn't know. "That was her mother," he said, "in the room with her. The cannibal."

Tredan stared at him. "The madwoman was her mother?"

"Yes. She told me."

"Did she tell you anything else about her family?"

"No. Just that her mother was likely dead by now."

"That is probably true, yes." Tredan paced the room, pulling at his hair and tossing the free strands into the fire. The room smelled briefly acrid. "It's possible her mother's affliction was believed to be hereditary. Or contagious. It's possible someone believed Cassie might follow in her mother's footsteps." He turned back to Alrick. "Did you notice any odd behaviors? Did she seem mad to you?"

"No," Alrick said. "Well, yes—but nothing beyond what might be considered normal, given what she's experienced. Who wouldn't be a little bit mad after all that?"

"True. Fair. Still—it's a troubling revelation. We'll have to keep an eye on her, watch for any signs of…unquietness."

"Tredan, she'll be spending her days with Nelda."

Tredan laughed. It was humorless, a bit hysterical. "Yes. Well. I haven't got a better plan, at the moment. But we have a few weeks. A lot can happen in that time. We'll make a proper lady of her."

"By then I suppose this new butler will have trained us all into proper ladies and gentlemen."

"He's a butler, not a magician, Alrick."

Merry cackled. She had just entered from the hall, carrying a stack of fresh sheets and towels. "Well, he's already ordering us lot about. If he's a magician, that poor young Shepherdson is the pigeon up his sleeve."

"I'll take those, Merry." Alrick claimed the stack of linens and headed for the stairs.

"Let me know if he becomes a problem, Merry," Tredan said.

"Oh, he will be. I can already tell," Merry said. "But there's nowt you can do about it right now."

Do something about it.

"We'll do what we can," Alrick said.

She bobbed and made to exit, but turned back. "Oh, m'lord—I'm sure Elizabeth meant to come back and let you know how your gifts were received, but she's busy just now tying bows and cutting patterns. And now I've got no one to beat the rugs, thanks to you." She laughed and left.

"It sounds like it went well," Tredan said.

"Should I go and help Merry? It sounds like I've left her shorthanded with the new butler watching."

"No, Alrick. Merry is fine. She's a force. You must see to your studies. We need to go over our notes from last night."

The evening's horrors rushed back to Alrick. "Tredan, Aemon knows what we're doing. That we're helping Nelda contact the spirit of their mother. He was talking to her last night—his mother, through Nelda—after you were in bed."

"It's possible he knows a great deal more than we do. And he encourages her into dangerous behaviors because it works in his favor. Because she's fighting on his side."

Alrick rubbed the sore knot on the back of his head. "Is that safe? It seems like Burgrune is getting…stronger."

"She is. And no—it's not safe. She's an angry spirit, Alrick, energized by how close she is to seeing her unfinished business fulfilled—her son taking his father's place. The Sibald line on the Aldane throne." Tredan followed Alrick as they started up the stairs.

"Aren't we working against our own interest, then, in bringing on these trances?"

They had reached the lab. Alrick carried the linens to the cabinet and put them away.

"It appears so. Which is why we're being allowed to continue."

"Why?"

"Burgrune is practice. A willing spirit, fighting to come forward. Calling her forth is easy, almost effortless, for someone as powerful as Nelda. She's eager to speak. She's teaching us how to refine these techniques we use to hear her. But they, and she, and you, Alrick, have forgotten an important point." He led Alrick to the wall of blue bottles. The wall of breaths. "If one spirit can be made to talk, why can't they all? What would your father say to all this? How would your mother respond to Burgrune burning you? What would my scratchlings like to say to Aemon?" He pulled a bottle down from the shelf and blew the dust away from an old label. "I intend to find out. I'm learning how."

Alrick reached out and touched the bottle containing his father's last breath. "I heard her. My mother. I've heard her a few times. Sometimes her voice slips out of Nelda's mouth."

"She's not far, Alrick. She's never been far from you. We have to help her grow stronger, bring her forward, raise her voice."

"How do we do that?"

Tredan pulled at his hair. "If we had something that belonged to her…did you say her things are up there in that attic?"

Alrick nodded.

"I'll have Merry choose something of hers to bring to us. To focus her, to help her come forward. The closer the thing was to her, the better. The more personal."

"Like her hair?"

Tredan paused. "Yes, Alrick. Something like that would create a very strong bridge."

Mama's hair. She needs it. Aemon needs it.

CHAPTER ELEVEN

Alrick chewed his buttered bread and watched his uncle pace, bread held forgotten in one hand while the other pulled at his beard. Nelda sat quietly tapping the side of her new teacup, watching the rings ripple across the cold tea's surface.

"So, Tredan, when does our guest arrive? The latest addition to the house of orphans." Aemon sorted dusty bottles of wine on the long hall table, making notes in his ledger.

"I only just sent my reply. I imagine it will be a few weeks, yet. They were not specific about her condition after her illness—she may not be fit to travel for some time."

"I suppose we should begin preparing soon, then."

"Indeed. I'm not sure if you have a room in mind?"

"There are several empty beds yet in the maid's chambers."

"Might I suggest, nephew, that if she is to be a companion for Nelda, that she take the room in the attic of the lady's wing? Her room would be similar to Alrick's, and she'd be close at hand should Nelda require her at odd hours."

"That room is used for storing old junk, now, as I understand it."

"It is. Likely things we don't need, or things that could be stored in the stable attics or an outbuilding. If we're bringing the house back to life, let's set the rooms back to their purpose. Merry can organize it all. Mister Shepherdson and George can carry away the heavy items."

Aemon tossed his pen on the ledger, leaving a spray of ink. "I have no argument against your logic, Uncle. Only my own feeling that a ward from Eleanor's family not occupy a place of honor in my house. If I weren't so sympathetic to her current position, I'd put her up in the kennel."

Tredan pursed his lips and drew a long breath. "The room has been used to store Eleanor's cast-off clothes for a generation. It's no place of honor. Indeed, with your train of thought, it could be said to be continuing in the same purpose."

Aemon laughed. "There's no point in arguing with a scientist. You've convinced me, Uncle. I'll speak to Merry."

"No need. Don't trouble yourself. I'm going to her now. I'll relay the plan."

Aemon nodded. He picked up his pen and blotted the splash of ink from the page. He did not see Tredan smile, or the wink that he cast Alrick's way.

Alrick wasn't certain that the arrangement was a victory. That room could only be accessed through Nelda's parlor. Would Cassie feel trapped? And what hours did Nelda keep but odd ones? Would Nelda be yet another mad jailkeeper between Cassie and her freedom? Alrick wondered if the strange smoke from Nelda's herbal fires would reach that attic. If Cassie would be subject to those toxins. He didn't think Cassie's resistance to medicines would be enough to protect her from Nelda's brand of pharmacy. Alrick would have preferred it if Cassie could stay with Elizabeth and Susan. Their quarters were cramped and spartan, but safe.

It occurred to him, like a punch in the gut, that he'd had no say in the matter at all—and that the decision should have been his in the first place. They were all falling complacent to Aemon's rule, including him. *Don't forget your purpose.*

Alrick followed after Tredan, intending to bring up his concerns about Cassie's room.

Merry was in the garden, taking advantage of an early spring thaw to hang linens. Alrick caught up to Tredan just as he interrupted her work.

Alrick bent to the basket of heavy wet linens and held them to the line while Merry placed the pins.

"Merry, I have a project for you and George. Include Shepherdson if you must, but I'd prefer the task be limited to those loyal to the house. The real house," Tredan said.

"Yes, sir?"

"Our new guest that will be arriving…" He raised his eyebrows and Merry nodded her understanding. "…will be taking the attic apartment in the lady's wing."

"Oh, dear," Merry said, shaking her head and tutting her tongue.

"Yes, I realize it requires a great deal of work." Tredan pulled a pencil from his pocket and spun it nervously in his fingers.

"Do you realize, indeed?"

"Merry—"

"I'll help," Alrick said.

Tredan turned to him, half obscured behind a sheet Alrick held on the line. "Alrick, your studies—"

"Must come second to the needs of my house," Alrick finished.

Tredan pinched the bridge of his nose and squeezed his eyes shut. "Yes, you are quite right."

"Uncle, are you sure Cassie will be safe in that attic? Above Nelda?"

"She will. What Aemon doesn't know is that it's the safest room in the house."

Alrick paused in his work. "How is that?"

"While your father was a very faithful man—besotted almost to a fault with his wives—your grandfather, my father, was not. He kept mistresses, brought on as ladies' maids, that attended to my mother and who slept in that room. To aid in their natural meetings, he had a secret door put in. It's hidden within a false headboard, and leads to a passage stair within the wall, down to the lord's chambers, and further to a back door near the kitchen gardens. The exit is in the cold store. I'm not certain your father even knew of it. I am certain that your brother doesn't. I'm sure Merry remembers it, don't you?"

Merry flushed and shook water from a sheet. "Those stairs are damn cold in the winter. But yes—Cassie may come and go as she pleases by them, safe as you like."

Merry's blush deepened. Alrick had never thought of her as anything other than the round, rosy-cheeked nurse he had always known.

"Merry?" Alrick peered around the sheet, and Merry stifled a giggle.

Tredan cleared his throat. "Merry, as you clear that room, I'll need you to set aside some things that Cassie can use. Items a lady would have. None of Burgrune's belongings—Aemon and Nelda might recognize them. But anything indistinct would be useful."

"And I bought some fabric as well, so dresses could be made up for her," Alrick added.

Merry's levity wilted. "Unlikely your girl can sew and mend with only one hand."

"I don't expect her to," Tredan said.

"Of course not, Master Tredan," Merry said. "Fortunately,

Elizabeth is good with a needle. Not up to a true lady's standards, of course, but there's nowt in this house but me that would know any difference. And my eyesight is not what it was."

Tredan nodded. "Let me know when the room is ready." He strode away through a patch of weeds toward the corner door to Burgrune's garden.

Merry rounded the sheet to look at Alrick. "That poor man hasn't realized yet he's got all his many purposes tied up in knots." She shook her head.

"What do you mean?"

"He can't have all his outcomes. He can't keep pulling all the strings at once, or the knot gets tighter. Sooner or later, he'll have to pick a line and follow it."

Alrick considered his uncle's puzzled ambitions—as well as his own. Drummond's passing had complicated Tredan's life as much as anyone else's. And perhaps less than Merry's.

Merry lowered her eyes. Alrick could see the shadows of faded bruises on her face. "Alrick, I've known that man longer than anyone else in this world. When he chooses his line—it won't be yours. Be sure you're the one holding onto the end of your own string, my boy, when the lines are chosen and the knots come undone."

The sun peeked out from behind the clouds and cast Alrick's shadow onto the sheet in front of him like he was a player in a puppet show.

As if I'm one of the puppets, held up by strings in others' hands.

He saw, also, in that bright light, that the sheets hadn't quite come clean. There was still blood on them.

CHAPTER TWELVE

So much dust filled the room that Nelda's fire had to be extinguished lest the air itself be set ablaze.

Nelda sat on her new chaise and watched the procession of dusty trunks and chests. She selected what she wanted from what passed, and those items split from the path and filled her room.

Merry, situated in the back of the attic, made a selection of the plainer, more practical pieces and secreted them into the hidden stairway to be carried, later, to Cassie.

Cassie had spent the previous week sat in one of Tredan's chairs by the fire, reading books on etiquette and making remarks about the stupidity of it all. She made it clear she believed their plan would fail—that Aemon would spot her as just another scratchling, just another orphan creature for the workhouse. Her hair had grown in, a soft yellow curled close to her scalp, and her wounds were no longer weeping, but her face still held the gaunt, sallow tone of deep suffering.

Alrick hauled another trunk down the attic stairs and past Nelda's chaise. She pulled a hat from it and deposited it on her head. She laughed deeply in a voice Alrick could tell was Burgrune's—the old spirit clearly delighted that her daughter finally possessed her old belongings, delighted that Eleanor's dusty old gowns were finally leaving the house. That they were likely to be stripped into rags or stuffed into a hayloft.

The room, in the wake of all the detritus and debris, was identical to Alrick's, but bare of furnishings and coated in considerably more dust.

Alrick wrapped a cloth around his face and offered one to George as they scooped piles of dust into pans and pulled down ropes of cobweb.

They stripped the cover linens from the old bed and scrubbed at the wood, beat and tightened the ropes that would suspend the new mattress that had just arrived from London.

"Help me move the bed, so I can clean behind it?" Elizabeth gestured to Alrick to take the heavier head of the structure.

Alrick pressed his hand against the tall board. The hidden doorway was behind it, and he wanted that secret to remain private, even from Elizabeth. "I think we should leave it," he said. "This is an important family piece. I don't want to risk damaging it if we try."

Elizabeth nodded, and swept her broom under the bed to chase the dust out that way. Alrick took a rag and reached down between the suspended ropes to scrub at any stubborn spots.

Alrick's own shirt had become a rag itself. Dust covered him and the pail he used to rinse the cloth was down to an inch of water so thick with grime it was nearly mud.

But the room was coming clean. Alrick pried open the stiff windows and let in a cool breeze that helped to rinse away the dust in the air.

George arrived with a bucket of firewood and one of Aemon's thick, new rugs slung over his shoulder. Shepherdson followed with a new chair that he placed beside the hearth.

"Did Aemon approve of these pieces for the room?" Alrick asked. He was surprised to see such fine things brought up for the cast-off orphan.

"Nelda insisted," George said. He rolled the carpet over the freshly scoured boards and set the wood in the hearth. "There's more to come, as well."

"Well, I think Elizabeth and I are finished here. Please let me know when you're done, so I can see it. And be careful of the bed, please. I don't want that piece so much as scratched."

"Yes, m'lord," George said. He saluted, and he and Shepherdson descended the stairs. Elizabeth and Alrick followed.

There was a cluster of furniture in Nelda's parlor, clearly intended for Cassie's room. A small writing desk, a wardrobe and dresser. Nelda had also collected an assortment of lamps and old books, and a painting of a young woman in a white dress.

Nelda emerged from her chamber and grasped Alrick's arm. The weight of her grip strained his aching shoulder. "You must come later, after dinner, and tell me what things my new friend likes."

Alrick was pleased, but a bit unnerved at Nelda's excitement. He knew Cassie wasn't one to enjoy much attention or fuss. He almost said so when he remembered her story—her ruse.

"I'm afraid neither Tredan nor I have even seen her since she and I were small children. But I'm sure she wouldn't want you to go to too much trouble."

Nelda pursed her lips into a smile and pulled harder on Alrick's arm. He winced.

"Just ask her for me, Alrick. If there's anything she requires. It will be easier for me to get things for her now than if she asks for them herself, later."

"I suppose I could write—"

Nelda pulled him around to face her. Her eyes searched his. The lavender blue irises were clearer than they had been in days. The sclera shone nearly white where the red had faded. Her pupils seemed normal, reactive. "Ask her for me, Alrick. Or I'll come ask her myself."

She knows.

Alrick felt the blood rush from his face in a dizzying tide, then return in heated blooms as his anger responded to fear.

"I'm sure she'll appreciate your kindness," he said. His voice came hoarse, tight. He hoped it would sound as though it was raw from dust and not from the mix of emotions he kept rigid under Tredan's cravat around his throat.

"It's nothing compared to yours, dear brother." She stretched up on her toes and kissed his cheek. "And find out her favorite color for me."

Alrick bowed his acknowledgement, fearing to trust his voice again, and left the room. His weary legs protested the rush. He was tempted to stop by the kitchens and request water for a bath but didn't want to ask anything else of the staff that day. They were likely more exhausted than he was, and still had an evening's work ahead of them. Everyone had put in extra effort to prepare for Cassie's arrival.

Everyone except for Aemon. And, Alrick noted with some irritation, he hadn't seen Tredan all afternoon, either. A foul mood had overcome his uncle after their talk with Merry, and he had gone off to brood or study something.

As if summoned, Alrick walked right into him as he entered their parlor.

"I'm sorry, Uncle," Alrick said, reaching out a hand to steady them both. "I was lost in thought."

"You look as if you were lost in a dustbin." Tredan brushed away a patch of dust from where Alrick had touched him. "What's the matter with your face?"

Alrick's face still burned—he assumed from the flush of anxiety at his suspicion that Nelda knew about Cassie. "Oh, Nelda upset me just now. Something she said. I'm certain she already knows about Cassie."

"No, you have a rash—just there." Tredan's finger hovered near Alrick's cheek.

"Probably reacting to something nasty in the attic," Alrick said, raising a hand toward his face. Tredan grasped his hand and pulled it away.

"Come," Tredan tugged him toward the stairs and Alrick knew he was going to be further delayed from his rest by Tredan's administrations.

"Could I bathe, first, uncle? The mark doesn't hurt. I'm filthy and aching."

"No, it's spreading just as we stand. Best to get to it quickly." Tredan still gripped Alrick's hand as he pulled him into the lab and over to the worktable.

Cassie sat in a chair by the fire. She had a book balanced open on her lap, but her eyes were fixed on the flames, unblinking. Alrick wondered if her oddness and Nelda's could coexist peacefully.

A hot, wet rag scraped his face, and splashed bitter-smelling water down the front of his shirt. It stung like acid across his cheekbone.

"It's blistering already," Tredan mumbled. "Were there any plants or dried herbs in the attic? Any flowers or leaves that might have touched your face?"

"Nothing has touched my face but dust and cobwebs," Alrick said. Then he remembered, and felt his face go pale again.

"What?"

"Nelda. She kissed my cheek."

Tredan paused at his row of apothecary drawers. "Ah. I see." He returned to his stores, now more precise in his selections. "Well, the bad news is, it's going to itch for a few days. The good news is, it will go away, soon."

Again, Alrick's face heated, and the warmth aggravated the spreading sting. "Why would she do that?"

"It was likely an accident. She may have been sampling from the garden and forgotten the trace was on her mouth. Or perhaps she was feeling wicked—her moods are mercurial."

"I don't think all of her moods are her own."

"I believe that is correct."

"Her eyes were clear, though—clearer than I've seen them in all the time she's been here. She seemed more…normal, than usual."

"It's possible whatever she was taking was to reverse her usual state, this time." Tredan handed him a small jar full of a paste that looked like porridge inside.

"What's in this one?"

"Oats. And some mint and willow, to help with the itching. There isn't a proper treatment, I'm afraid, once the oils have soaked into your skin. You'll just have to wait it out."

"It doesn't itch."

"It will."

"Why didn't she have a rash, then, if this was on her mouth?"

"That I do not know. We'll have to ask her. Not everyone reacts to all plants in the same manner. We've seen before that you appear to be particularly sensitive to many of them."

"I'm supposed to speak with her after dinner. I'll ask her then."

Alrick turned to Cassie. She gazed into the fire, book ignored. He strode over and sat in the chair next to hers. She didn't seem to notice.

"Cassie, I've been asked to learn your favorite color. And to ask if there's anything you might like to have in your room, beyond the basic requirements."

If it hadn't been for the slow rise and fall of her shoulders, Alrick might have thought her a statue, or a painting. Her hair shone bright and golden in the firelight, and the heat cast her face with a fresh glow of health.

"My favorite color is blue," she finally whispered, as if only realizing it now, herself.

"Is there anything we can get for your room? Something to make life easier? You'll have Merry and Elizabeth and Susan, of course, but if there's anything we can provide—"

"I can't even begin to recount the scope of my needs." She turned toward him, her eyes glinting in the reflected flames.

Alrick swallowed. "I can only imagine."

Her eyebrows twitched.

"If you think of anything, tell us. Make a list. I don't care if the list is longer than the hall itself, I'll do what I can." Alrick tugged at the knot in the cravat at his throat. He'd sweated through the fabric, and the silk knot had become immovable as a stone.

Cassie turned back to the fire. The book slipped from her lap and landed face-down on the carpet. It was not her etiquette book. It was a novel—the kind that would have fed the fire if discarded at school. The kind with a keep like House Aldane illustrated inside.

Alrick picked it up and thumbed through the pages. "You enjoy books? Stories?"

She reached out with her shortened forearm, realized too late what she was doing, and let her arm fall to her lap.

Alrick placed the book back on her knee. "I'll send for more books. As many as you want."

He stood and left her to her meditation of the fire.

Tredan stood bent over his table, peering through a lens at a sediment at the bottom of a jar.

"I'm going to have a bath, now. I'll see you at dinner," Alrick said. He made his way upstairs, feeling the ache in his legs with each step.

In his room, a full tub steamed in front of the blazing hearth. He nearly wept with gratitude.

"Oh, thank you. Thank you," he whispered. Alrick stripped and slipped into the tub, hoping his hidden helpers had offered him privacy as well. Dust and grime lifted from his skin, skimming the water's surface and drifting in the current of his breath.

He finished washing, dressed in fresh clothes—noted that most of his clothes were missing and assumed they had been whisked away to be laundered, either by Elizabeth or the scratchlings.

He still had time before dinner, so he sat at his desk and began composing a new order from the clothier, adding several measures of fine blue fabric.

He reapplied his medications before heading down the hall.

Since the arrival of Mr. Skillson, dinner had become a quiet, formal affair, full of meaningless pleasantries and proper forks. Only Nelda appeared immune to the social pressures of propriety.

Alrick suspected she was baiting Aemon with her behavior. Aemon ignored her, but she persisted. She toyed with the candles and told fortunes from the herbs floating in their soup. The harder she tried, the more fiercely Aemon ignored her, engaging Tredan in conversation about managing the tenant farms for the spring.

So it was only Alrick who saw that the salt well slid, independently, toward her plate when she wanted it. That the candle lighting Aemon's plate winked out when she hissed at it.

Alrick's food cooled on his plate as his gut twisted. More things across the table moved and twitched at her call. His face itched fiercely under the oat plaster as he began to sweat.

When his own peas began to roll across his plate, he stood and excused himself. Nelda's giggle followed him from the room.

Perspiration trickled down his back, dampening his fresh shirt. He made his way to his wing, to the stairs. The door to the lab was locked again. Tredan was being extra cautious to keep Cassie a secret from their new staff. Alrick felt sure most of them could be trusted to see Aemon for what he was—that they could be allies in their plan to oust him—but he knew he must be cautious. That trust must first be earned. If Aemon knew that Alrick was determined to prove his father's true wishes, he'd be packed off to a school or left to fend for himself on the streets of London. And he was certain he'd lost the offer of Mr. Legan's employment. He'd no doubt end up a scratchling himself, but without the mercy of a doctor like Tredan.

He tapped softly at the door, not wanting to disturb Cassie if she was resting.

Merry ascended the stairs behind him, carrying a basket of linens. The ones he had helped her hang. "Evening, m'lord. Did you need something?"

"I was just checking in, on my way up. I had a question, earlier—I wanted to see if there was an answer yet."

Merry reached past him and slid her key into the lock. "Well, come, then."

They entered, Merry opening the heavy door just wide enough for Alrick to slip through.

Cassie had clearly been awaiting Merry's return. She stood on a stool by the fire, draped in shapeless cloth studded with pins that caught the firelight. A nest of crumpled fabrics surrounded the stool.

As Alrick drew closer, he could see that the fabric draping Cassie's small form was in fact a dress—pale pink, its neckline studded with small pearls. Alrick's eyes widened. He couldn't say how he knew, but he remembered the feel of those pearls under his fingertips, the smoothness of them comforting as his own head rested against a warm shoulder.

"It's been a long time since I worked this piece," Merry said, returning to Cassie and pinning a side-seam to fit. She glanced at Alrick. "It was your mother's."

Alrick stepped closer, picked up a piece of powder blue satin from the floor and rubbed it between his fingers.

"I'm afraid they're not much in the modern style, but I'll do what I can." Merry bent to the hem of the gown and pinned a good four inches of fabric.

"They're beautiful," Alrick said. "I think they will suit her very well."

Cassie blushed and fidgeted anxiously on the stool. "I've never had anything so nice," she whispered. "I'm afraid I'll ruin it."

"Nonsense, dearie. There's nowt you could do to these dresses that I can't undo." Merry pulled another candle closer so she could see her stitching.

Alrick let the satin fall back to the floor, like poured water. He struggled to regain his voice. "Cassie, have you thought any more about things you'd like for your room? I'm going to speak with Nelda soon, to finalize the plan for furnishing it. Of course, we can always add anything, at any time."

Cassie tugged at the belled lace cuff of the dress, drawing it over the wrapped bandage at her forearm. The blush of the gown matched her scars exactly, matched the flush of Alrick's cheeks. *Rosebud.*

"I don't know, Alrick. I don't think I'll know what I can do until I try. I don't know what I need, yet."

Alrick nodded. "The invitation is always open. Anything you

need—or want. It isn't just about needs. Anything that would make you…happy."

"If I ask for a looking glass on a stand so that I might comb my hair when it grows back—would that ease your conscience?"

Alrick's heart dropped. *Is this what she thought? Is she right?*

"I don't mean—" Alrick stammered, cleared his tightening throat. "I'll see that it's done," he said. He turned to go and realized that he still held the blue fabric clutched in his fist—he could have sworn he'd dropped it, watched it fall—the satin dampened and crushed in his grip. He spread it out over the back of a chair, smoothed it as best he could, and fled.

He *did* feel guilty. He wanted to make it better—do whatever small measure might gain any ground of her happiness. But guilt wasn't the only motivation for his kindness. He wouldn't have wished Cassie's suffering on anyone. He simply wished to unmake some of the cruelty of the world. And this was the opportunity before him. But if she thought he was all guilt and pity…He could not help her if she didn't trust him. He wasn't sure how he could win such trust, or if he even deserved it. Cassie had no reason to trust anyone, and he didn't blame her for it.

Alrick returned to his room and splashed water on his face. He applied more of the oat medicine to the blisters on his cheek, and the salve to the burn on his neck. The scab there had thickened, embedded well into his flesh. The tender layer of new skin forming beneath it itched, but didn't hurt as often now. The balm kept the wound supple, kept it from peeling away at the edges and exposing the rawness beneath. He put a fresh plaster over it and re-tied his cravat. Alrick didn't like always having the knot at his throat. It was always hard enough to breathe, to speak. Further obstacle seemed ridiculous to him. But his wound was ugly. The scar would be frightful. *And what of Cassie's scars?* He remembered her tugging at the lace cuff of the dress.

Neither of them had anything to hide. He picked at the tight knot and pulled the silk from his neck, tossing it over the back of the chair. The cool air felt good against his skin. He took a deep, unobstructed breath.

He dreaded his meeting with Nelda, and whatever spirits attended her this evening. He wondered if their discussion would be fraught with small objects twitching all around them. He slipped his pen and notebook into his jacket pocket. If Tredan needed data about the ways in which his sister interacted with the spirit world, he'd have done well to observe her at dinner, instead of debating the merits and downfalls of field boundaries.

He had time, still, before dinner finished. He'd wait until he heard Tredan return before he set out for the lady's wing.

Alrick fitted a lens into his telescope, spun the knobs, and swept his view across the darkening sky. Early spring clouds masked the stars. He found himself longing for the cold, clear skies of winter. The most he could see was a lantern glowing in the distant stable window—likely George tucking the horses in for the night.

Then the light jumped. It jerked out of sight.

Alrick panned his view and saw the lantern speeding away from the house. It hadn't been in the stable window, but affixed to a carriage that vanished down the road.

Light feet sounded on the stairs. Elizabeth's figure appeared in the doorway, winded, her candle flickering in her shuddering breath. "Your uncle sent me to tell you—he's had to rush to the village." She paused to gulp air.

"What's wrong?" Alrick approached her, offering a hand to the seat by the fire.

She shook her head, braced a hand on the doorframe. "The physician in town is ill—very ill, from the sound of it. There's no one else to tend to him."

"Does Tredan need my help?"

"He said to pack his kit and send it along with George. You're to stay here and watch the family."

Alrick's heart slowed and cooled. Tredan didn't want his help any more than Cassie did. Did anyone trust him?

Elizabeth must have seen the disappointment in his face.

"He said he couldn't risk exposing you, as well as himself, to whatever's taken over the physician. He said at least one Aldane must always be in the house."

Alrick took little comfort from the excuse. He'd been willing enough to send him into the cells at the hospital. "Thank you. I'd best see to his wishes."

Elizabeth curtsied and vanished back down the stairs, her breaths still puffing as she ran.

Alrick hurried to the lab. He didn't knock this time, but fitted his key and burst through the door and across the sitting room. Cassie must have returned to her room. Merry tutted his intrusion as she folded the mess of fabrics spread around the chairs. Alrick ignored Merry and propped Tredan's bag open on the stool, tossing in the essential jars and vials. He tucked a bit of cloth over them and placed the roll of surgical tools on top before squeezing the latch closed.

He hurried from the room, calling to Merry as he ran, "Tredan was needed in the village. I'm sending his bag along."

George waited by the door, his jacket pulled tight, ready to leap on his horse.

Alrick handed him the case, and George spurred off down the long drive toward the village.

Alrick sighed. Without Tredan, the house felt somehow alien. Tredan was the last remaining constant that made House Aldane what it was. Without his uncle, this was Aemon's house. *No. It's mine. As it was my father's and his father's, and his.* It was said that this land held traces of occupation since the first houses existed, and for all Alrick knew, those occupants had always been Aldanes, one after another after another. He tried to imagine those roots, branching out beneath his feet, deep into the earth, peppered with the very flints his ancestors might have used to protect this land. As he would.

Alrick stepped back from the door and swung it closed.

With his errand done, he had nothing left to do but keep his promise and speak to Nelda, and pray he did not fall victim to another of her noxious plants.

CHAPTER THIRTEEN

The woodsmoke in her room smelled normal. And while a musty cloud of dust still hung in the air from their cleaning, much of it had settled—onto the carpets and chairs, the candlesticks and baubles—as if the room had been abandoned all over again instead of having been revived.

Alrick didn't see Nelda at first, in the dim light, but he heard soft singing.

He had hoped he might find her asleep, worn out from her antics at dinner. Her voice sounded weary. Faint, like breath came hard.

"Nelda?" He stepped toward the chair by her fire, figuring he'd sit and wait till she approached him.

But she was there—sitting on the floor inside a ring of chairs. A large frame spread across the floor in front of her, the glass shattered. Dusty fragments glowed across the carpet. Fray lay curled on the rug beside her, his tail idly whipping through the mess.

A canvas lay behind the broken glass, patterned with dark embroidery in myriad shades of brown, black, gold, russet, and silver. They'd been stitched into the shape of a branching tree that reached from corner to corner within the frame, and trailed to the bottom in an intricate root system.

Nelda pulled strands from the canvas, plucking them at the root and unbinding them along the twisting branches. She tucked the strands into her hair and tied them there with the bright ribbons that Alrick had bought for her.

She continued to sing under her breath as she turned to him, her lips bright lavender, eyes fully black. When she smiled, her teeth were stained red as the ribbons at her temples.

Alrick lowered himself into the nearest chair and slid his hand into his pocket, toying with the cap on his pen, pulling the notebook out and clutching it in his lap. He tried to think scientifically. Every moment now was data. He forced a shield around himself with the clinical stoicism he'd seen Tredan adopt in a crisis, pushing from his thoughts the fact that his sister sat before him—his kin, her body wracked with poisons and angry spirits—angry with him, and vengeful of his heritage. The fact that he'd failed to bring a vial of antidote vexed him. He didn't even have one ready, and half of what he needed for one had sped away down the road toward the village.

Nelda stopped her song. A long sigh escaped her lips, like a growl. It went on for too long, and the air of it seemed to feed the fire so that the flames grew and brightened, illuminating the mess spread across the floor. Fray joined in the growl, his own low timbre harmonizing with Nelda's.

The curling, dark embroidery was hairwork, Alrick saw. The locks of deceased Sibald women, woven together and bound into that leafless tree. A dead tree. Or a winter one, waiting for spring.

Nelda's curls bristled with knotted ribbons and the twisted, broken hair she'd pulled from the picture. It stuck out at odd angles, winding like the branches, as if she had become the tree itself.

Alrick flipped open his notebook and began to write, but kept his eyes on Nelda. His scrawl slid over the paper, and he hoped he'd be able to read it later.

He tried to speak—to ask her if she was okay—but his voice caught on the dryness at the back of his throat. Alrick swallowed and tried again. "Is...did you find your mother's hair?"

Her gaze snapped to him. He felt her appraisal on him, heavy and bitter.

"It's all mine. All of it mine." She dragged her nails over the fine cloth and a tatter of dry, torn hairs sprang free. "Generations of curls and locks and braids—all stitched as one."

"Who are you right now?" Alrick kept writing, though his hand shook, smearing ink across the side of his palm, dragging a haggard line across the page.

"We are Aldane."

The hair on the back of Alrick's neck and arms stood up. It prickled as though singed by the air itself. Soft spattering drew his eyes to the mantel. A candle melted its wax down the carved surround and into the carpet.

"Burgrune?"

"Yes?"

"I want to speak with my mother."

Nelda's head lolled on her neck, then rolled, and snapped back, mouth agape, throat swelling. A distant keening sounded from the well of her mouth, like someone lost on the moor. Alrick couldn't make out the words, but the voice was sad, familiar.

"I can't hear you..." Alrick leaned in, straining his ears for more of that distant voice.

A low growl overpowered the quiet call. *"It's a long way to come from that stinking churchyard. And I don't want her here. You should have buried her on the grounds, like a proper Aldane. But then, is she even an Aldane?"* The coarse voice laughed.

"You're buried here, on the grounds, Burgrune. Is that why you can't leave?"

"I'm everywhere. I'm in every stone. I'm the heart of this house."

"Is my father here?"

Nelda's head snapped forward, driving her teeth together with a crack. Blood ran down her chin.

"He cannot speak," she whispered, blood spattering from her lips.

"Why?"

"He has no breath."

Alrick shifted in his seat, leaned toward Nelda's mask of a face. "Since when does a spirit need breath to speak? Can he use your breath?"

Nelda lifted from the floor, ribbons and tattered curls trailing behind her, toes brushing the shards of glass in the carpet, then rising, higher, till the crown of her head nearly touched the beams above.

"I won't allow it," the growl tumbled from the rafters.

"I'm speaking to Nelda, now. Nelda, could he speak? Through you—could you give him a voice?"

A shriek split the air and every scrap of glass in the room shattered. Nelda's pale, clawed hands rose to her throat and dug themselves into the meat of her neck. She twisted against their grip. Vibrant welts trailed from where her nails scraped.

Alrick leapt for Nelda and wrapped his arms around her knees, pulling her down, reaching for the savage hands that tore at his sister's throat.

Fray jumped up and grasped Alrick's ankle in his teeth, pulling, tearing the hem of Alrick's trousers as he tried to drag him away.

Aemon and Merry burst into the room.

"Grab her hands!" Alrick shouted.

The three of them pried her fingers away from her neck. Aemon wrapped her in his arms, pinning hers down as Merry pulled the wild hair from her face so Alrick could inspect her wounds.

Nelda coughed weakly, her voice a faint wheeze that terrified Alrick. She choked on the blood that pooled in her mouth where she'd bit through her tongue.

"Lean her forward," Alrick said, and Aemon tipped their sister so that the blood ran onto the floor instead of down her throat.

The scratches on her neck were ragged. Deep for fingernail scratches, but not, Alrick thought, something that threatened her life. He was more concerned about the crushing, the bruising, and the squeaking way in which she drew breath.

"Can you carry her to the lab?" Alrick asked.

"I can barely hold her," Aemon grunted.

It was as if she possessed all the strength of House Aldane as well as all its voices.

"Tie her arms down with your belt," Alrick said. "I'll fetch my things."

Alrick dashed to the lab as Aemon and Merry wrestled the gasping Nelda toward her bed.

The twisting halls rocked underfoot, threatening to buck him to the floor and slide from beneath his feet. He would no sooner gain his footing than he would fall again, as if the stones and boards tossed him like a rowboat in a storm. He half-crawled to the base of the stairs, where he saw Cassie's pale face staring down at him.

"What's wrong?"

"Nelda. Help me gather my kit."

Tredan had much of what Alrick needed in the bag he'd sent to town. They searched the lab for spare supplies and tossed them in a basket Merry used for washing.

"Thank you," Alrick shouted over his shoulder as he raced back down the stairwell.

Aemon, Merry, and Elizabeth were tightening Nelda's bonds to the bed posts as she thrashed in the sheets, spattering blood across the linens.

Alrick pushed through to her side and fished the chloroform and gauze from his basket.

He pressed the soaked gauze against her face. Hot blood soaked though the fabric against his palm.

Her movements slowed, but would not stop. The growling ceased, and Alrick swore he still heard the keen of the lonely voice.

She was calm enough, at last, for him to get to her wounds.

"Help me get these away," he said, pulling a ribbon wrapped in broken hair from the tar-like blood at her throat.

Elizabeth and Merry cleaned away the nest of hair while Alrick cleansed and bandaged the gouges in her neck. They weren't deep, but he knew the tender skin would have trouble knitting itself together if he couldn't keep her still. He could do nothing about her tongue. She'd nearly bitten through the tip, which writhed, red and angry, struggling to speak.

He gave her medicines for pain and swelling. Soon, her breathing evened, though it sounded as though it were being forced through a torn paper screen.

Aemon stood by the fire, picking at the wax on the mantel. "When does your cousin arrive, Alrick?" One hand rustled in his pocket.

"Soon. Very soon, I think."

"Good. I can see that my sister is very ill. She'll need to stay bound here in her room. Your cousin's assistance will be most welcome." His voice was quiet. Not the booming lord of the manor now, but a concerned brother. He broke off a slab of wax, crushed it in his fist, and tossed the pieces into the fire where they hissed and smoked.

"I'll see to her till then, m'lord," Merry said, drawing a chair to Nelda's bedside.

Alrick nodded. Aemon's gaze never left the fire. He hadn't seen that Merry had addressed Alrick.

"Good," Aemon said. He strode out of the room.

Alrick felt exhaustion settle on him like a rough skin rug. "Come and get me, Merry, if you need anything. At any hour."

"Yes, m'lord," Merry said. "Don't worry. I've watched over her on nights like this before, when she was just a little thing."

Alrick stared at his sister's twitching form. She looked little, now. "She was like this before? Even as a child?"

Merry sighed. "Takes after her mother."

Elizabeth looked to Alrick with an eyebrow raised. "Shall I bring you hot water and a cup of wine, m'lo—Master Alrick?"

Alrick nodded and almost couldn't raise his head again. "That would be perfect, thank you."

He turned to leave the room, then remembered his notebook left beside the chair. He searched for it, found his pen—capless, nib bent—but the book was gone.

Then he remembered the rustle in Aemon's pocket. Had Aemon taken it? If Aemon read his notes—if he learned that all the ghost of his father needed was his voice, his breath—

Alrick rushed back to the lab, burning his last store of energy, as if he were one of the candles on Nelda's mantel.

When he reached it, the door was locked and barred. Alrick fumbled with his keys, till he heard his name whispered through the keyhole.

"Alrick?"

"Cassie?"

Locks and bolts ground open. Cassie peered from around the door.

"Did he come? Was Aemon here?"

Cassie nodded. Redness ringed her eyes.

"Did he see you? Are you hurt?"

Cassie shook her head and stepped back, opening the door wide. "I hid. But…" She pointed to the lab's entrance.

Alrick hurried in, but stopped short when the crunch of broken glass sounded underfoot. Tredan's shelf of bottles had been pulled down. Blue fragments lay scattered across the floor. Every bottle broken, their torn labels tattered like old leaves. All the collected last breaths of the Aldane clan, lost. The air in the room smelled of sepsis and old teeth. It hung cold and moist against his face.

CHAPTER FOURTEEN

Alrick tried to seal his throat against the unnatural humidity. Against the subtle rankness of breaths that were stale even when they were new. He recalled the diminishing fog that had glazed the inside of his father's jar. He'd expected Tredan to stare at it through some lens or scope—to study it for some sort of secret. Not feed it to his sister so she might speak with his father's voice. He didn't expect to need his father's voice again—not in this way.

His chest ached. He finally broke and sucked in a long, slow breath. He didn't have his sister's gift. *Maybe it will be enough. Just to have set the breath free. If Father's spirit can find it….*

Cassie stood behind Alrick, watching him. She held her hand to her mouth, observing his struggle with the sudden consciousness of his own breathing.

"Let's clean this up," he whispered, wondering whose breath he had just sent swirling ahead of his words. Whose breath he had used to form them.

They plucked broken glass from the carpet and swept it from the wooden boards. They contained it all in a corner of the room, in case Tredan might still make use of any of it. If some useful residue might still remain.

Alrick's exhaustion stretched beyond his experience. "I need to retire," he said.

Cassie nodded. "If Tredan returns tonight, I'll explain."

"Send him up to me, if he does. I have more than just this to explain. Things more critical, even."

"All right," Cassie said.

Alrick could tell from her furrowed brow that she wanted to ask more.

"Lock the door again behind me. In case he comes back."

She nodded, and Alrick returned to the stairs and climbed to his room. He found the tub full, the water cooling to tepid. The fire burned low.

He sunk into the chair at his desk, pulled out a new pen, and began to write everything he could remember of the evening—all of Nelda's unsettling words, his missing notebook, the broken jars.

Alrick heard soft steps on the stairs, and the glow of a candlestick grew in the doorway, till Merry's face appeared, shrouded in a nightcap. "Miss Nelda's asleep, now, m'lord. I'll be retiring to bed, now, myself."

"Is there anyone with her? Merry, I don't want her to be alone. Perhaps we can trade shifts."

"No need to fret, m'lord. Her mother is looking over her." Merry turned to go.

"Merry—" Alrick stood. His legs shook beneath him.

"Get some rest, yourself, m'lord," Merry said as she disappeared around the turn in the stairs.

Alrick followed after her, grasped her shoulder, and spun her around to face him. Even in the glow of the candle, her eyes were dilated.

"Did you eat or drink anything in Nelda's room, Merry? Did you notice any strange smoke from the fire?"

Merry's face contorted in confusion as some part of her fought to resurface.

"Merry, tell me so I can help you!"

"I…I had a sweet from the box."

"Did Nelda tell you her mother was there?"

"No. She's been sleeping. But I saw her. Plain as day in the chair by Nelda's bed."

The black rings of Merry's eyes twitched. Her chin quivered. "Alrick…what's happening?"

"It will be okay," Alrick said, guiding Merry down the stairs back to Tredan's door. "You just accidentally took some medicine. Nelda hides it in her food."

He unlocked the door to Tredan's rooms and led Merry to the lab.

Cassie's brow appeared around the edge of her closet. "What else has happened? What's wrong now?"

"Merry accidentally took one of Nelda's homemade doses. I'm not even certain what. Let's hope this works." He pulled a vial of general remedy that Tredan kept pre-made, on hand for Nelda's transgressions. It wasn't the antidote, but he recalled some overlap of ingredients. He held the vial to Merry's lips and tipped the liquid over her tongue.

"It should work fast, if it works at all." He guided her to a chair and pried the candle from her fingers. "Will you watch her a moment, Cassie? It might make her sleepy. I need to go check on Nelda."

"They're all watching me," Merry mumbled. "So many…The poor dear hearts." She buried her face in her hands and her shoulders shook as she sobbed. Cassie rushed to her side and wrapped her in a hug.

Alrick grabbed the bottle of remedy and hurried to the opposite wing, his alarm giving him a renewed energy that he knew would leave him even more exhausted when it was burned out.

If Nelda has stores of her poison hidden around the room...

He paused at the large wooden door to Nelda's private sitting room, which was almost always left open. Cold air emanated from the wood and a haze of frost coated the metal hinges. The ice burned his hand as he gripped the latch.

Alrick leaned into the door to break its frozen seal and hurried past the struggling fire and into the bedchamber.

Nelda lay still tied to the bed, her breath misting like rapid steam—rising then falling to settle around her face, which peered palely from a nest of brambled hair.

No one else appeared anywhere in the room.

Alrick knelt down to the bed skirt and lifted it, whispering into the darkness below, "Go for Tredan, if you can. I need him here. We need him."

The only reply was Fray's growl.

A scrape and a stir sounded from the dark space below the bed. He added a log to the dying fire, hoping to banish the chill that had settled over everything.

Alrick turned back to his half-sister and pulled the vial of remedy from his pocket. He slipped the medicine past her pale lips.

The muscles of her face slackened and the pace of her breathing slowed.

He fed her more of the remedy, and wondered what chloroform dreams did when overcome with the forces Nelda had summoned. What world did she dream in?

Alrick scanned the room till his eyes settled on a small tin box on the opposite bedside table. He pried the lid off and saw rows of sugar-lavender buttons stuck to wax paper. He slid a fingernail under the edge of a tablet and pulled it free of the paper. It crumbled between his fingertips, releasing a bitter floral scent. He pressed it to his tongue before it could disintegrate any further. "If it worked for Merry…"

He watched Nelda's even breaths as he waited for the pill to take effect. Her breath continued to cloud the air around her face—the column of mist growing taller and broader as the shadows of the room brightened and shrank away. He stared through the mist into the darkness of the corner when he realized the mist watched him back.

The plume had coalesced into a face and a curving figure in a sweeping skirt. A slash of darkness, an absence of vapor, suggested a crooked smile.

"Burgrune?" Alrick asked.

Nelda let out a sigh and the mist scattered.

Footsteps sounded behind him and Alrick spun in his seat—back toward the doorway. A shadow stood there. He rose and it moved away—into the sitting room and across to the stairs leading to the attic.

Alrick grabbed a stub of candle from the mantel and lit it in the fire. He followed. His legs weighed him down like anchors dragged through a storm tide. The shadow glided up the stairs; the sound of its soft footfalls echoed off the plaster walls of the narrow stairwell.

He followed the shadow into Cassie's prepared chamber. It paused at the center of the rug, and Alrick felt, distinctly, eyes upon him.

"Who are you?" he whispered.

The shape didn't have the same aggression as Burgrune's spirit. The air felt sad and cold—not hot and violent.

Shadows slithered from the corners—drawn to the dark figure—and coalesced there as its form grew more distinct.

Vague features took shape in the face. A curve of neck. The

sweep of an insubstantial skirt. He didn't feel the wave of dread that Burgrune's spirit called forth in him.

"Who are you?"

This figure had no voice.

It shuffled, now, instead of glide, as if its own substance grounded it, to the back of the room and the ancient bed. The ropes groaned. The coverlet mussed under its touch.

And then it was gone—sunk behind the broad panels of the headboard. Alrick stared at the spot where it had disappeared.

The poison had fogged his mind, crowding logic and memory into some inaccessible chamber.

Something about the bed. He fumbled for his thoughts.

The passage. This was the mistress maid's room.

Alrick ran his fingers over the boards at the back of the ancient bed until he found a loose edge. He pulled and the plank swung down on a stiff hinge and laid across the mattress, exposing a hollow in the wall and a short tunnel through the stone. It led to a cramped and crooked staircase inside the structure of the thick wall itself.

Turning sideways, Alrick wriggled through and moved along the stairs. Each step plunged steeply, sloping down to the master's chambers in the main keep.

The passage bent itself around the shape of the house, and Alrick ducked under the crisscross of drains. He stepped quietly. Anyone might be on the other side of the wall. Anyone could be listening. At any moment, he might find himself at the entrance to Aemon's room.

That moment came soon enough. Another wooden panel lay set into the wall in front of him. Would it open down into the face of a sleeping Aemon? The stairs spiraled away, descending into darkness. He could follow them to the cold store, to the back door and the cool, fresh air of the garden. But what he needed was here.

Alrick shifted his position, but it was almost impossible to move inside the wall. He pressed his fingertips against the board and pushed gently. The hinges rasped, but did not squeak or groan. He peered around the edge of the board.

He looked into the sitting room, not the bedchamber. Fading embers reflected off lacquered chair legs. The room stood empty; Aemon's bedchamber door closed.

Alrick pushed the panel all the way open and slid through, crawling onto soft, new carpet. He righted himself and gazed around the room.

Something stirred in the shadows beside his father's ornate desk, and Alrick's heart thundered. Papers fluttered on its surface, though there was no breeze.

Alrick crept over the floor, his feet sinking into the rich carpet, the groaning of ancient boards muffled under its padding.

The fire bloomed brighter just as he reached the desk.

His notebook was there, atop a messy pile of letters and ledgers. He slipped it into his pocket. The letterhead on a paper beneath it caught his eye. It was from the Crumpsall Workhouse in Manchester, acknowledging the receipt of "nine orphans of ill health." Alrick's hand shook as he lowered the paper back to the desk. The scratchlings. But at least now he knew where they were. *Do something about it.* He would.

Beside it, Aemon had been drafting a letter of his own, this one addressed to the doctors of the Prestwich Lunatic Asylum. Nelda's name practically glowed from the page as a heat of anger rose in Alrick's face. He pulled the letter from the desk and tossed it in the fire. He would not allow this. He needed to hurry, to stop Aemon before he destroyed everything.

Alrick sneaked back to the tilted panel and climbed into the dark passage. He scraped his way through the interstitial walls to Cassie's attic room.

The presence, the opaque figure, had vanished. The space now felt quiet and cozy. As close to comfortable as an ancient attic could be—and certainly more so than his own chambers. Cassie had earned this comfort. Alrick hoped it might help heal some of her past torments.

With wide pupils adjusted to darkness, the room looked lighter.

Something stirred behind him. He spun, saw a pale hand dart from under the bed, drop a sheet of paper, then vanish back into the shadows.

Alrick retrieved the paper from the floor. Tredan's swift writing swept across the sheet: *Alrick, When I return from town in the morning, I will bring your cousin Cassandra with me. Please deposit the item we took from the London hospital along the road, halfway between the house and village. I will need it for our arrival. Tredan.*

He was bringing Cassie so soon? Alrick's heart clutched, nervous for her. He didn't think she was ready. Alrick would need to get her ready, quickly, if he was to leave her by the side of the road for Tredan to pick her up and pretend they'd come all the way from the village. He didn't like this plan—or that he had been left out of the forming of this plan. He crumpled the note into his pocket.

Alrick crept downstairs into Nelda's sitting room. The fire had grown so hot that the hairs springing from the old embroidery singed and crumbled to the carpet. Alrick picked up the broken frame with its tattered fabric and fraying blossoms. With the medicine coursing in his veins, the stitches appeared to move, swooping in and out of the linen, drawing themselves taut in a trail of long-dead locks. Redrawing the tree. He could almost hear the whisper of the fibers pulling through the fabric, the pop of the needle puncture. The hissing and popping blended into words and then he felt lips against his ear, cold, but with hot breath.

"They are everywhere now. They are all free."

Alrick dropped the frame and staggered away. He looked around for the source of the voice.

Nelda lay in her bed, breath misting the air as if she were a kettle about to scream.

He fumbled in his pocket for the remedy bottle and pried the lid free. He swallowed eagerly, hoping for fast effect.

The room grew more dim as every second passed. He prayed it was his pupils cinching and not an array of shadows filling the room.

But even Nelda's breath steadied as his own heart calmed.

He walked back into the bedchamber to her bedside, careful not to stumble in the growing dark.

She seemed more peaceful. Her eyes unmoving beneath two pale crepe lids, her breath even. Alrick reached out and curled his fingers around hers. They flinched a light grip in return. She seemed past the worst. Well enough that he could leave—let her rest, while he broke the news to Cassie. He undid the belt from her wrists and set it aside, rubbing her skin where the leather had chaffed.

Alrick stepped out of the room, and as he passed the door, he felt more than saw the marks on the wood, mapping his childhood, as if the lines there dragged across his skin like cobwebs.

His legs ached with the strain of it as he climbed the stairs to the lab. The door was shut fast again, and he was certain he heard soft movement inside. Too tired to sort through his keys, Alrick tapped on the door.

Merry answered, her frazzled hair coming out from under her bonnet. Her eyes had returned to normal, though with an exhausted cast that stirred Alrick's guilt. She clutched handfuls of clothes in her hands and bustled away from the door, stuffing them into an open trunk by the fire.

"Did he leave a note for you, too?" Alrick asked.

"That foolish man will get a taste of my temper when he returns, no doubt about that, m'lord. Imagine the nerve, springing this on us all like that, poor girl can hardly stop shaking for nerves."

Alrick did not see Cassie. The door to the bedchamber remained closed.

"I'll have to take her well before dawn, to drop her off and return before anyone notices, Merry."

"Of course you will, my boy. Go. Get rest. I've told her the same. I'll have her packed and ready when you come for her."

"Thank you, Merry. Take tomorrow off, please. You need rest, yourself."

"Ha! I'm sure his lordship will love that. Don't worry about me, love. I'm no stranger to a sleepless night caused by Tredan's foolery. And neither will you be. Go, rest while you can."

He climbed all the way up to his room. His bed had been turned down, with the heated brick placed at the foot. He stripped and sank into the linens, trying to force his body to release the evening's tension. Ignoring the acrid stench of burnt hair and the dust from inside the walls.

"Could you wake me at three?" he said to whatever scratchling might be listening. He'd need to rise early to see Cassie to the road where Tredan would claim her.

Alrick closed his eyes and slid under the blanket. He felt as if he were still moving—still rushing, and his breath would not slow. He pulled in a deep breath and held it straining inside him, like one trapped in a jar for centuries. *They're all free.*

He sat up and gasped. A cold mouth pressed to his ear again.

"It's three."

CHAPTER FIFTEEN

Alrick spread a shawl over Cassie's shoulders. Tredan said he'd be by at dawn, but the early spring air carried with it a bitter cold, and Cassie shivered uncontrollably. Alrick couldn't stay. He needed to be seen back at the house.

"Will you be okay?" He added his own jacket over the shawl and rubbed her upper arms, which she clutched against her sides. His horse pawed at the ground near where her small trunk lay in the dirt.

"I won't be, if he doesn't come," she said. Alrick knew from the moment he'd fetched her and her trunk from the lab that she didn't like the plan any more than he did. It was too reckless. If Tredan was delayed, she could freeze.

"He'll come," he said. "He'd have sent word ahead if he wasn't."

"To the house? Where there's no one to receive it?"

The chill ached in Alrick's tired joints. "If I don't see the carriage from my window in two hours, I'll ride back and get you. I promise."

She pursed her lips, but he couldn't tell if it was from cold or frustrated disapproval. Likely both.

"And when Tredan is back, I'll feed him the worst thing I can find in the lab," he said.

She didn't smile.

"I'll see you soon, either way." He climbed back up onto his restless horse—its sides still hot from their rush out onto the moor. His face burned like the horse's flanks as he turned away and left her there in the empty road.

Alrick paced the uneven boards of the hall, his exhaustion accentuating the vertigo in such a way that it felt as if the whole house had floated off on rough seas.

Every ten minutes he pulled open the heavy door and stared through the early dawn light to the ribbon of road across the fields.

Anne came and went from the hall, hauling wood and candles and setting the table for breakfast.

Alrick's anxiety grew when he saw the extra setting next to Nelda's.

The two-hour mark was approaching. His thoughts raced. He could claim he was riding out to meet them, in case they'd thrown a wheel. He could pretend he'd received a letter to fetch her in the village.

He ran out to check the road again, but saw nothing save his breath freezing in the air before his face. He cursed Tredan's plan and sent the cloud of breath billowing.

Alrick pulled his notebook from his pocket and tore a page free before running back inside.

Anne scrubbed the floor by the hearth.

"I need to fetch Cassandra in the village. Something came up for Tredan—he'll be delayed." Alrick waved the sheet of paper in the air as Anne glanced his way, then stuffed it in his pocket as if it were a passing note. He dashed out the door before he could be questioned. "I'll be back soon," he called back as he drew the door shut behind him.

He ran across the yard to the stable, where he'd left his horse Loki saddled and ready. Alrick drove the horse at a gallop along the lane. He'd forgotten his gloves, and his white knuckles soon numbed to the chill. He feared Cassie was much colder. Feared he'd find her slumped by the side of the road, succumbing to hypothermia.

His worry grew as he passed the crossroad where he'd left her. An impression of her trunk remained in the dirt, but there was no sign of Cassie.

Alrick rode up and down past the spot he remembered till he found a furrow in the road where something heavy had been dragged.

He gritted his teeth against the anxious rage blooming in his chest and followed the trail over a rise in the road.

His horse reared at the hill's crest, and Cassie scrambled away from its thrashing hooves.

Alrick's frozen fingers failed him and his hands slipped from the reins. He landed with a grunt across Cassie's trunk.

Cassie grabbed Loki's bridle and led him off the road.

Alrick lifted himself carefully, hoping that the sharp pains at his back and side were only superficial. It took him a moment to reclaim the rhythm of his breaths. When he could stand straight again, he looked to Cassie. She was fixing her trunk to the saddle.

"You were going the wrong way. I was worried." He panted past the pain radiating through his chest.

"Was I?" She raised her eyebrows, climbed up into the saddle.

Loki shifted anxiously under an unfamiliar rider. Cassie leaned uncomfortably in the saddle alone, but she turned the horse around to the direction she'd been walking—away from House Aldane.

Alrick took a step after them, and Cassie nudged the horse, hastening his stride.

"Cassie!"

As he followed her over the next rise, she pulled up the reins. Tredan's carriage approached them at last. Alrick took advantage of the distraction and seized the bridle.

He led Loki from the road as the carriage pulled alongside them and stopped.

Tredan emerged, pale and unshaven. "Tie Loki up to the back of the carriage. We should all ride inside. We need to talk."

"Yes, we do," Alrick said. His anger still bloomed, still kept him warm.

Cassie sniffed. She was clearly furious. Alrick didn't blame her, and hoped her rage warmed her as well.

She slid from the saddle, flinching as her slippered feet met the road. She climbed stiffly into the carriage.

"Uncle, where were you?" Alrick asked, hands shaking as he tied Loki's lead rope to the back of the carriage.

Cassie let out a muffled squeal from inside the carriage. Alrick hurried to the door and leaned through.

Sleeping children lined one bench, drenched in fever sweat, rags clinging to their bone-thin limbs.

Alrick's throat tightened. He grasped the blanket that had slid from their laps and covered them. He felt Tredan's hand on his back urging him into the carriage.

"Drive on, straight home," Tredan called up to George before climbing in after them.

"Aemon is waiting for you. Everyone is. How do you expect to sneak them inside?" Alrick could feel Cassie's shoulder trembling against his as they all squeezed onto the bench opposite the children.

"Merry will bring them in from the stables while the rest of us are having breakfast. They'll be too distracted by Cassie to notice."

Alrick turned to Cassie, but she stared resolutely at the carriage curtain as if she could see through it to the damp fields outside. To what might have felt like freedom. *She was riding away.*

He reached for her hand, but she pulled away.

"I'm sorry, Cassie—"

"We have bigger concerns, with Mister Legan," Tredan interrupted.

Alrick wished, for a moment, that he could stop caring about houses and lawyers and lineage. He wanted to mend things with Cassie. But he knew that by caring for the house, he was caring for her, if indirectly.

"What now," he asked.

"Aemon is apparently eager to marry. To produce an heir and write you out of the family altogether. He's been making inquiries in London about eligible ladies of society—and wealth."

Alrick sighed. He wanted this growing, thriving family line—but not under Aemon's dynasty. Still. The house had come alive again. Voices rang in its halls, and not just the whispers of the dead, anymore. If he succeeded in supplanting his brother, the house he'd take would be better than the one his father had left just weeks ago. If only he could let go and give up. Take Cassie and run back to London, or maybe to some small farmhouse where he could run his own clinic.

But what About Nelda? Tredan? And he could never forget the bruises on Merry's face. Or the scratchlings hiding in the house. It wouldn't take Aemon long to discover them and send them away to workhouses and orphanages with the others.

There was duty to consider. And not all of the voices in the Aldane halls were happy. Frightened maids. Cries of anger. And the dead. So many voices out of their bottles.

A draft brushed his cheek. He turned toward it in time to see Cassie turn away.

The road roughened as they neared the house.

"We had some difficulty while you were away. I'm going to need your help. Nelda isn't well."

Tredan frowned. But they were too close to home, now, for a full explanation. Tredan woke the scratchlings, their bleary eyes over-bright with fever, and had them crouch near the carriage floor. Cassie drew her dusty slippers away from them.

They could hear Aemon's voice before the carriage even slowed. He barked orders at the assembled staff as they lined up and awaited the new arrival.

The carriage lurched to a stop and the horses shuddered. Loki stopped behind them, pulling at his rope.

Tredan sprang from the carriage, holding his coat wide to block the view in a gesture of welcome. Cassie followed him, and Alrick slipped out behind them, closing the carriage door on the small figures hidden inside.

Tredan formally presented Cassie to Aemon. She looked thin and pale in her scavenged silks, her cropped hair growing in like golden gorse escaping her bonnet at reckless angles.

Aemon's smile was pinched, but appraising. He appeared genuinely pleased to be welcoming someone, or at least to be performing the ritual of welcoming—to play the role of the lord.

Alrick was surprised to see Nelda at his side. She was upright and seemed no worse off than any other day. She had bright ribbons wrapped around her wrists where her bindings had been, a silk scarf covering the wound at her neck.

Nelda abandoned all decorum and rushed to Cassie, taking her hand. "We are instant sisters," she said, and led Cassie to the door.

Merry caught Alrick's eye as all else turned away to follow Cassie. She raised her eyebrows and glanced at the carriage that was already being led away toward the carriage house, suitcases piled in the dirt in its wake.

Alrick nodded and held up three fingers.

Merry shook her head and her shoulders rose in a sigh that Alrick echoed. How Tredan planned to continue his secret foundling hospital in a house now full to the rafters was beyond his comprehension. Would these children spend their young years hidden under beds and in closets? If he were lord...When...

Alrick followed the group inside.

Cassie was pressed between Nelda and Aemon, her hand draped over Aemon's forearm, and her wounded arm, encased in a muffler, clasped gently to Nelda's chest. They led her around the hall, presenting its features, extolling its virtues. They rose and fell over the sloping floor, pointing and exclaiming like whalers in a spear boat.

Tredan hung back with Alrick. "Couldn't have wished for a warmer welcome," he said, a smile creeping up out of his beard.

"She'll need the warmth, after that cold wait on the road."

"Why were you with her, Alrick? That wasn't part of the plan."

"You were late. I couldn't just let her freeze to death out there. I came back for her."

"I apologize for the delay. My errands took much longer than I anticipated."

"She doesn't want to stay here, you know. When I came back for her, she was walking away. Setting off on her own, instead of returning to the house." Alrick fought to keep the rising anxiety from his voice.

"Well. Perhaps that will change now that she's not having to hide away in a closet."

Nelda helped Cassie into a chair at the breakfast table, and Aemon took his seat.

"I suppose at least she had the closet to herself. What are you going to do with three, Tredan?"

"I don't know, Alrick. I didn't have much choice. But we'd best discuss it later." Tredan strode over to the table and took his seat.

A breeze continued to tickle the side of Alrick's face, nudging his gaze ever closer to the wide hearth that was piled with blazing logs despite the growing warmth of the day. It was for display, Alrick realized. A statement. We have wood to burn.

Everything burns, the breeze hissed against his ear.

He clasped a hand to the side of his face as Nelda's eyes whipped to meet his. The cheerful flush drained from her cheeks and Alrick felt his own pallor cool to match hers. That voice—it was new. A man's voice. Edged with reckless rage. Not his father's deep, warm rumble, but a growl eking out through strained cords.

"Hush!" Nelda shouted to the rafters. "Not now. Haunt us later, if you must." She pulled Cassie's wrapped wrist closer. "You must be starved—up all night on the cold road." There was a smile in her eyes and Alrick wondered if she knew all—if the voices of the house had whispered Cassie's story. Whether she knew or not, she didn't seem to care. She poured Cassie's tea.

"Allow me, Miss," Merry said, hurrying over from the entrance to the kitchens in a sweat, huffing. She took the pot from Nelda and began to pour for the table. Her apron was filthy—the grime of London ground deep into the linen.

Alrick glanced to Aemon, but he hadn't noticed. He was smiling strangely at Cassie, who sat quietly and allowed herself to be waited on.

Alrick took his own seat as a parade of hot breakfast trailed from the kitchen to the table.

Nelda did not eat but spoke endlessly to Cassie, as if all the loneliness of her life sought an instant cure. As if anyone's life—even Nelda's—could be as lonely as Cassie's had been.

Cassie smiled and nibbled demurely at her breakfast, humming sounds of interest at intervals.

Aemon's jaw tightened as the meal wore on, till he finally slammed his cup of tea against the saucer.

"Enough, Nelda! You will talk our guest to death. She's here to rest. You'll exhaust her to her grave. You'll exhaust me to my grave."

Nelda chewed at her lip and glared at Aemon.

Cassie pursed her lips and flushed. For a moment, she almost looked healthy.

The meal continued in silence save for the hiss of whispered voices that brushed Alrick's ear, that made Nelda twitch and cock her head like an owl on the hunt.

Nelda held her tongue till the slow progression of Cassie's birdlike manners cleared her plate, then Nelda pulled her from her seat. "Come—I'll show you your room. There's a gift for you on the bed. I made it myself." They disappeared down the hall to the lady's wing.

Aemon sent Elizabeth after them. "Please see to it that Miss Cassandra is settled comfortably and allowed to rest from her travels. Stand guard at her door if you must."

Elizabeth hurried away as Merry began to clean the table.

"Come, Alrick," Tredan said. "My absence has interrupted your studies. But I did bring you the lenses you requested." He headed for their wing.

Alrick followed. He glanced back to the table. Aemon stood behind the chair where Cassie had been seated. He ran his finger over the rim of her teacup, then brought it to his mouth.

Alrick stumbled as if the floor had tossed him. Hot breakfast surged in his throat, fire behind his teeth.

Tredan's hand clasped down on his arm and pulled him forward. "Come, now."

He dragged him all the way to their parlor. Alrick gripped the back of a chair and shook. "Did you see…"

"Yes."

"Does he…Is he going to…"

"He might."

"But what if he…"

"It's not up to you, Alrick. It has nothing to do with you."

"It does if it happens in my house!"

The fire in the hearth extinguished in a rolling cloud of smoke that blanketed the carpet in soot and singeing embers.

My house, they all seemed to hiss as they stifled in the blackened wool.

Tredan stepped on the smoldering embers, snuffing them under the toe of his shoe. He turned to Alrick, and Alrick saw his own anger reflected there.

"It's not your house until you take it back."

Alrick's heart lurched.

"And even then—that does not give you rule over the people in it. Not the living or the dead."

Tredan stomped up the stairs, his shoes leaving soot prints on the steps.

Alrick sank into a chair. His face cooled. The carpet smoked.

CHAPTER SIXTEEN

There was to be a welcome party for Cassie. A banquet, a dance. Neighboring families assessing her place among them. She protested, of course, but Nelda had taken to the idea with all her relentless passion, determined to "present" Cassandra, and dragged her into the garden to teach her to dance.

The new lenses broadened the range of Alrick's telescope so that he felt he could count the eyelashes on a deer across the overgrown park.

He could count the petals in the rosebuds that Nelda pinned to Cassie's bonnet as they walked the garden. Count the buttons that ran up the back of her dress.

The garden wall was gone, now a pile of broken stones and twisted metal that Aemon was repurposing into a path winding among the plants. Rows upon rows of green spikes poked up from the earth in every shade of green and gold and purple. Some plants had been fitted over with glass boxes, like small greenhouses, engineered to be moved from plant to plant as needed.

At the center of the radiating rows of greenery stood a cluster of headstones. The old family plot. Alrick hadn't known that the older cemetery had been located in Burgrune's garden. The newer plot, where he'd laid his own father, was behind the other wing. In the center of the cemetery below was a robed statue, a mournful figure like a wingless angel, face hidden in folds of delicately carved cloth. The plants around its base grew richer than those elsewhere in the garden. Speckled leaves unfurled where others were still tight spikes guarded against the cold nights of early spring.

Alrick watched as Nelda bent and plucked a bloom from a small plant and placed it on one of the graves. She peeled away the leaf and popped it in her mouth. He shuddered to think what ancient Aldane bones fed those plants that in turn fed his sister.

Alrick pointed his telescope skyward, where the faintest crescent of moon could be seen against the bright blue backdrop of sky. Its face was as scoured and pocked as a scratchling's—as if the stones that beat at the celestial heavens had also rendered those children miserable.

As if summoned, quiet footsteps sounded behind him. Alrick turned to the small girl who set about straightening his bedsheets.

"Would you like to see the moon?"

The girl looked at him but didn't answer. Her pale face was spread with a film of poultice—something Tredan had no doubt invented to help cure the furrows in her flesh that pox had left behind.

"Come, see how beautiful it is."

The girl took a hesitant step toward him, then overcame her fear and skipped over and peered into the eyepiece as he held it steady.

"Where does the rest of it go when the moon is broken?" she whispered.

"It isn't broken," he said. "It's still there, just beyond the light where we can't see it." He smiled. "Hiding in the shadows, in plain sight."

She smiled as if she liked that explanation, then skipped away to her work.

Alrick glanced back to the garden. Cassie and Nelda sat by a squat plant that didn't seem to have survived the winter. Nelda plucked at its leaves and placed them in a handkerchief spread across Cassie's lap.

Alrick sighed and wondered what new demons Nelda intended to unlock with whatever it was she harvested. He hoped Cassie wouldn't be drawn into Nelda's experiments. Hoped she wouldn't be frightened by them.

He turned away from the telescope and made his way to the stairs. He'd fill his pockets with vials of antidote. Carry it with him always, ready to administer a cure at any moment.

The door to Tredan's chambers was locked. A high wailing leaked through the cracks in the boards of the door. It seemed to soak into the plaster walls, and Alrick felt more of it crumbling away beneath his palm as he bent to listen.

It was a child's cry. One of the new scratchlings, no doubt. *Or the ghost of one.* Riding out whatever terrible illness wracked their small body.

There was no other sound inside. Alrick knocked lightly. The sobs continued, unchanged. There was no answer.

Alrick set off down the stairs. Where was Tredan? It wasn't like him to leave his charges wholly neglected. Where was Merry?

He found them, all of them, assembled in the hall, standing in ranks before a seated Aemon, Mister Legan at his elbow. Aemon's lip curled at the sight of Alrick entering the hall. He'd clearly not been invited to this meeting. Neither had Nelda or Cassie, for that matter.

"Pardon my intrusion." Alrick could not keep his irritation entirely out of his tone. "Uncle, may I have your keys? There's something I need to see to in the lab." He had his own key on him, of course, but he needed Tredan to know that something was wrong.

Tredan's face blanched slightly as he fumbled in the pocket of his waistcoat. He handed Alrick the keys without making eye contact.

Alrick took them and hurried from the room, whispering to the tapestries as he passed, "I want to know everything they say."

The tapestries rippled in response.

"I suppose you'll want to know what that was about," Tredan said.

Alrick's hand jumped and the scratchling's eyelids fluttered. He hadn't heard Tredan come in. He'd stopped expecting him almost an hour ago. The scratchling's fever still burned, but at least now he slept. Alrick dabbed the boy's dry lips with a damp cloth.

"It all seemed less important to what was going on in here, to me."

"Thank you," Tredan said. He sat and took the cloth from Alrick. He sniffed at the basin of water. "Good choices. You're an excellent student."

"I couldn't bring the fever down."

"No. Neither can I."

"What's the matter with him?"

"His blood is infected. No matter how much I bleed him, the corruption spreads. I dare not take any more."

Alrick saw the bandage wrapped around the boy's forearm. "What's going to happen to him?"

"I suspect he won't make it through the night. The best we can do is keep him comfortable, so it doesn't hurt."

"He was crying. Sobbing. You just left him here." The heat in Alrick's face flared.

"I have to pretend he isn't here, remember? I can't say I'm busy tending my patient when there isn't supposed to be a patient."

"Patient? Just one? Where are the others?"

Tredan pulled a dark bottle from his pocket and poured a milky honey over the boy's lips.

"Where are they?"

Tredan sighed. "There is another plot on the grounds. One you wouldn't remember, and I doubt your brother does, either. Only servants and animals were buried there. It's well into the trees beyond the carriage house."

Alrick stood and listened to the boy's breathing slow.

"I can't save them all, Alrick. For many, it's too late before I even arrive. That is, perhaps, the hardest lesson I have to teach you."

"What is that in the bottle?" Alrick whispered. He didn't trust his throat to release the voice that felt trapped there.

"An opium mixture. He won't feel any pain. He'll sleep peacefully through it all."

Alrick nodded, though his uncle's eyes were turned to his doomed charge.

"Will you help me?" Tredan asked.

"Of course. What can I do for him?"

"Help me bury him. In the morning, early. Merry has been up with me these last two nights and I dare not ask her again."

"You should have asked me to begin with, Uncle."

"I know. I suppose I wanted to protect you from this part a little longer."

"I'm not a child."

"No, you're not. Which was, incidentally, what part of that meeting was about."

"What do you mean?"

"Aemon has removed you from the line of succession. You are no longer his heir. He says the land and title will pass to his future offspring, or his sister's."

"But there aren't any…"

"He must have plans. More advanced plans than I imagined. Which means we have less time than we thought."

"He's better at this scheming than I am, Uncle. I don't know how to stop him anymore."

"We need your father's will. We need his word that you were his sole heir."

"I've been looking. The scratchlings looked. No one has found anything."

"No, and I don't know that we ever will find it. We can assume it was destroyed."

"Then how do we—"

We need his word. It doesn't have to be written. We have his breath. We have his voice. I just need your sister to ask him—in front of witnesses, at Cassie's party."

"You had his voice. You saw the jars, Uncle. They're smashed. The breath is gone."

"I had it in the jar, yes. The jar was smashed, yes. Now—now, the breath is everywhere."

CHAPTER SEVENTEEN

The woods behind the carriage house were moor woods—trees covered in thorns, rooted in split boulders, twisted by relentless, wailing winds.

In meandering crevasses between sheets of stone was earth soft enough to bury the unfortunate dead. Their names were crudely carved into the stones already present at their places of rest. The landscape itself became their headstone. And where there were no names, the stones simply read "boy" or "girl." All punctuated with spreading lichen.

"Keep going till there's an empty spot in the stone," Tredan instructed. He carried the boy, swaddled in a sheet of bedlinen. Alrick led with the lantern. He ducked thorns and traced shadows over the fading names of the dead for what felt like a mile before the rock appeared smooth at his feet. The ground beside him was already disturbed, freshly turned, with "Michael" and "Ella" carved into a space that had been cleared of lichen.

"Here," Alrick said.

Tredan laid the boy on the ground and pulled a shortened spade from behind his back. He dug a trench in the hollow, deep enough, until it met another shelf of rock below. The earth smelled of ice and limestone, but with a rich, green promise the deeper he dug.

Tredan lowered the boy into the trench, and Alrick caught a glimpse of dirty sheet through the wall of the grave—the adjoining burial. They were so close. At least they'd have each other for company. Alrick covered the boy gently with the dark earth while Tredan set to carving "James" into the rock's surface.

"At least these ones have names," Alrick said.

"They all have names, Alrick. None of them need them anymore."

The response stung.

"You don't know that. Somewhere, some of these children might have a mother. One who presses toxic flowers under her tongue and calls for them. We can still use their names."

"I would never take a child from their mother, Alrick. I only take the orphans."

"You took Cassie."

Tredan paused in his carving. "I suppose that's true. But there was nothing left of her mother, there, really."

"She lost her mother twice." Alrick smoothed the dirt over the grave.

"In any case, we can suppose the scratchlings remember their own names, whether we ever learn them or not. Come. We'd best get back before breakfast."

"Shouldn't we say some words? Lay him to rest?"

"That's superstition, Alrick. If words laid spirits to rest, House Aldane would be a much quieter place."

"I saw the other graves—the old plot in Burgrune's garden," Alrick said. "It seems the Aldane dead are buried everywhere."

Tredan stilled but did not answer.

"Whose graves are those?"

Tredan seemed to consider his answer, then finally whispered. "Those were Aldane babies that died in infancy. Burgrune's children, born after Aemon and Nelda. None of them lived more than a year."

Alrick swallowed against the knot forming in his throat. He hadn't known there were other children, other siblings. "And did they have names? What were they?"

"I'd rather not discuss this now, Alrick." Tredan slung the spade over his shoulder, picked up the lantern, and began to follow the path of graves toward the lawns beyond the trees.

Alrick watched the glow of the lantern recede. "I'll see you back at the house, then, James," he whispered to the dirt.

"Alrick, come," Tredan's voice slithered through the trench of graves.

Alrick followed the light into the thorns. He didn't want to step on the soft burials. Nor did he want to step on the carven names. But he had to walk somewhere, bound to earth as he was.

"I need more ribbons," Nelda insisted as Alrick handed Tredan the list of supplies they needed from London. "Not hair ribbons. Ones for the hall. The chair backs and bannisters and door handles—"

"You'd have the house looking like a doxy's birthday cake," Aemon cut in. "This is meant to be a sensible, sophisticated party."

"You said yourself I'm the lady of the house, Aemon. And it's the lady's duty to plan the parties." Nelda's voice rasped with agitation. She'd been manic for days, making enough plans for a whole season of festivals.

"There are two ladies, now," Aemon said, smiling and raising Cassie's hand to his lips. "Perhaps Cassandra would like to have a say in the plans."

"Oh. I think I still prefer there were no party at all," Cassie said.

"She's a lady's companion," Nelda said, taking Cassie's hand away from Aemon. "You know nothing of parties, do you, darling?"

Cassie shook her head.

"I'm here to help you," Nelda said. "But Tredan, I need ribbons. Fat ones, for rosettes."

"I'll see what I can do, Nelda," Tredan said.

Nelda turned to Alrick. "Can't you go? You always find me ribbons."

"Not this time, Nelda," Alrick said. He waited till Aemon turned his smug smile back to Tredan, then leaned toward Nelda and whispered, "Don't worry; you'll have them."

Nelda smiled, giggled, and squeezed Cassie's hand again.

Alrick swallowed. He needed to keep Nelda happy. He needed her alliance for what he was to ask of her. He hadn't dared to ask yet, but he'd promised Tredan the matter would be settled before he returned from London.

Nelda pulled at Cassie's hand. "Come. There are trunks and trunks of my mother's dresses, and some of your aunt's too. We'll find something to make over for the party that will have every lord in the room courting you."

Aemon's head whipped back around to Nelda. "Modesty, sister. I won't have either of you dressed as trollops."

Nelda cackled. "Cassie, I think he just called his own mother a trollop!" The ladies disappeared down the hall to their wing.

A tapestry crashed to the floor, rod and all. It was the fox hunt scene Aemon had picked to hang behind his seat at the head of the table.

Aemon spun too slowly to see the small shadow dart from behind it to the shadows beneath the table.

The crash set Aemon to barking orders. Tredan slipped out of the door as Alrick backed into the kitchen stairway. He needed supplies. He had cooking to do. New recipes to brew with ingredients from Burgrune's garden.

If it was daylight, Alrick wouldn't have known it. The layer of steam in the lab coated the windows. Condensation clung to the lenses that pressed into the flesh around his eyes. But it must be well past dawn. He'd replaced the candles twice since he'd locked the door. He vaguely remembered ignoring Merry's knock, but didn't know if she'd bade him goodnight or offered him breakfast. It must be dawn at least, because the reduction was complete.

The beaker bubbled slowly with a substance that smelled like honey but looked like tar. He dipped a rod into the goo and dabbed it onto wax paper, making pellets no larger than apple seeds. He spread the dark pills across every table and surface in the lab to let them harden.

Alrick blew out the candles, peeled the goggles from his eyes and the soaked strip of cloth from his mouth and nose, and staggered to the tattered chair by the fire.

He supposed there might still be enough of the drug in the steam to take effect, but he was so tired he thought not even a pill to wake the dead could make him stir.

But in House Aldane, the dead always stir. He slipped into dreams as if he was pulled.

Scarred children filed from the woods in a wavering line a mile long. Their mouths gyrated in silent screams, their voices bursting like gunshot in his mind. A litany of names—too many to count or even remember—more names than even the stars could ever know.

He whispered the names. Called them out. Tried to commit as many as he could to memory.

He felt the splintered wood and rough weave of the chair eating away at the insides of his hands.

"You called, m'lord?" Cold lips blew moon wind into his ear. His face ached with the chill of it and his eyes shot open.

He sat in the center of concentric rings of scratchlings, their fever eyes on him, their names falling from his mouth in a frantic prayer.

He gasped and his eyes focused and the sea of scratchlings blurred and condensed, narrowing into one pale, scarred face before his own.

"Did you call me, m'lord?" the child whispered.

Alrick searched the shadows of the room for the others. There were none. Just this small figure in stained linen.

"What's your name?" he asked.

"Alice, m'lord."

"Are you happy, Alice? Do you like it here?"

She pursed her lips.

"I just want you to know some happiness, Alice. Here, or anywhere."

Alice pulled a small rag doll from the pocket of her shift. "Small Alice is happy," she whispered. She smoothed the doll's tiny smock and wool hair and tucked it back into her pocket.

Alrick felt as if his heart was in his mouth, finally stifling the tide of names that wanted to keep rolling from his throat. He tried to swallow, failed, and felt his chin wet as he spoke. "Please tell me if there's anything Small Alice needs. Whatever she wants that will make her happy."

The girl curtsied, the callouses of her bare feet catching on the rug. "Is that all, m'lord?"

"Yes. Thank you."

Alrick pulled out his handkerchief and mopped at his chin, and at the water pooling in his eyes, and when he looked again, she was gone. A steaming breakfast sat on the table.

There were ribbons tied to the chairs. Bows on the thick links of chain that suspended the chandeliers. Strips of satin trailing from the candlestick holders. The number of candles in the room had doubled—pushed into pools of their own dry wax to keep them from rolling down the slopes of the crooked surfaces. The floor was newly polished, the dust shaken from the tapestries and swept away.

Alrick stared around the room, memory tickling in his throat. The house looked more alive than he'd ever seen it. It had color again, like a face emerging from illness.

He started as Nelda crawled out from under a table clutching a fistful of ribbons. He saw, then, that even the chair legs had been decorated.

Nelda hopped up and ran to him, planted a kiss on his cheek, right on the dry patch that was still healing from her last kiss. "That's for the ribbons, brother."

He smiled. "It looks beautiful, Nelda."

She smiled and spun her ribbons in the air. "Aemon says it looks like a whore's room."

"It has color and life. This was just what it needed."

She giggled and tied a ribbon to his coat button.

"Where's Cassie?"

Her smile slipped. "She went with Aemon. He said he had a gift for her out in the garden." Nelda stared into his face, her expression grown serious.

Alrick's jaw tensed. He knew there was no hope of hiding his feelings from Nelda.

"I do think she likes him, Alrick," she said.

Alrick exhaled slowly, and Nelda pulled him into a hug.

Should he be happy? Cassie deserved happiness, comfort. A scratchling that might do more than just live, beyond mere survival. But would she be happy?

"And what about Aemon?" he asked. "Does he like her? Truly?"

Nelda pulled away and her expression darkened. "I think he's in a hurry."

Alrick felt his pulse catch, and the rosebuds spread across his face. "But would he be good to her?"

"He wouldn't even buy ribbons for her party." She let the tangled clump of satin fall to the floor. Her mood was storming and the whole room cooled, the color of the ribbons faded.

Ribbons or no, Alrick knew the answer.

"Nelda, do you care about her? About me? Our home here, our family?" Desperation roughened his voice.

She stepped close again and pressed her cheek to his. "I always have. More than anyone. That's why they talk to me. They're listening, now."

Ribbons all around the room trembled in a breeze Alrick couldn't feel.

"Nelda, we have to stop him." He felt the muscles of her face shift into a smile. "Will you do something for me? For Cassie—for all of us?"

The ribbons in her hair tickled his face as she nodded.

"It…may ruin the party," he said.

"It's not a real party unless everyone is invited."

"Can you invite him? Bring him forth? Do you think you can find him and use his voice—his breath, here, lost somewhere in the house? Can you speak for him?"

He could feel the pounding of her heart against his arm.

"I'll try, brother."

Alrick lifted his shaking hands and squeezed her narrow shoulders. "Thank you."

He pulled back and looked into her eyes. They were clear, bright—their color as intense as the ribbons.

"Alrick, if you win—if you beat him, what happens to me? Will you 'care for me as befits my station?'"

Alrick smiled. "I'd set no such limits on your care, Nelda. And I don't believe in stations."

"I know. Aemon knows it, too."

"What is Aemon's gift? What is he giving Cassie?"

She pursed her lips. "He's planted a rose laurel." Fury laced her voice.

Alrick frowned, confused. "I don't understand."

"He's put it on the east lawn. He ripped it from Mother's garden, and he's put it by the apiary."

Alrick shook his head.

"Oleander. He'll make honey that will be the death of her."

Nelda's eyes roved, her mind slipping away again. She stooped to retrieve her fallen ribbons. "There's a reason Mother's garden is so far from the bees. And why children always say that mean little girls are as sweet as Oleander honey. Poison." She sped away down the hall, leaving a trail of bright bows in her wake.

Alrick wanted to run to the east lawn, to see Cassie, to see this tree. Instead he ran to his room, his attic, to his telescope.

The tree on the east lawn was no twig of a sapling—it was small, but already budding, promising blooms.

Alrick scanned the yard. There was a rough patch of stirred earth in Burgrune's garden, just behind the robed statue that stood at the center of the infant graves. A bright swath of plants reveled in newfound sunshine. The tree had been relocated. Why hadn't he given her the tree where it had stood? Why move it, especially so near the apiary? Did he intend to poison their honey crop, or was it done in ignorance?

Alrick watched as Nelda crossed the yard to the turned patch of earth where the tree had been. She curled up in the damp dirt and poked holes in the ground, finger-deep, and pulled something from her pocket. It was a small bundle of tied cloth. She opened it, pulled something from it, and dropped it into a hole, before covering it up. Seeds, Alrick presumed. What sort of seeds did Nelda keep in her pockets?

He swiveled his view back to Aemon and Cassie. She was smiling. Alrick stood straight and let his telescope lower.

She seemed happy. But was she safe? Was it any of his business? No. But it was his house, and Aemon was his business. His problem.

He hurried down the stairs to Tredan's door. His uncle had returned from London in the wee hours and had been resting into the early afternoon. Alrick knocked, and Tredan opened the door.

"She said yes. She's going to help us." Alrick pushed past him to the lab, to the tables where the dark pills of his concoction still sat lined along the strips of wax paper.

He put on his gloves, fetched an empty jar and a pair of tweezers, and began to pull the pills from the paper and fill the jar. When he'd collected them all, he sealed the lid and put it in his pocket.

"You won't need all of those. Three, at most. Four would be dangerous. More might be deadly. How many did you make?"

"There are fifty. They're not all for Nelda."

"She may be the only one here with the tolerance for this dose…"

"This ends tomorrow. Aemon needs to leave, and he needs to

hear it from my father. Our father. They all need to hear it—everyone who comes."

"Alrick—"

"Do you have enough antidote?"

"For all that? No, of course not."

"Then we must make it, tonight."

Tredan turned to his cupboard and pulled open a drawer full of stoppered vials. "I suppose we must."

He spun back to Alrick and held out his hand. "Give me those tablets, Alrick. Whatever you have planned, it's madness. It isn't safe."

"Can you make the rest of the antidote tonight, yes or no? We'll need it. Whether we have it or not."

"Give me the tablets, Alrick."

"Tredan, he's going to hurt Cassie. I know it. Nelda knows it. That's why she agreed to help us."

Tredan lowered his hand. His brow furrowed. "What do you mean?"

"He wants to marry her. He gave her one of Burgrune's old Oleander trees. He pulled it right out of the ground and moved it."

Tredan reached a hand into his pocket. It fidgeted behind the fabric. "You're going to need a stronger antidote for that. I'll have it done." He turned to his table and began pulling jars and beakers into service.

CHAPTER EIGHTEEN

Nelda's hands stuck planted in the earth, fingers like roots seeking something. The curls of her hair wove around and through clumps of dirt. Fray lay alongside her, his shaggy black fur caked with mud and dried leaves.

The infant graves were all around them, small stones poking out of the dirt like crooked milk teeth. He knelt and ran his fingers over the names. William. Edward. Alfred. Arthur. Henry. They were all boys' names. Brothers' names. He'd have had so many brothers if they had lived. And among them, the deep scar where the tree had been.

"It was your mother's tree," Alrick said.

Her eyes darted to him, then back to the grey sky. "It was my tree. They took it."

He knelt by her and saw, then, that her pupils had widened again. An over-sweet floral scent hung on the air. A cascade of barbed seeds tumbled from her pocket into the dirt at her side.

Alrick picked one up and pulled at its husk, peeling back the woody skin to the tender, pale kernel inside. His fingertips tingled.

He raised it to his nose and sniffed. His head spun and his throat relaxed into numbness. He placed the kernel on his tongue and the numbness spread. He crushed it between his teeth and an acrid wave slid down his throat and his mind slipped into a fog. The rushing sound of high wind filled his ears, though he could not feel any breeze. It seemed to carry a thousand voices, though he couldn't pluck any words from the mass of it. He wanted to see what Nelda saw, needed to hear what she could hear.

He lay down in the dirt beside Nelda and sunk his fingers into the earth beside hers.

The ground seemed to conduct the wind of voices, concentrating them. He felt a pull on his eyes toward the tall statue of the weeping woman that stood just to their right. It leaned slightly.

Try to stop him if you can, it will only cement his cause, the legacy is set, the line will be secured, there is no place for you here anymore, this house is ours...

"Do you hear it, too?" Alrick struggled to form words. His numb mouth felt like it was not his own. It wanted to speak the wind's words and not his.

"I hear her," Nelda said.

"She's going to try to stop us."

"Yes."

"Is there any hope, then? Any point in trying?" The seed's bitterness crept back up his throat.

Nelda didn't answer.

"Do you remember these babies? The lost ones?" Alrick dug his fingers deeper into the earth. He could hear them, he thought. A faint crying on the wind.

"They weren't lost. They were taken."

"What do you mean?"

Nelda began to sing, a low hum deep in her chest. Then her lips parted. "I have a deadly nightshade, so twisted does it grow. With berries black as midnight and skulls as white as snow." The rest of the rhyme was lost as she pressed another seed between her lips.

Alrick's head spun. The soft cries, the ghostly whispers swirled around him in a vortex. "We can stop her. Tell me what you need."

"I have what I need. I always have."

"I made you pills. More potent than before. We'll all take them. I'll put them in the wine. If you bring him, we'll all see him. Everyone will hear the truth."

"But will they care?"

"What do you mean?"

"The house is well. The lord is well. The line is secure. Why would the living obey the dead? They will hear him. He's here. He'll speak. So will she."

"The line isn't secure yet."

"It is."

"Moving a tree and whispered intentions isn't the same thing as securing a lineage."

"The tree is just a symbol, little brother. Of other growing things. The line is secure."

Alrick curled his earth-bound fingers into fists, compacting the soil against his palms. "But...how?"

Nelda laughed dryly. "You didn't learn that at your fancy school?"

Alrick sat up, ripping his hands from the ground and the clumps of hardened dirt with them. He rushed back toward the house.

Nelda called after him, "Be careful in there. She knows."

The fog in his mind flooded and receded so that he seemed to wake intermittently, each time closer to Nelda's quarters.

He raced past the door with penciled measurements, past brambles of tangled ribbons, dried flowers, and strewn dresses, up the stairs to Cassie's room. He pulled the door open and then suddenly was at her bedside.

The bed was unmade, sheets twisted and tossed. The scratchlings and maids appeared to have abandoned these quarters. Or had been ordered to keep away.

Alrick reached for the pillow, dropping the fistfuls of dirt he still carried, and pulled the pillow forward and saw that the board securing the passage to Aemon's chambers was askew, the dark tunnel behind it cracked open like a black grin. The whispered wind in his mind seemed to pour from it.

He shoved the bedding aside and crawled in. His mind fogged again, and he surfaced to the sight of Aemon's sitting room table, still set for breakfast, for two. Cups with cold dredges of tea, bowls scraped of porridge.

He sank into one of the chairs.

The line is secured. This house is ours.

Fog filled his vision again, then coalesced, solidified, shaped itself into a figure in the other chair. The wind, too, condensed into a single voice. Alrick could feel a gaze emanating from the deep shadows in the face of the form before him. He could feel its smile.

House Aldane is alive and well.

A teacup flew from the table and crashed into his lips. The bone china shattered against his teeth and hot blood flooded his mouth, poured over his tongue, down his throat, and over his chin. The fog advanced and filled his vision, filled his mind.

The line is secure this house is ours get out get out get out…

Alrick could not move his fingers. He peeled his eyes open, but snapped them shut as pain lanced through his brain. He tried to lift his hands to his eyes, but they were stuck fast, aching with immobility. Cold.

He pulled at them and something gave—a crumbling. He pulled again and felt some pressure release. He smelled it, then. Damp earth. His hands came free from the dirt. He shook the grit from his palms, rubbed it from his nails, and brought his hands to his face. He remembered, then, the fog, the teacup. He ran his tongue over his teeth. They were intact. No blood filled his throat. His lips were whole, untattered. Had he ever even gone inside?

He struggled to sit, his head spinning, aching, and slowly opened his eyes.

The sun was low but bore down on him like knives.

Nelda leaned against a nearby tree neatly braiding long flowers and ribbons together. She smiled at him with soft sympathy.

"Did I go inside? Have I been here the whole time?" he asked.

"Yes. Both."

Alrick rubbed his face again. "She hurt me, but I'm not—"

"Stay out of the house as much as you can until tomorrow night." Her eyes flickered toward the lawn. Aemon strode across the grass toward them.

Nelda held up the wreath she'd woven. "Do you think Cassie would wear this tomorrow night?"

Alrick could hardly think. He wanted to attack his brother. He wanted to go inside and get cold water and wash his vision away.

"It's beautiful, Nelda. If she won't wear it, you should," Alrick said.

"Oh, no. I've no use for this. She'll wear it and wear it well."

Aemon had reached them.

"I saw what you did to the hall." His eyes cast blame at both of them.

"It's a very special occasion, isn't it?" Nelda stood and tied the wreath to her belt. "Welcoming Cassie to our family. To our home."

Aemon sighed. "No matter. Merry will set it right."

Nelda's eyes flashed.

"Is Cassie's dress ready?" Aemon asked.

"Why are you asking me if my lady's maid has finished my companion's dress? I should think even you would know the status of her clothing better than I would."

"Forget it. You are less than useless today. Now get out of the dirt and get cleaned up for dinner. We have much still to plan."

Alrick stood, steadied himself, and made to follow Aemon back to the house, but Nelda grabbed his hand and squeezed, the dirt between their fingers scraping his skin. She pulled him closer.

"Go to the woods and gather the little ones. They'll follow you. We'll need them."

"But what about the dirt?"

Nelda laughed. The sound was pain.

The path through the stones was somber, even in daylight. The sun cast the rows of carved names into dark relief. The words seemed like they were in a different season from the rock in which they were set. Earth had sunken in around its delicate charges and left the ground uneven in a tactile way that reminded Alrick with every step of what lay below.

He climbed up onto a broad stone that sloped above the grave trench and looked down at the subterranean river of bodies.

"I'm sorry," he whispered to the still air. "You're far from home. This wasn't the better, safer place it was meant to be."

The sun dipped behind the trees toward the horizon. The blue of the sky deepened.

"I do want to make it a better place. A safer place."

The wind echoed in his ears again, a rush he didn't feel against his skin or in his hair.

"Will you help me?"

He could almost feel the wind against the wetness of his lips.

"I can't save you. But there are so many others."

If the wind he heard had been real, it would have been a gale that dashed him from the rock and pinned him to the dirt.

Alrick tried to listen. He followed the traces of fog still clouding his thoughts, and the voices he heard in the breath behind the wind. There was rage, there. And pain. Confusion—a searching for home, for mother, for a drink of water.

"I want this home for us. This can be your home. Our home. You are welcome here."

He made a promise, unspoken, of protection, of guardianship, of belonging. He felt the wind commit. Concede. He knew the scratchlings would come when he needed them. When he called. He did not know if he could protect them from Burgrune.

He would protect them, or he would join them.

The full jar of black pills was an anchor in Alrick's pocket. The other pocket was weighed down with several dozen small vials of Tredan's new antidote. In both pockets, there was dirt. There was dirt in his hair and shoes, and under his nails. It was as if the soft patch of turned earth in the garden had swallowed him, as if it were a grave, and he another lost son of House Aldane. *Not lost. Taken. Black berries.* The patch of dirt beneath the tree had been just the size to fit both him and Nelda, as if it were meant for the both of them. Perhaps that would be where they would rest, if it all went wrong. It would make sense to rest in the old family plot, where the ground was already soft.

CHAPTER NINETEEN

A train of guests filed through the door, dressed in fine clothes—stiff jackets and flowing gowns, rich with embroidery, satin slippers, and beaver-pelt hats.

Alrick didn't remember them from his childhood. They regarded him quickly enough, then turned away. Whether they didn't recognize him or were stricken with the awkwardness of his fallen station, he didn't know. But they clearly didn't think him important enough to approach.

"Is this what it was always like for you?" Alrick asked Tredan.

"Not always. Once word about my research got out, though, it was worse. And better. People were either fascinated or horrified. I found I didn't care for either kind of attention. I'd stay up in my lab at parties. I prefer it even now."

Alrick smiled. "Tonight, this is the lab."

"Be careful, Alrick."

"Careful won't win this."

"But is winning worth the cost?"

"What cost?"

"War. Will you still have a brother, when all this is over?"

"Do I have one, now?"

"You might, in time. With patience and healing. All healing takes time. No medicine is instant."

Alrick remembered Merry's warning—that, in the end, he'd have to control his own fate. Pull his own strings.

Alrick sighed. "Time also corrupts. Infects. Wastes away."

"Do you think your father and I never quarreled? Take care to not break things past the point of mending them."

"This is more than a quarrel, Uncle. This would never have ended well."

Tredan hung his head. "If that's how you truly feel, Alrick, then you are right."

"Speaking of time..." Alrick slipped a hand in his pocket. "It's time for me to see Merry."

He made his way through the crowd to the kitchen stairs, past a frazzled Shepherdson, and down into the heart of the house.

Merry, Anne, and Martha were in a frenzy, finishing courses, preparing dishes, arranging temptations on broad trays. Mister Skillson stood in the corner barking orders.

Alrick approached him. He cut his tirade short but couldn't hide his sneer of irritation. "What can I do for you Master Alrick?"

"The hall is overheated and it's causing the candles to burn too quickly. They already need switching, and the windows need to be opened."

"Right away, sir." He headed upstairs.

Alrick pulled the bottle of pills from his pocket. He laid a line of pills on the workbench and crushed them with the flat edge of a knife till they were a fine purple powder. He pressed his fingertip to the pile and sprinkled it over the cheese on the tray. Over the slices of dark bread. He dropped a fine fall of powder into each pitcher of wine that lined the long table, ready to be taken up and poured.

"Alrick?" Merry bustled over, her face red and slicked with sweat and flour that had blended into a dough-like mask.

"Is there anything else I can help with, Merry? I feel awkward out there."

Merry cooed and gave him a half hug. "I can't let you be seen serving, love. But thank you."

Alrick hugged her back. "That's a silly rule," he said.

"My aching back agrees with that, m'lord." She laughed and returned to the frenzy at the stove.

Alrick returned to the hall. He didn't know how many guests Aemon had invited, but it didn't appear that many more would fit. Even at its heyday, House Aldane was a smaller hall. Because it was older. More ancient. Exclusivity of age and of space. It had been a distinguished honor to have a seat in the hall—his father had said that the Aldanes had only made room for the best.

But Aemon had invited everyone, and the honor had become an inconvenience. Once all were seated at the long tables, dinner would be an intimate affair. They'd almost have to eat with their elbows linked. If they even made it to dinner at all.

Aemon circled the crowd, chatting with lords and landowners. Building his empire.

The clocks had all spun to different hours, one marking six, another eleven, some at odd intervals. Intermittently, one would chime, and a few confused heads would turn and then drift back to whatever scintillating conversation held them.

Is this even really what I want? To preside over a room of wealthy gossips? If the room were mine, they would not be here.

Another clock chimed. Whatever the hour, Cassie must be due to join them soon. And Nelda.

Elizabeth and Susan soon appeared with trays, Shepherdson with pitchers of wine. They began circling, serving. Hands reached, grasped, darted to mouths. Glasses lifted, throats worked, swallowing down.

Alrick watched and waited.

Aemon stepped to the head of the room and gestured for attention.

The room hushed. Eyes that were beginning to blink and squeeze turned to him.

"Welcome, friends and neighbors, to the reopening of House Aldane."

A hushed ripple of happy murmurs and a few claps resonated through the room.

"It is good to see you all here for what I hope is the first of many times."

A few raised their glasses and drank deeply.

"As part of our celebration of the continued prosperity of my house, I would like to invite you to welcome the newest member of our household—a cousin of my dear half-brother, Alrick."

Alrick forced a smile toward the sudden flash of eyes his way.

"And my bride-to-be—"

There was a collective gasp and exclamation. Alrick felt his throat tighten. He'd suspected—knew, even—but hearing it aloud was fresh torture.

"Cassandra."

Alrick placed a black pill on his tongue. It melted and spilled its medicine around his teeth. It helped to numb the heat rising in his face. The thumping of his heart echoed in his ears.

The crowd had already begun to sway as Cassie stepped from the shadowed corridor of her wing. *Her wing. The Lady's wing.*

Nelda stayed in the shadows behind her.

All eyes in the room fixated on Cassie except for Aemon's. He glared at Alrick.

Alrick held his gaze through the sensation of his stretching pupils. The light in the room blurred and doubled, and everything radiated, as if every face in the room was a lantern.

Cassie wore a blue lace dress that swept to the floor in tiers of crisp filigree. The trailing lace of the cuffs hid her missing hand. Her carefully sculpted smile did not hide the tension in her face. The wreath of flowers Nelda had woven while Alrick lay in the dirt dreaming of Burgrune's revenge lay delicately atop her curls.

Nelda stepped up beside Cassie and clasped her arm as the crowd made a display of their welcome, cheering and toasting the new Lady Aldane.

Where Nelda had stood in the hall, a shadow remained.

Some of the crowd gave up on standing and had sank, kneeling, to the floor. Some swayed where they stood. Aemon clasped the sides of his face and groaned.

Cassie's brow furrowed in concern and confusion as Nelda led her into the wilting party.

Cassie and Nelda each took a cup of wine from the footman.

The shadow figure in the hall moved closer, or grew larger, Alrick couldn't tell which.

Cassie hurried to Aemon's side. He clutched at his face. More guests sank to the floor. Wind pulled at them and their fine clothes, causing the feathers in the ladies' hair to dance.

The dark figure stepped from the corridor into the glow of candlelight, but remained a shadow, the only thing in the room unlit by the strange, pervasive light that filled Alrick's vision.

Nelda appeared at Alrick's side. Her hand fished in his pocket and lifted the burden of the bottle of pills. Her hand flashed to her mouth, then again, and a third time.

Nelda's eyes became as black as the figure who faced them.

She pressed her fingers to Alrick's lips and bitterness flooded his mouth. Light filled the room, flowing from every candle, luminescent, as if snaking in between the bricks of the hall itself.

Liquid light illuminated the features of the figure in the hall. A broad, pale forehead, dark eyes, a full mouth stretched in a dark smile. Long hair curled away from the face. Alrick felt Nelda tremble beside him.

The hall quieted. All guests turned to the figure that drifted into the room.

Alrick scanned the crowd for Cassie. She stood by Aemon, her face buried in his neck, hand clenched at his chest. She'd abandoned her cup of wine, and Alrick felt a wave of relief rush through the fear and adrenaline that overwhelmed his thoughts.

Aemon's face froze in a rictus smile, his forehead creased in concern.

Nelda moved toward the figure. The guests stared at the two women, uncannily matched, who towered over the kneeling mass.

"Lade Aldane," one murmured, and the whisper spread. They remembered her. They knew her face.

"Children," the figure said. The wind increased. Candles guttered and extinguished, leaving only the light that seeped from the faces of the crowd, from the walls. The figure a shadow, even in the dark, but its outline began to waver. To fade.

The sound of retching filled the darkness, and the smell of wine and bile choked Alrick.

Bitter cold brushed his side—a passing scratchling.

Aemon wailed. "Tredan! Uncle, our guests are ill. See to their needs."

Nelda's cold lips pressed to Alrick's ear as her hand slipped into his other pocket. "These men have drunk too greedily. They've taken too much and are losing it all." She pressed a vial of antidote into his hands.

"Is it too late?" Alrick asked. "Can you call him? Can he speak?"

"Not now. They won't hear, not with the drug spilling out of them, all over the floor."

Alrick felt his hope sinking, as the wine bled into the flagstones.

"She used so much of herself to be seen, here. Her energy. She'll be weaker, now, for a while. She used nearly all the strength of the whole house for this trick."

"Trick?"

"They all saw her. Recognized her," Nelda said.

"Her ghost."

"Most of these men don't believe in ghosts, Alrick. They saw Burgrune."

"But they won't think—"

"They might. They'll question. They'll wonder where she's been all this time."

"She's been underground. In her grave." Alrick fought to keep his own throat from spilling the medicine, and everything else in his stomach, onto the floor.

"Are you ready to prove it, Brother?"

"Alrick, help me!" Tredan called from the darkness.

Alrick lifted the antidote to his lips to drink, but Nelda pushed his hand down. "Save it for these fools. You may need to see in the dark a little longer. Not even a match will strike, now."

Alrick nodded and saw Nelda smile, dark-on-dark, so much like her mother's.

He waded into the sea of groaning guests to help.

House Aldane had not been built to house guests. Lords and ladies too ill to complain of the indignity were laid out on bed rolls in the hall and parlors. A few of the least indulgent of them were quickly set to right with Tredan's medicine and left in silence, but clearly brooding over the sight of the long-dead Lady Aldane. Not the new Lady Aldane, as Aemon had hoped.

Alrick felt a small but shameful relief that the announcement had been overshadowed.

He sat on a parlor rug, spooning water into the mouth of a sleeping lord whose name he had already forgotten.

I'm not fit for heraldry, anyway.

"But you are well suited to the healing arts," Tredan said, joining him, "though it would be better if you had not made them ill in the first place."

"Uncle?"

"You write your thoughts across your face, Alrick." He moved to tend to his own patient in one of the chairs in front of the hearth. The fire would not light.

"They think they really saw her," Alrick said.

"Of course. Wouldn't you, if you didn't know otherwise?"

Alrick sighed. "What will they think, then? About father? My mother? What will they think of me?"

"I imagine, Alrick, that they will think your father a philanderer. They loved your mother, so will perhaps assume she couldn't have known that her husband might still have had a living wife. Whether or not they do blame her, though, they will consider you a bastard."

Alrick's hand shook and the water in the spoon dripped into the anonymous lord's beard.

"I'm sure that was her intent. Her plan. To eliminate any claim you might produce," Tredan said.

"I don't know how I can prove otherwise, when they've the evidence of their own eyes. Would they ever trust my father's voice, then, even if I could summon it?"

"If we could prove that there are spirits walking here, we may convince some of them. We could introduce the idea that Aemon might have hired an actress. I could say it was a hallucination caused by bad wine—a mass illness. Perhaps a contamination of ergot. Common and innocent enough."

"And all of them happening to have the same hallucination?"

"I could say we have a maid who resembles her. Don't give up hope, Alrick. This plan didn't work. But we can cast doubt on this new shadow."

Nelda slipped into the chair behind Alrick's shoulder. "You could show them her body."

Alrick spun to her. She hadn't taken any cure for herself and was clearly still riding the effects of Alrick's over-potent pills.

Tredan paused in his work to stare at her from where he sat on the floor. "We already have an angry spirit on our hands. I don't think disturbing her grave is a good idea. It might serve to make her stronger."

"She'll be weaker for a few days. She won't be able to stop us. I can't even hear her, now. It's almost like she's gone. I can breathe."

"There are other ways to cast doubt at this charade without desecrating the family grounds."

"You don't need doubt, you need proof," Nelda said. "Else Alrick is a bastard and Aemon will send him away. The county would soon forget that there ever was a second son of Aldane."

"And your family will prosper," Alrick said.

Nelda's eyelids constricted across the yellow sclera and wide pupils. "I'm trying to help you."

"How do we know that spectacle wasn't your doing?" Tredan stood. "That you didn't call her forth and lend her your own strength, and bring all this about? You were meant to call Drummond. You took enough of that poison to kill a man, overdosed the whole room. How do we know that that specter didn't come from you?"

"None of this comes *from* me, Uncle. It comes *through* me. I have less control than you might think."

"If it doesn't come from you, then where does it come from?" Alrick asked.

"From the garden," Nelda said. "My mother's garden." She smiled. Her teeth were the color of blood. "Why give them only doubts when you can give them knowledge?"

They'd sent the last of their guests home by the following evening, some into the hands of caring butlers with vials of Tredan's concoctions in their pockets. All of them as good as telegrams for spreading rumors throughout the county.

Aemon was already drawing plans for a new hall—a new wing large enough to host guests more fashionably, more suited to a modern lord.

Alrick hadn't seen Nelda since Tredan had accused her. She and Cassie remained secluded in the lady's wing, Merry delivering their meals at the chime of a small brass bell that hung on the kitchen wall. Fray sat outside the parlor door, growling the announcement of anyone who approached.

Alrick and Tredan kept to their own quarters, replenishing their store of medicines.

"We're going to need to return to London again already. This event has set my supplies back a month."

"I understand, Uncle."

"I think you should come with me."

"You don't want to leave me here alone with them?"

"Precisely. This has all gotten well out of hand, Alrick."

"If I'm not safe here, neither is Cassie. I can't leave her here."

"Alrick, she's with Aemon now. She's chosen her side in this."

"The winning side?"

"The dangerous side, Alrick. Though your reckless plan that poisoned half the nobility in the county has given them a good run for that title."

"Nelda was helping us, remember. I won't go if Cassie doesn't. That's settled. We could say that family has written and requested her to visit."

"She won't go, Alrick. She won't want to."

"We could say her sister is dying of the fever that almost claimed her. She'd have to go. If she refused, it would be suspicious. She won't want Aemon doubting her story. Our story. If he knew where she really came from, he'd send her to a workhouse. If he didn't kill her outright in a rage."

"Threats and blackmail. Yes, that would probably work, if that's how you want it to."

"I'm trying to protect her, Uncle. She doesn't know what he's like!"

"She doesn't know what's best for herself? And you do? Do you really know Aemon better than she does?"

Alrick's hands shook too much to measure the fine powder he was working with and it sprinkled down the front of his waistcoat.

"I'll posit she knows him better than you do, Alrick. And she chose him. Now go clean yourself up before that eats through the wool to your skin. And pack your trunk. We'll leave in the morning."

"You'll have to go without me, Uncle." Alrick stepped into the stairway and climbed.

"Suit yourself," the answer followed him up the stairs.

Alrick clutched an ewer of tea to his chest. His room was cold without the fires of Tredan's lab below. He should be sleeping. He wanted to sleep. But shouting in the hall kept him awake. Nelda and Aemon, back and forth.

He stirred from his seat and set off downstairs, down the dark twisting corridor now as familiar as a song. The shouting condensed into words as he grew closer.

"How long do you think, then, before they start to wonder if you knew all along? How could you not have known? This rumor will take you down with it unless you put it to rest!" Nelda's voice was clearer than Alrick had ever heard it. It held a richness and tone of its own, as if she finally spoke for herself and not for the ghosts in her throat.

"They'll believe what I tell them to believe," Aemon said. A lilt of joy tinged his shout. He was enjoying the fight.

Alrick hung back in the shadow of the corridor, certain Nelda would have sensed his approach, but she didn't acknowledge him. Perhaps she was too distracted by the argument.

"You're too young in that seat to begin lying now. You've built no trust to fall back on. Call the illusion a sign from God if you want, but name it an illusion!"

"What would your plan prove, anyway? Dig up a grave and find a body. Sure, there's a marker with her name, but it won't have her face. The house is seven hundred years old. There are probably a hundred Aldanes in that earth."

"Half those lords were here for her interment. Remember them?

They'll remember her. They remember you—what you did to Alrick. What you did to all of them."

"What *we* did."

"I was only a child."

"You knew."

There was a sharp retort of flesh on flesh. Then silence. Alrick was ready to spring forward, to defend Nelda if he must, but it was Aemon's voice that came in a low growl.

"You'll regret that."

Alrick felt the air pressure shift and his ears popped. It felt as if he were being dragged into the hall. He grappled for purchase, pressing himself against the crumbling plaster of the wall.

"It's time you stopped underestimating me, brother. I'm not a child anymore. I'm my mother's daughter." Nelda's voice emanated from the stones themselves.

The pressure built unbearably. Alrick's ears rang, popped again, flipping his balance, spilling him to the floor. He felt as if he had fallen to the ceiling and clung to the floorboards as if he might plummet in any direction. The house spun.

"Merry!" Nelda shouted. "Please come. My lord brother is unwell."

Her words traveled through the halls like a song and the whole house awoke as if from a spell. Nelda turned to the shadows where Alrick lay and stared through the darkness straight into his eyes.

"You'd best wake the lab, Alrick. It's time to see what you've learned."

Aemon's tall frame collapsed into a heap at Nelda's feet. Aemon and Alrick, both with faces pressed to the floor, glared at one another through the deepening shadows before their eyelids slid shut.

CHAPTER TWENTY

I t was the smell that woke him, or the pain in his head, or the jolt of the carriage wheels on cobbled streets. All three combined into a wakeful klaxon that pulled Alrick from oblivion into nightmare.

He was in the city. He knew it from the way the air clung to his throat. But it wasn't London. He coughed and regretted it, the sound cutting through his head in a bolt of agony.

"He's awake. Speed it up."

The man's voice was low and unfamiliar, its tone unsure of its command. The carriage jolted forward and the hammer-blows of the rough street stones knocked Alrick's head into the carriage wall. He tried to raise his hands to cushion the blow, but they were stuck fast, bound tight behind him, his fingers burning with the needle pricks of lost circulation. He twisted his wrists and felt unforgiving iron.

Alrick peeled his eyes open, flinching at the light. The man who'd spoken sat across from him, his suit dusty, his legs bent as far from Alrick's as they could get, heels practically climbing up to the threadbare cushion on the peeling wooden seat. This was not an Aldane carriage, and the man was not a family acquaintance.

"Stay calm now, lad. Almost home."

"But we're in the city," Alrick croaked. His throat grated, raw.

"That's right."

"Who are you?" Alrick shifted in his seat to release some of the pressure against his hands. Bilious panic rose in his throat.

The man inched farther away—as far as he could, pressed against the door so that its hinges strained against the latch. "No one of consequence. Just a hired man." He leaned his head out the window. "Faster, Jerry!"

But instead of speeding up, the carriage stopped with a jolt that sent Alrick tumbling into the man's lap.

"We're here," a voice called from above.

"Who hired you?" Alrick asked as the man flailed and shoved him back onto the opposite bench. He didn't answer. Instead, he popped the carriage door open and dove out into the street.

A large man, who must be Jerry, the driver, appeared in the open door.

"Can you walk, lad?" he asked.

Alrick tested his knees, head spinning as he stood. He leaned into the wall to help him upright, then a strong hand gripped his upper arm.

"Come along, then."

Alrick was dragged from the carriage, and even the fog-filtered green light of the city felt like daggers to his eyes. Still, he arced his gaze upward to the brick façade that towered overhead.

A tall gate bared its bars at him like clenched teeth. The man who had shared his carriage stood at those bars and pulled a cord that dangled there.

Confusion, exhaustion, and pain overwhelmed Alrick's curiosity, and he let the man gripping his arm take a little more of his weight.

Alrick's back snapped straight when the rusted hinges of the gate screamed open. He was dragged forward, off the edge of rough cobbles and onto a muddy path threaded with dry weeds, through the mouth of the Crumpsall Workhouse.

Worn stones formed the unsteady foundation of a courtyard around which a U of narrow-windowed walls embraced the empty space. Threads of smoke unwound from spindle chimneys and hung low over the rooftop in a storm of its own making.

Alrick smelled the hall before the door was opened. Smoke and phlegm, fever and putrefaction. Bodies in distress. A smell that had grown familiar, but no less distressing than his first encounter with it.

The porter who had opened the gate—an older boy with a shaved head and a limp, hurried past them to the central door of the building, a passageway that seemed too small for the façade that surrounded it. The boards stuck as he pulled, grating splinters against the ground, and Alrick was pushed inside ahead of his hired captors.

He did not ask them again who had hired them. It was clear in their manor and destination that Aemon had made true on his threat.

Rage and despair welled in him. He thought of Merry and her bruises, of the new staff trembling at Aemon's drunken outbursts, of Tredan's recklessness with Nelda. Of Nelda. A bitter taste rose in the back of his throat. She'd given him an extra pill, talked him out of taking any remedy. Had she drugged him on purpose? He tried to raise a hand to his pounding head, forgetting the shackles. *Cassie. I need to get home to Cassie.*

"Well, let's get those off you." A short, round woman in a black dress appeared from a dark doorway off the entrance hall. She snapped her fingers at the man who held Alrick's arm.

"Beg pardon, Matron, but the family says this one's prone to violence."

The woman planted her hands on her hips and raked her eyes over Alrick. Her eyes were small and buried beneath white brows, but they glittered with shrewdness. "No, he isn't."

"You know him?"

"No. But I know a thousand-thousand boys, and I can tell." She snapped her fingers again and the man pulled a key from his pocket.

"We're to hand him over to the Guardian," the smaller man said. He pulled a paper from his vest. "Need a signature for proof of delivery. Then we'll be on our way."

"He's giving prayers right now. Let me get this boy in uniform so he doesn't miss breakfast, then the Guardian will see you." She plucked the key from the man's hand and pulled Alrick's arm loose from his grip. She twisted the key in the lock and let the shackles fall to the ground, leaving them there for the men to pick up.

"Come along," she said. "We'll get you checked in and fed."

Alrick followed the woman through the doorway from where she'd appeared. He rolled his shoulders, stretched his arms, rubbed his wrists. He had never been restrained before. He hoped he never would be again.

Through a labyrinth of passageways, they emerged in a laundry room humid with steaming wash tubs. The woman stopped him by a rack of hanging linens. She ran her hands over the fabric of his jacket.

"Normally the clothes you come in go to scrap, but these are finer things. Poor lad. Where have you come from, and what have you come to? Long way to fall."

Alrick could tell he was not meant to answer. He didn't have it in him to answer, anyway. The only question that mattered to him was how he was going to get out.

The woman's short fingers made quick work of his buttons, then he was pushed behind a hanging sheet.

"Everything off, and toss it all to me. I'll set it aside for you in a box in storage, should you ever need it again."

Should he? He would. He must.

He threw his clothes over the hanging sheet, and a parcel of clothing sailed back over, landing right at his feet. They were roughly spun, but soft from over-washing, with loosely stitched patches on the knees. At least they were clean. He pulled them on and shivered at the promise of future cold.

"You can put your own shoes back on, and be glad of them," she said. "We've no extras to spare."

He was glad of them. And ashamed of how seldom he'd thought to be glad of them before.

The matron looked him over when he emerged, clucking her tongue at the length of ankle showing between the hem of the trousers and the tops of Alrick's shoes.

"So, you're fourteen, then, lad?"

"Actually, I'm sev—"

She moved forward and pressed three fingers to Alrick's lips. Her hand was rough, calloused, and smelled of lye. "Fourteen is such a rough age. No longer a child. Not yet a man." She gave him a pointed look before withdrawing her hand.

Alrick nodded, the scent of lye lingering on his lips.

She led him outside, then, to a side yard piled with refuse, and had him sit on a broken stool that tipped unless he balanced it with his foot.

"I'm sorry for this, love. But it must be done," she said, pulling scissors and a razor from her apron pocket. "You're not crawling now, but you will be, and this will make it easier."

Alrick watched his hair fall, the small strands clinging to the dampness on his face. There was no breeze to carry the mess away, so when he stood, it was in a ring of himself.

"Birds will be happy with that," the matron said, and pulled him to his feet, brushing shorn hair from his back and shoulders.

Alrick felt numb as the matron shuffled him back inside, through the maze of rooms, and pushed him through the door of a long, narrow room lined with cots, the floor strewn with filthy straw. A chipped, overflowing chamber pot leaked in the corner.

"Wash up there in the basin, then come back downstairs for breakfast. The hall is just off the entry where you came in." She disappeared in a swirl of black skirt.

The basin was to his left—a pottery bowl that had once been white, an inch of grey water swirling with debris at the bottom. The pitcher on the shelf below was empty. Alrick turned away and hurried from the room.

He'd give anything for a pitcher full of tea. Warm. Washing himself in bergamot.

Perhaps there will be tea at breakfast.

He wasn't hungry. Panic had turned his stomach sour, and the smell of the dormitory had turned his stomach even more. It was so like, and yet so unlike the dormitory he'd slept in at school. A dark twin—a shadow version of his past.

Dim light from a barred window lit the hallway, casting striped shadows at Alrick's feet.

Alrick pressed his face close to the glass, peering through the layer of grime at the rows of brick buildings. A bell rang somewhere, and the grounds came alive with the movement of hundreds of figures. Lines of scrawny men trailed from the chapel doors, passing under the steeple's shadow, to other narrow structures, while nurses pushed wheeled baskets of infants through filthy courtyards.

A cacophony filtered up the stairs as an army of boys returned to the lonely building.

Alrick hunched his shoulders and made his way down the staircase, following the noise to a large room set with six long tables surrounded with benches that filled with boys of all ages, all in the same worn brown suits, all with shorn heads.

Scratchlings. All of them—him included. And he realized with a gasp that some of them might even have come from House Aldane; that this was where Aemon had banished them. He didn't know if, or how, he would recognize them. But they might recognize him. He stared out over the crowd and saw round, hollow eyes stare back. They were all the same here. All ghosts.

Alrick let his hunched shoulders relax as he saw he was not the tallest boy there. He would not stand out. He didn't know if Manchester boys grew taller than their southern counterparts, but he suspected the matron had a habit of saving young men from the hard labor expected of the adult inmates.

Alrick sat at the end of the bench closest to the door. The boys paid no mind to him, the stranger among them. He realized it was likely common for new faces to come and go. Appear and disappear.

Tables were dismissed one by one to the front of the room where an old woman in a white apron and cap ladled lumpy porridge into bowls and handed each child a cup of watery milk.

No tea, then.

Alrick blushed at his disappointment. Had he become so spoiled that he'd expected tea at the poorhouse? His face glowed with shame.

Rosebud.

He shook his head clear and stared at his food while the others ate quickly and silently around him.

He didn't want it.

But it was all he had. All any of them had.

He ate. And he planned. He would get out of here. And this time, he knew, he would not be leaving anyone behind.

CHAPTER TWENTY-ONE

A mound of rough rope lay at the end of the long table. Children lined the benches along the table length, heads and shoulders bent over piles of bristling fibers. Small, reddened fingers plucked at the coils of rope, leaving piles like rodent nests that were swept into sacks and hauled away.

A place appeared for him on the bench as small bodies shifted without pausing in their work.

Alrick sat and laid his hands upon the rope, its fibers rough and dry as nettle.

In silence, they picked and plucked, and there, with all the others, Alrick unraveled.

By evening, blisters wept from his stiff fingers. He stared at the bowl of dirty water in the dormitory and dreamed of Tredan's jars of salves and rolls of clean bandage.

The others suffered similarly, and Alrick wondered if the task grew easier with time—and if anyone lasted here long enough for that time to pass.

If he was going to escape—if they were all going to escape—he would have to act before the workhouse sapped his strength.

The boys had set places among the beds in the room, not through official assignment, but through some invisible agreement. There was no bed for Alrick, nor for half the boys assigned to the room. Still, they piled two or three to each narrow cot, the remainders clustered on the floor.

Alrick's mind wandered back to the crowded hospital rooms, how his heart had ached as he peered through narrow barred windows at the suffering inside. These boys' bodies were piled like the corpses he'd seen in the morgue. But the corpses, at least, had had sheets.

This was, Alrick knew, an un-survivable place.

He did not lie down on the floor with the other children. He left the dormitory and crept down the stairs to the entryway.

A dim glow flickered from the rooms where the matron had been. Everywhere else was dark. Alrick used that glow to inspect the door. A thick bolt had been drawn across it. He ran his sore fingers over the metal rod, felt the roughness of it—knew it would be loud if he were to draw it open—a scraping creak that would pull figures from the shadows.

This bolt was his first obstacle. There would be more, he knew, beyond the door.

"Come, lad. You have a visitor." The matron gripped Alrick's shoulder.

Waking hurt. The ache in his back and arms, the sting in his hands. Sleep had been a welcome freedom, and now the squeezing grip at his shoulder came again.

"Up, now. He's in a hurry, best not keep him waiting."

Alrick pressed his palm against the filthy floor and pushed himself up, arm shaking with fatigue. It took another minute before he could stand, his floor-stiffened body slow to uncurl from the fetal position he had slept in, tucked in a corner as far from the other coughing inmates as he could get.

He stumbled down the hall, descended the narrow stairs, and followed the matron to a small office. A narrow wooden desk and three chairs filled the space. Tredan sat in one of the chairs.

Alrick nearly wept with relief, his legs giving way just as he reached the chair beside his uncle's. Tredan reached for him as he collapsed into the seat.

"Alrick, I need you to listen to me," Tredan said, gripping Alrick's knee. "I can't stay long. And I can't take you with me."

Alrick's relief melted into rage. "What do you mean?"

"Aemon can't know I've been here. And these are his people, Alrick. They don't know me here like they do in London. I can't just take you away with me. But you must listen." He pushed a soft parcel into Alrick's lap. It was a blanket, rolled up and tied with Nelda's ribbons. "This was all they let me bring you. I need you to find a way out. Get out and get home. And hurry. I have to get to Nelda. They've taken her to the asylum. I will get her out, and then I must get back to Aemon. He isn't well. Whatever she did to him, before he sent you both away, is slowly killing him, and I need both of you home to help me."

Alrick's heart felt as cold and hard as the dormitory floor. "To help you what, Uncle?"

Tredan sighed and raised one hand as if to silence Alrick. But Alrick had nothing more to say. "To help me save your brother."

Alrick stood, legs steadied by anger, and tucked the blanket under his arm. It was the softest thing he'd touched in the three days since he'd woken in the carriage. It took all of his self-control not to bury his face in the fabric and weep.

"Get to Nelda," Alrick said. "Get her safe. I'll be there soon. But not for Aemon."

He heard the heavy workhouse door swing shut behind him as he climbed the stairs, heard the shriek of the metal lock slide into place.

Tredan hadn't even brought him a salve. Alrick would trade a hundred blankets for the greasy mint-willow medicine for his blistered hands. *Grease.* The other boys had rubbed the fat from their sinewed stew meat on their wounds. The sharp squeak of the metal lock still rang in Alrick's ears. It needed grease.

Alrick hesitated before spreading his soft blanket on the filthy dormitory floor. What would Merry say? She'd have wept. Not for the blanket, but for him. There was no sense in trying to preserve anything here.

The blanket offered a thin shield against the cold, the hardness, the putrefaction around him. The scent of Aldane air was still trapped in its fibers and Alrick breathed it in. He lowered his face to the fabric and inhaled deeply. Another scent tickled his memory. Clean linen, cold stone, clothesline breeze—and something else. Floral, medicinal. Alrick pressed his face against the weave and felt the soft crackle of something crisp inside it. His heart hammered.

He swept his gaze around the room, but the boys all around him slept, or suffered too much to care if others slept.

Alrick traced his fingers over the seams of the blanket till his blistered fingertips found a narrow pocket tucked into the stitches. Inside was a sachet of leaves. Herbs.

But not medicine.

Tredan had sent him poison.

CHAPTER TWENTY-TWO

It was hard to earn the trust of the hopeless. Trust is a promise, and to the children of the workhouse, all promises were lies.

Alrick drew on his own anger and desperation to summon the strength to earn their trust the only way he could—by easing their burdens. He shared his food with the starving, finished the work of the weary. Soon, several of the boys had offered him whispered names. Ethan. Sam. Jude.

Alrick tried hardest to befriend the porter, the boy with the limp who had opened the gate for him when he arrived. If the meat grease worked on the door's lock, he would still have the gate to deal with. He needed a friend with a key. But the workhouse had made their choice deliberately, and the porter did not seem interested in friendship. But he was interested in Alrick's shoes.

Alrick's bare feet learned every seam in every floor, every splinter on every stair. Soon his feet hurt as badly as his hands did. But he had won the porter over. By the end of his first week, he had a way out. But he still needed a way back to House Aldane, and he needed a plan for the rest of the scratchlings.

He knew he would not be able to free the entire workhouse, as he had hoped. He had learned, in his wanderings, that there were over two thousand inmates across the complex. Men, women, girls, and boys all housed in separate buildings, different dormitories. And there was a whole neighborhood of buildings just for housing the starving Irish. He could not return to House Aldane with a starving army of thousands of typhus-ridden scratchlings. More arrived every day. And souls departed every night.

Jude had a way with words. Alrick employed him to talk to the other boys and get an understanding of where they stood. If they would follow. Some were too lost in their fate to dream of a life beyond the gate, but others soon joined their quiet ranks.

Alrick woke one night to the soft puff of breath against his face. He nearly screamed, but rough, foul fingers pressed against his lips. Wide brown eyes stared into his. "I'll follow you, m'lord. I'll help."

Alrick's heart stuttered. "You're one of ours. An Aldane scratchling." His eyes roved over the scarred face. It was familiar. Alrick brought his hand up to the child's cheek. "I'm going to get us out of here. We're going home."

"When?" the boy asked.

"Soon. Very soon. Be ready."

Alrick paced in the entry hall. He was supposed to be at prayers, but he had slipped out of line and hidden in a closet till the building was empty. The Guardian's office was locked. He wanted in.

The men who had brought him had carried papers—proof of delivery. They had spoken of payments and letters. Somewhere in the Guardian's office, there were letters from House Aldane. If he could get inside, get those pages, and wash the old ink away, he could compose a new letter. He could summon the hired carriage again to bring him and his scratchlings home.

He had picked at the lock with a pin pulled from a bench, but with no luck.

His time was short, and in his desperation, his thoughts turned again to the leafy sachet tucked inside his blanket.

There was enough Atropa Belladona there to kill, yes. But he didn't think his uncle intended that for him. If he only nibbled one leaf, a dried berry—would it be enough to channel the dead of the workhouse? There were more dead here than at House Aldane. More lost souls here than on a battlefield. Could they help him? Or would those raw leaves send him to join them?

He thought of the scratchling spirits at House Aldane. He had sworn to them that he would protect them or join them. Here, he would have the chance to keep his oath. Should the worst happen, it would be better to die quickly in a toxic fit than to waste away from cholera on the dormitory floor.

Alrick climbed back into the hall closet to hide as the chapel bell sounded. There was a day's hard work ahead of him. And at night, he would meet with the dead.

CHAPTER TWENTY-THREE

I f he'd had water, he'd have brewed a tea, or boiled a concentrate, created a measured dose. Instead, he did as his sister did, and chewed a leaf whole, letting its bitter flakes stick to his teeth and gums.

He sat on the floor, legs crossed, in the place he knew would have the highest concentration of spirits—the hospital dormitory. The air was heavily scented with sickness, blood, excrement, and vomit. Children moaned in fever all around him. No adults came, not even the matron. No nurses tended to their suffering through the night. The dead would be collected in the morning, tallies taken, beds freed for new bodies.

Alrick's anger heated his face. His mouth felt dry. He struggled to swallow the leaf that stuck to his hot throat. But it was working. The room seemed to grow brighter as his pupils stretched, details springing into his vision. The texture of the tattered blanket covering a still form. The peeling plaster on the wall. The gathering of shadows in the corners of the room.

The air felt heavy. A knot formed in Alrick's stomach. A cramp.

He stood, as if to ease it, as if to try and lift the weight of shadows off his shoulders.

The wave of voices hit him like the speeding of a train. Agony. Grief immeasurable. The very air was haunted with such a density of ghosts that Alrick felt smothered in their writhing effluvia. He could not breathe without sucking in the fogged form of a wailing soul. He squeezed his eyes shut and focused, concentrated on his own glowing spirit locked in his body. He felt hot and dry, as if he were leaning over an oven. His hands shook. He had taken too much. But Tredan hadn't sent any antidote. He was running out of time.

"Listen to me," he whispered to the spirits, his breath sending their shapes billowing in front of him. They did not stop screaming.

"I want to end this place. End the suffering. I need to free us all, but I need your help."

The writhing around him continued, but a few forms stilled, turned to him.

Alrick.

Lord Aldane.

His name echoed in his ears, then around the room.

Alrick's breath stuttered. The scratchlings. The ghosts here knew him. Because the children Aemon had sent away had died.

Alrick wailed with the spirits, then, his own keening cry joining theirs. A haunted harmony.

As his name circled the room, the spirits slowed. They turned to him, lining up in concentric circles that weaved like the braids in Nelda's hairwork.

The tears on Alrick's hot cheeks turned to steam. "I couldn't save you. I'm sorry. I was too late." His whole body shook until exhaustion forced him to stop.

"But there are others," he whispered. "Help me help them." He lifted his head to a sea of glowing eyes turned to him. They were listening. They were ready.

A deep cough sounded behind the wall of spirits. A rasping rattle. Light flared from a figure in one of the beds. The spirits rearranged their circle to center on the small form. The child shook on his cot, dry voice crying out wordlessly as another cough stole his breath.

Alrick stood and ran to the child's side. The water pitcher was empty, the washcloth dry and hot on the boy's fevered brow. His eyes stretched wide and glassy in the dark as his breathing grew shallow, shallower.

Alrick squeezed the boy's hand and leaned over him. "I'm here with you. You're safe," he said, as the boy exhaled his last breath, his pneuma, and Alrick breathed it in.

The boy's body blurred in Alrick's vision. The edges of his form seemed to shimmer as the boy's body fell back limp against the pillow, and his spirit sat up.

The ghosts stood silent as the boy joined them, his ephemeral hand still clinging to Alrick's.

Alrick broke the silence. He did not have an eternity, as they did. He may only have minutes. "I need to get into the Guardian's office. There are papers there I can use to help get us out of here. To get us home."

It was easy for the spirits to open a door. They moved through the building as water runs through sand, unstopped by matter, soaking through the most infinitesimal space.

Alrick panted hot breath as he rifled through the papers in the Guardian's office. He did not worry about order or mess. There was no order; it was all mess. But he found it at last—the letter Aemon had sent notifying them that he would be sending them more charges, and a copy of the hired coach's invoice.

He took the papers, as well as a pen and inkwell, and headed down the hall to the laundry room, where he knew there would be water.

The steam felt cool on his hot, dry face as he leaned over the pots that still simmered over their last feed of firewood.

Aemon's letter washed easily. It was good paper, sturdy stuff that Tredan had selected for its quality. The ink ran away, leaving the sheet damp but intact, ready for a new message. The hired coachman's invoice provided the address he needed.

The spirits watched him work. They had returned to their weeping, but it had changed. As if the souls had followed Alrick into a new stage of their grief.

He hid the papers, pen, and ink beneath a dusty box in the closet where he often hid himself. The sheet would need a day to dry before he composed his letter. He'd have the porter slip the letter into the mail—the Aldane stationery to the carriage company, summoning them to pick them up. He hoped it would work. He hoped that filling the carriage with scratchlings would not send the hired men into a panic. They'd seemed uncomfortable enough when it was only him.

The last thing he needed to do was pick a day.

Alrick turned to the circle of spirits that orbited him like dust motes in a sunbeam.

"What day is the best for leaving?" he asked them.

A small spirit stepped forward—one of the Aldane scratchlings. "The Guardian goes home on Mondays," the boy's spirit whispered. "Only the matron will be here."

Alrick nodded. "Be ready next Monday. We're going home."

CHAPTER TWENTY-FOUR

Word spread quickly through the building, from dormitory to dormitory, until Alrick knew that one carriage would not be enough to carry them all away, not even if they swarmed it and drove it themselves. But most did not want to come to House Aldane. They simply wanted to leave, to melt back into the city or run to their own homes. Alrick would open the gate to freedom, and they would choose their own fates.

Hope gave them all strength. Fewer boys sickened in the week that followed, fewer bodies were carried out the back door and loaded into carts. For the living, there was something to live for, and the dead eased their way. Clocks sped up as meals approached and slow while they rested. The canes used to beat tired workers broke in their masters' hands. Rain came to quench their thirst when they worked outside, and cool breezes drafted their way into hot rooms.

The porter confirmed that Alrick's letter had arrived, and that the appointment was set. The carriage would be there Monday just after the noon meal. The matron would be busy with the women workers clearing the halls and re-stoking the fires for the afternoon shift. With luck, they could slip away and be a mile down the road before anyone took notice of their absence.

Alrick instructed them all to set aside their bread in small amounts for the day they'd spend on the road. He did not know how long the ride would be, as he'd been unconscious the whole way here, but he knew it would be at least the length of a day.

Monday morning dawned to an atmosphere that buzzed with tension. The children were slack in their work, distracted by the greater task at hand, and the ghosts ran rampant with agitation. Candles would not stay lit, fires guttered, and objects seemed to slide off tables as if the room was tilted. It worked to their advantage. The matron was so agitated by noon that she did not notice the boys skimming fat from their soup to ease the lock, or pocketing bread. She was more than happy to dismiss them after the meal, and shut the hall door behind them so she could clean in peace.

Alrick did not hesitate.

He spread soup fat over the metal lock, while Jude and Ethan slathered the door's hinges.

A small crowd had gathered in the entry, all pressing forward, ready to rush out into the courtyard.

Alrick worked the lock slowly, adding lubricant until it slid free with a scrape quiet enough that he was sure no one beyond the entryway would hear it.

They flooded through the door to the gate. The porter was there, bobbing anxiously in Alrick's shoes as he swung the heavy iron open for them. He did not join them.

Alrick stood by him as boys scattered into the Manchester afternoon, silent and secret, but with their shouts of joy writ clean across their faces.

"You're not coming?"

The porter shook his head. His name was John, a voice whispered in Alrick's ear.

"I can't keep up," he said. "And at least here, I have meals."

"There's room in the carriage," Alrick said, gesturing to the shabby coach that waited for them on the cobblestones.

Jerry the driver sat agape in his seat, flustered as boys scrambled through the door.

John shook his head again. "For what it's worth, this is home. I'll stay. But I won't tell them which way you gone," he said, granting Alrick a shy smile.

Alrick reached out and shook John's hand. "I'll write to you. My name is Alrick Aldane, and you're always welcome at my house."

John's eyebrows raised. He nodded and backed away, vanishing into the shade of the porter's cabin.

Alrick climbed into the carriage, squeezing himself onto the tattered bench alongside seven other boys. Jude, Ethan, Sam, and the Aldane scratchling were there, along with three others who had decided to follow him home.

It was far from the mass freedom he had wanted for the people of the workhouse. But it was a start, and it would grant him the freedom he needed to finish what he'd started.

The driver drove them quickly, almost recklessly, from the city, but Alrick didn't complain. The small man wasn't with him this time, as Alrick's letter hadn't warned of any need for backup. They made fast time into the countryside, and the workhouse scratchlings were soon nodding asleep as the sun crept lower toward the rural fields.

As dark fell and only the coach's lantern light seeped through the seams in the door, Alrick reached into his ragged coat pocket and broke off a small corner of Belladonna.

He sighed deeply as he chewed, reaching his thoughts out for the spirits he hoped were following him. He felt them. They were silent, like trailing ribbons tied to the back of the carriage.

The driver stopped the carriage, as instructed, at the crossroads just out of sight of the house. In the grey pre-dawn light, Alrick could see the verge where he'd argued with Cassie, see the groove cut in the dirt where she'd dragged her trunk. His heart constricted. He'd been away for weeks, unable to keep an eye on her or anyone. He didn't know what he might find at the house. He didn't even know if Tredan had succeeded in bringing Nelda home. If not, he would go himself.

Alrick sent the coach away, and the scratchlings with their entourage of spirits made their way toward the house on foot, bare feet combing through the tall grass beside the road.

As the house came into sight, Alrick led them around to the side, so they could approach from behind the carriage house, through the garden to the cold storage, where they could slip into the passage to Cassie's room.

She wouldn't be there, Alrick knew.

His eyes stung as the house came into focus, his chest tight with emotion. There had been nights, shivering on the workhouse floor, that Alrick didn't think he'd see House Aldane again.

But it was his house. He knew that now more than ever.

Aemon could not cast him out so easily.

Tredan could not discard him.

He was Lord Aldane, and the house, and its spirits, were his. All but one. And her reign would soon be over.

CHAPTER TWENTY-FIVE

Alrick swayed in dizzy relief when he saw Nelda asleep in her bed.

They had crept through the passageway into the attic, and the Aldane scratchling had led the others into the secret corners of the house while Alrick made his way to Nelda's rooms.

Her head tossed restlessly on her pillow, as if she was aware, even in sleep, of the house filling with new voices, new spirits come to call new halls their home.

He crept from her room, through the keep, into his own wing, and up the stairs to his room. A hot bath awaited him, and a pitcher of tea. Fresh, clean clothes lay across his bed.

Alrick fell to his knees and wept.

He knew, now, why the dead never left House Aldane. It was home. It was sacred ground. He would never leave it again, not in this life or the next.

He peeled his workhouse rags from his body and tossed them in a corner, taking the pitcher of tea with him into the bath. He drank deeply and let the water soak his aches away.

Both the tea and water had turned cold before he moved again.

He did not remember dressing himself or crawling into bed. Sleep carried him there, a deep oblivion as close to death as he had ever been, except for once. Except for the time Aemon fed him berries.

"Open your mouth."

Alrick twisted his face away from Nelda's cold hand.

"Trust me. It will clear your mind." Her nails raked at his lips and something hot and sour flooded past his teeth. He coughed as it stung his throat. "Give it a minute, then try to stand."

The spinning in his head slowed. His heartbeat evened. Light lanced his eyes as he tried to force them open. It was midday light. He'd slept a long time. He forced himself to look at her as he sat up, training his eyes over her face and hands.

"You're okay? He got you out?"

Nelda nodded grimly. "And you are not okay. He did not get you out."

Alrick shook his head.

"There are so many of them," she said, her voice shaking. "They're screaming."

"I know," Alrick whispered back.

Her eyes were clear, though, and her lips were pale, unstained with her usual toxins.

"I need your help, brother. With Aemon."

Help me save your brother, Tredan had said.

"He's still ill?"

Nelda nodded.

"Where's Tredan?"

"In London, restocking his medicines. He's tried everything."

"What did you do to him, Nelda?"

She didn't answer.

"If I'm to cure him, I need to know what's wrong to begin with."

"Well, I suppose you'd better examine him and make your diagnosis."

Alrick slowly pushed back his blanket. "How long have I been sleeping?" His stiff joints ached as if he'd slept on a cold floor again.

"Since dawn. It's afternoon, now. I couldn't wait any longer."

Alrick pulled slippers onto his feet. "Is Aemon awake?"

"Not fully. He speaks, but not to us…"

"What did you just give me? Did you try giving him any of that?"

"A waking tincture. I did. That's when he began speaking."

"A waking tincture."

"Yes. My mother made it for midwives to take during long births, to help them stay alert. I always keep some on hand."

Alrick squeezed the last bit of dizziness from his eyes. He grasped a beam in the wall and steadied his hands. Nelda supported him down his stairs, across the empty keep and up the stairs to Aemon's, *Father's, My,* chambers.

Aemon tossed on the bed. The same bed where Lord Drummond had entered eternal stillness.

George and Merry stood at the foot of the bed, Merry wringing her hands so hard that they'd gone bone white. She screamed when she saw Alrick and ran to him, throwing her arms around his shoulders. "Thank all the spirits of the house, you're home," she said.

Alrick squeezed her back, but his attention was on Aemon.

Aemon mumbled as he writhed. The blankets had all twisted away from him. Alrick wanted to, too. Instead, he leaned in, placed his ear near Aemon's face.

"The more you eat, the sweeter they get. Just like candy from London. Like an orphan from London. Just like an orphan. Never an orphan. She'll always be here."

Alrick leaned back again. He gripped Aemon's face in his hands to still it. His eyes roved, one dilating and constricting, the other fixed wide.

"What do you think, brother?" Nelda thumbed the corners of an envelope in her hands.

"I don't know. His eyes…I've never seen that. I'll go start the lab fires. I need to make new medicine, but we're out of so much."

"Is he going to die?" Merry's voice quavered. She'd seen him born, known him in the sweetness of his childhood. Maybe even helped deliver him. Maybe tasted the waking tincture that night.

Alrick looked to Nelda again. She didn't seem worried.

"George," Nelda said.

"Yes, m'lady?"

"I need you to ride hard and fast for London. Take this letter to the solicitor Mister Legan. Tell him to come at once. Find Tredan if you can. Be sure to check the gutters."

George nodded, took the letter, and raced down the stairs.

"Mister Legan?" Alrick asked.

"My brother needs to add his new bride to his will. And I want Legan here tomorrow when we exhume mother."

New bride. They'd married officially, then.

"Where is Cassie?" Alrick asked.

"She's resting," Nelda said, though she looked at Merry while she said it.

An ice wind circled the room and the lamps guttered. Merry gasped.

"And you're going to exhume Burgrune?"

"We must do it soon. While she's still weak."

Aemon moaned.

"Go light the fires, Alrick. Bring all your arts to boil."

Tredan had left a mess. Beakers let to cool without rinsing, now blackened and sticky. Alrick searched the shelves for clean ones. He poured shards of blue glass from them, from when the jars had been shattered. He washed out the dust as well as he could.

The jars and compartments of Tredan's cupboard were nearly bare. He pulled out the small drawer for willow bark and tipped what was left of it into a vial, hoping it was more herb than sawdust.

None of the standard, familiar ingredients remained in any quantity, and Tredan had taken his book of recipes to the White Lily. Alrick wracked his memory for any note of usefulness. *Anise for the heart, menthol for breath…*He threw it all into a brew. The alertness from Nelda's tincture helped, though it also amplified the anxiety chewing at his heart.

He didn't know how long he'd been in the lab when he finally had a smoky syrup to pour into a long vial. He set it in a cup of water to cool.

Something tugged at his coat. He turned to see a scratchling—a living one—with a bowl of soup. His stomach cramped with hunger as aromatic steam rose to his face.

"Thank you," he said, and drank the soup standing in place. When he lowered the bowl, the scratchling stood there, watching him. He handed her the empty bowl.

"Will you be the lord? If he dies?"

Alrick stared at her. "I…Yes, I think I would be."

"Betsy could come back, then. They could all come back."

Alrick didn't know what to say. But he felt himself nod. *She might already be here. You just can't see her.*

"You're trying to save him?"

He nodded again, slower this time.

"Why?" Her head tilted, stretching the scars of her face.

"He's my brother."

"He killed you."

"He what?"

"With the berries. When you were a baby."

"I'm not dead."

"Not anymore. Just like me. Like us."

Alrick felt the soup fighting its way back up his throat.

"Do you need anything else, my lord?"

Alrick shook his head. He squeezed his eyes shut. When he opened them again, she was gone. He grabbed the vial from the water. It still felt warm in his hand, but it would do.

Alrick raced down the stairs and through the corridors, across the hall. With the sour alertness alive in his veins, the floor seemed unusually still.

Aemon lay just as Alrick had left him—roving, reeling, ranting to something unseen. Alrick leaned in with the vial and Aemon's mumbling lips sealed shut, drawn in past his teeth so hard Alrick could see the outline of each tooth against his whitened lips.

"Come help me," Alrick called over his shoulder to Nelda and Merry, who sat in chairs by the window.

Merry came. "Now, Master Aemon, you open up and take your medicine like a good lad," she said, stroking his face as she must have done when he was a baby.

The groaning from behind his sealed lips intensified, became a muffled howl.

Nelda rose and walked to the foot of the bed. She reached under the blanket to the twin peaks of Aemon's feet beneath the cloth. A sharp crack sounded from beneath the blanket.

Aemon's pupils shrunk to pinpricks before spreading back to wide, black pools. His mouth popped open and a hoarse scream shredded the air.

Alrick slipped his thumb between Aemon's black back teeth and poured the vial's contents into the hollowness of his cheek. It spluttered and gargled its passage down his throat. But down it went, and down those back teeth came onto the joint of Alrick's thumb.

Another crack, and Alrick's scream echoed Aemon's. He wrenched back, though he'd have done better not to. His skin broke and tore against a tooth edge. The flesh peeled away as his body fell backward into Merry, who caught him against her apron. The scent of bread filled his nostrils, then blood.

The pain followed. Worse.

Blood ran down Aemon's chin, mixed with the smoky potion that hadn't made it past his thrashing tongue.

Alrick looked at his hand. His left thumb—the skin peeled back like a budding flower, meat shining out from behind a veil of seeping blood. The nail was gone, somewhere down Aemon's gullet.

Alrick panted. He tasted Nelda's hand on the air before he felt it pressed to his lips, pushing one of her own powders into his mouth.

He shoved her away and spat. "Enough! Do you even know what you're giving me? Or how it might blend with what I've had already? Have you done any study at all besides the hell you inflict upon yourself?"

She only smiled and looked to Aemon.

He had stilled. His eyes closed and his lips lay in repose, Alrick's blood settling into the creases of skin at the corners of his mouth and drying there.

"He'll sleep now, for a while. He'll feel better when he wakes. I suppose we'll never know if it was your medicine or your blood that cured him, Brother." Nelda straightened the blanket over Aemon, over the crooked lump of the toe she'd broken to make him scream. "Merry, please tell Cassie the danger is passed and all is well."

"I'm going back to the lab to see to my hand," Alrick said.

"Do you want me to help you?" Nelda asked.

"No!" Alrick shouted.

Merry jumped.

"I'm sorry. No. I'll be fine. I'd like a little more rest, myself. Fetch me when he wakes."

Alrick made his way back to the lab, knees as weak as the dry stalks in Nelda's garden. He whispered to the stones as he went by, "I didn't want her help, but I do want yours."

He couldn't hear any steps behind him, but he could feel the small, dark eyes on his back. Sense their silent presence.

When he reached the lab, he collapsed into a chair by the fire and held out his hand. He covered his eyes and felt the butterfly touch of quick, icy fingers upon him. An excruciating abrasion of water. The pinch against his stripped glove of skin, then the prick of a needle, the flooding warmth of numbness and the pressure of a bandage.

A hot cup of tea pressed into this right hand. He opened his eyes as he raised it to his mouth and thought he saw the fleeting haze of ephemeral children—or maybe it was the steam from his tea.

He looked at his thumb. It was expertly bound and wrapped in a length of lace from Cassie's wedding veil.

CHAPTER TWENTY-SIX

A child's fingers on his face woke him—cold and sharp as needles. His eyes sprang open and pain opened behind them. The light from the fire in front of him drove straight through the back of his skull and pinned him there as if staked.

The cold fingers vanished before he could see the arm or face behind them. He sat up in the chair and squeezed his eyes shut against the blaze of light, as if he could stifle the pounding in his temples with the muscles of his face. He couldn't.

And the pounding was soon echoed by the light tap of footfalls on the stairs.

Elizabeth entered the sitting room. "Are you awake, m'lord?"

Alrick cleared his groggy throat. "Yes. Only just. How is Aemon?"

"Better, I think. But not himself."

"That sounds better, indeed."

He caught her flash of smile before she stifled it and cast her gaze down. "Tredan and Mister Legan are on their way. They should be here in an hour or two."

"Thank you, Elizabeth. I suppose I better make a few things ready."

"Merry's taken care of the arrangements, sir, but we supposed you might like some time just the same."

"Yes. Quite. Thank you. I'll go see Aemon now. Then I'll bathe and change."

The maid curtsied and her footsteps retreated down the stairs.

Alrick stood, testing his tired legs. He had slept off all trace of Nelda's alertness tincture. He followed Elizabeth's fading footsteps through the halls, saw her candlelight disappear down the kitchen stairs as he made his way up to the lord's chambers.

No one was in the room except Aemon, stretched out on the bed, his blankets now askew where he'd tossed and turned in his sleep. His eyes were closed and peaceful. Mouth, since cleaned, now slack and restful.

Alrick walked to the window and looked down at the early dawn garden. Shadows weaved through the plants, dark shapes beneath the tangled canopy. Every time his eyes settled on a form it vanished into the uncertain grey light. One of the shadows resembled Fray, maybe hunting rabbits for his breakfast.

"Did you come to finish the job, brother?"

Alrick jumped, and when he blinked, the garden shadows vanished.

"I came to see how you were doing. To see if the medicine worked."

"I'm alive."

"I can see that."

"But I'm weak. If you wanted, you could end this now."

"Don't be ridiculous."

"You can't tell me you haven't thought about it."

"Maybe. Briefly. Especially when you bit me."

Aemon's smile glowed in the faint light. Alrick wondered where his thumbnail was, now. *Maybe it will stay there, stuck in his craw forever, like a thorn in a lion's paw.*

"You're like a disease I can't get rid of. Take your shot if you like, Brother. Even the score."

Alrick remembered the berries, then, or at least he remembered the stories about the berries. He didn't remember the event at all.

You died. Had he taken his place, however briefly, among the Aldane dead? Was that why they all seemed to know him? Why he could see them, hear their voices on drafts?

"I've no need to harm you, Aemon. I want us to be brothers. Will you still be my brother when the truth is found?"

"We live in different truths, Alrick."

"You're living in an old truth. What will you do when father speaks? Where will you go when everyone knows what you've done?"

"The only ones who know are dead."

"Ah, but this is House Aldane, Brother. The dead speak, here. You should know that.

"Nelda's little parlor tricks prove nothing to anyone."

"This has gone far beyond Nelda's gift. Tredan's science is behind it. Everyone at the party saw it. We all hear it—and see its effects. Maybe not everyone will believe, but enough will."

"Those fools at the party saw my mother. The only thing it proved to them is that you're a bastard."

Alrick smiled. "Her body will be exhumed within the hour. Then that rumor can rest with her."

Aemon laughed—a wet, choking sound. "The best of luck to you with that plot, Alrick. *Brother.* Now go. And send Elizabeth. I may not be able to stand, but I want to watch this from the window, with my bride, who carries my heir." He grinned wickedly at Alrick.

Alrick felt his face redden, but he ignored the bait. He left, satisfied that Aemon's energy was returning to him and that danger had passed. Aemon hadn't seemed worried about the exhumation. Alrick supposed it didn't matter, in the end. Burgrune's body might prove that Alrick was not a bastard, but it wouldn't prove that he was meant to inherit. The only ground he would gain would be enough to put him back to where he'd been two weeks ago: still lost, with hardly any footing left to fight on.

He found Elizabeth in the hall, setting the table for guests.

"Aemon would like Cassie brought to him so they can watch the exhumation together from the window," Alrick said.

I don't think that's a good idea," the maid said, shaking her head. "Tredan told us not to move her."

Alarm spiked in Alrick's veins. "What? Why?"

Elizabeth pursed her lips. "She hasn't been well since the party, either. It's nothing serious," she reassured him. "She's okay. But they're worried about the baby."

Alrick stumbled back. He closed his eyes. Where was she? She had not been in her rooms, nor Aemon's. A tug in the air pulled him toward the kitchen. Merry's room. Merry had likely been watching her, day and night. He rushed down the stairs to the warm bedroom off the kitchen.

Cassie sat up in one of the beds, a book spread across her lap.

"Cassie, are you all right?" Alrick rushed to her bedside.

She paled and flinched away. "You're back."

Alrick nodded, stopping himself from reaching for her hand. "Do you need anything?"

"You smell like the hospital," she whispered.

Alrick nodded weakly. He supposed it would take more than one bath to wash away weeks of the workhouse floor. "I just wanted to check on you. Aemon's asking for you."

Her face creased in anxiety. "Is he dying?"

"No," Alrick said. "He's much better, actually."

"You cured him?"

Alrick nodded.

"You're better than your uncle," Cassie said, drawing her feet out from under her blanket.

Alrick glanced away to grant her privacy. Her white lace wedding dress and veil lay draped over a chair in the corner. The flower wreath that Nelda had woven lay wilted atop it. Alrick frowned. He walked over to it, picking up the crown. He recognized the leaves, now. And the bell-shaped flowers from Nelda's rhyme. Atropa Belladonna. Nelda had given her a poison crown. No wonder she felt ill.

Alrick swore under his breath and hurried from the room, taking the crown with him. He tossed it out the kitchen window before heading back up to his room.

The fire in his hearth blazed before the metal washtub, its surface skimming steam that smelled of bergamot. He supposed the scratchlings also smelled the suffering clinging to his skin.

Alrick stripped off his rumpled clothes and slipped into the water, feeling the knots in his muscles melt in the heat, careful to keep his injured thumb dry.

He scrubbed at his face and hair to keep awake. "Don't let me sleep," he whispered to the room. He wanted to be alert for this meeting with Legan.

Alrick lounged for as long as he dared, then climbed out into the cool air, dried, and put on his best suit. His funeral suit. He supposed this was a funeral, of sorts. They would, of course, have to rebury her.

CHAPTER TWENTY-SEVEN

Alrick sat in the hall, watching a candle gutter and glow in some untraceable draft. The sound of hoofbeats and carriage wheels clattered on the gravel outside. He stood.

"Merry! Mister Skillson!" Alrick didn't wait for them; he dashed to the door.

Tredan was already helping Mister Legan from the carriage. The lanky scribe, Eames, followed.

Mister Legan nodded to Alrick but did not display any of the frivolity or familiarity of his previous visit. "And where is my client, Lord Aldane?"

"He's taken ill, I'm afraid," Alrick said. "He won't be joining us. But he has professed his desire to watch us from the window."

"Would you be liking a cup of tea, sir, to settle before you start?" Merry had come up behind Alrick. She shot him a glance, to remind him that he was receiving a guest.

"Of course, my apologies, Mister Legan, do come in." Alrick stepped aside and the lawyer and his clerk entered the house. Tredan followed, staring at Alrick.

Alrick met his gaze and held it.

Merry served a simple tea on the new china.

"This is a most unusual business, Tredan," Mister Legan said.

"I quite agree. I have never once in all my years heard anyone demean the good reputation of my dear brother until now." Tredan scowled into his tea.

"I beg your pardon?" Mister Legan spluttered toast crumbs into his mustache.

"The rumors circling the county are appalling. I want them put to rest immediately. Apparently putting them to rest requires disturbing the eternal rest of my dear departed sister-in-law."

"It was my understanding that it's the boy's reputation that's at stake, not the honorable Lord Drummond's!" Legan shot a sideways glance at Alrick.

"What is being said, Mister Legan, is that my brother took Alrick's mother into his home while Lady Burgrune still lived. Because they believe they saw her just last week in some illness-induced hallucination. It was, in fact, my niece they saw. She does resemble her mother. But to imply that my brother would have done such a thing—betrayed a woman he loved so dearly and taken a lover—is a slight that will not be borne by House Aldane. Do you understand?"

Mister Legan let out a dry, unintelligible reply that caught in the toast in his throat. He nodded.

"Well. If we are all fortified, we'd best get to it."

The earth over Alrick's father's grave had not yet settled into shape. It remained loose, tossed, and free from fresh grass. As if nothing could rest, nothing could grow so long as the truth lay buried.

George took up a spade, and Alrick and Tredan helped. Nelda stood at a distance, beyond the boundary of the small plot, as if she meant, at any moment, to dart into her garden.

Mister Legan's gaze traveled from the growing pile of earth to the windows above them.

Alrick couldn't see Aemon through the rippled glass, but he knew he must be there.

Mister Legan's scribe had perched his writing slope on a nearby headstone, a fresh piece of parchment rippling in the breeze.

As they dug lower, the earth became softer. It had all been disturbed when Lord Drummond's grave had been dug, and it eased their mission now. They'd buried Lord Drummond so close to his late wife that they could have been holding hands, at rest. Alrick remembered the scratchling's graves. Hoped they found as much comfort in one another. His own mother's resting place, the village churchyard, seemed far away and he wondered if she was lonely there.

They reached Lady Burgrune's box much quicker than planned, and Alrick felt a lump of uneasiness forming in his gut.

"Bad business, bad business," Legan mumbled to himself as he saw the old box appear.

The wood had warped from its twenty years in the earth. Alrick supposed the lady within would be, as well. He supposed it wouldn't be as bad as seeing the bodies in the hospital. It would not be as bad as seeing his own father's body, nor the tortured small bodies in the workhouse.

Tredan climbed down into the hole alongside the coffin and planted a prybar beneath its rim.

The box did not require prying, however. The lid came free easily.

It was nothing but a broken box.

Its side had come away and the space within had filled with dirt.

Silence overcame them as they all stared into the empty grave.

The scribe's pen scratched furiously across the page.

"Stop. Stop!" Tredan climbed from the hole and snatched the pen from the young man's hand. "She was buried here. I saw it myself. Many people saw it."

"Sir, did you see her buried, or did you see the box buried?" Legan asked.

"I saw her in the box. I helped seal this box. I helped lower it into the earth, myself. She was here."

"Where is Lord Aldane? I daresay he was here that day. Let us hear what he has to say about it."

Alrick looked around. "Nelda. She was here, too." He nodded to her distant figure.

She backed away from them, slowly, toward the garden, with Fray at her heels.

The garden.

Alrick looked into the grave at his feet. "The earth here. It was soft. Like it had been recently dug."

"Don't be ridiculous, boy. The surface was undisturbed."

"Here, yes. But not there." He pointed at his father's fresh grave beside Burgrune's. "They could have come in from the side and taken the body."

"They? Who are you accusing, boy?" Mister Legan began to twitch in agitation. The scribe pulled a spare pen from his box.

"Nelda said her mother's power came partly from her proximity to the house. Burgrune would have wanted the power—the prestige—of a proper Aldane burial."

"Please explain yourself, Alrick," Tredan said.

"Burgrune isn't here because she's been buried in the real Aldane plot. In her garden. In the fresh earth where Aemon moved the tree. Where the babies were buried."

As Alrick whispered this, Nelda turned, as if she'd heard, and ran into the garden.

Legan and Tredan stared at him.

"Come. George, bring your spades." Alrick strode across the lawn to the broken-walled garden where Nelda had disappeared among the fresh foliage of spring.

Nelda lay with her hand pressed into the dirt up to her wrist, her fingers writhing beneath the soil so that it churned as if rich with worms. Fray pawed at the dirt and buried his nose.

"Nelda," Alrick said, kneeling at her side, "Is your mother here? Did Aemon put her here?"

Nelda pulled her hand from the dirt and slipped her fingers into her mouth. Her lips were lilac, her eyes black. She pushed her hand further and further into her mouth, till her fist split the seams of her lips and blood began to shine in the fissures.

Alrick reached for her wrist, but her other hand got there first, slender fingers wrapped around her fist, trying to pull it free. Alrick clamped his hand over hers and pulled with her till her fist slipped from her mouth and shook with the effort to return there.

Nelda panted. "She's here." Her lips didn't move as she spoke. The whisper came as if through the leaves themselves.

George stepped forward with the spade and began to dig. Tredan joined him.

Alrick looked up to the dark window where Aemon had watched them. Did he watch now? Was he dragging his weak body through the halls, hoping to stop them in time? Alrick picked up a shovel and joined in the effort.

Nelda slunk away into the shade of a dark sapling speckled with raw buds. An Oleander. Perhaps the offspring of the missing tree.

It didn't take long for them to reach bone. There was no box, that having been left behind in the proper grave. Burgrune was raw within the earth, her bones mingled with the tendrils of root left behind by the transported tree.

She had been placed carefully, joints posed as well as was able. Her desiccated hands crossed her chest, a tatter of lace still visible at her wrists. In her hands, clutched in brittle finger bones, was a blue bottle. One of Tredan's bottles.

Tredan reached for it, but Alrick was faster. He pried it free from the ancient hands and turned it around in the sunlight. *Burgrune Aldane* the label read. *December eighth, eighteen-fifty-six.*

"That was not buried with her," Tredan said. "That was in my lab. On my shelf, until…"

"Until Aemon came in and shattered them," Alrick finished. "All but this one. He saved her breath. He gave it back to her."

"I breathed it back into her," Nelda said, from her perch in the shade. "I sucked it from the bottle and mingled it with my own and breathed it right back through her lips."

Alrick thumbed the dry cork at the top of the bottle. Its wax was gone, its seal broken. It moved loosely inside the mouth of the glass bottle. He pushed it free. The cork fell into the dirt and mingled there, scattering like a rotted tree.

He expected a blast of air from the bottle, or a scream, or a black cloud to envelop him in darkness. But the bottle was ordinary. Not empty. A folded sheet of paper lay curled inside, along with a scattering of rusted nails, fragments of bone, a twisted key, and dried herbs and flowers.

Alrick slipped his hand into the bottle and pinched an edge of the paper, working it out of the glass.

"What is it?" Tredan asked.

"A witch's bottle." Nelda smiled weakly at Tredan. He shot a quick glare at her in return.

"A curse?" Tredan peered through the glass still clutched in Alrick's hand.

Aemon's voice came weakly from across the lawn. His words were indistinguishable, but their intent was clear. He wanted them to stop.

Alrick hurried. He pulled the paper free and unfolded it. It was a thick sheet of old, fine parchment. He held it out for Tredan, Legan, and the clerk to see.

"This being the last will and testament of Lord Drummond Aldane..."

The clerk scribbled frantically, his lap desk perched on his bony hip. Mister Legan's moustache quivered and his feet involuntarily edged back from the loose dirt that reached for all their toes.

Tredan took the paper from Alrick. "Well. Here it is, at last. Did I not tell you, Mister Legan, that I knew of a more recent will? That—yes, here—names Alrick the heir to all? And witnessed by several such names, mine included, as well as two other local lords."

Mister Legan had edged nearly out of the shade of the garden. "Most remarkable. I swear I had no knowledge..."

"We know you didn't, Mister Legan," Alrick said. "Because you were not my father's lawyer. You are my brother's lawyer. I suggest you go see to your client. He's going to need you now more than ever."

Aemon had made his way across much of the grass, his legs buckling every few yards so that he sank to the ground and renewed his shouting from a prone position. Mister Legan eyed him, then returned his gaze to Alrick.

"I imagine it could be quite ruinous to champion the wrong side in a scandal," Tredan said. "This will certainly make the London papers."

Mister Legan's clerk's pen had slowed, then stilled. Tredan reached over and tore the pages from his lap desk, causing the whole device to spill to the ground, soaking the dirt with ink.

"Come, Eames." Mister Legan and his clerk took off across the lawn toward the front of the house and their carriage. They passed Aemon in the grass, pretending not to see him as he berated them from the mud.

CHAPTER TWENTY-EIGHT

Alrick ran his fingertip over his own name, in his father's hand. Here was the acknowledgment he sought. Here was the victory for which he hadn't even dared hope. The impossible solution in his own hands. *Why do I feel sick?*

There was no sense of pride or victory. There was relief, but it was drowned in concern.

Nelda lay beneath the tree, her dirty fingertips back at her lips. Aemon lay in the grass, his hope and his body exhausted.

"Tredan, George, help me get them inside." Alrick tucked the paper into his jacket and leaned down to Nelda.

"But…but m'lady…" George indicated the open grave at his feet.

"Leave it for now, George. Let us see to the living." Alrick slipped an arm behind Nelda's back and hoisted her to her feet.

Her breaths came shallow and hurried against Alrick's cheek, scented with something bitter and floral.

George and Tredan lifted Aemon from the grass and guided him back to the kitchen door which stood open, Elizabeth and Cassie just inside it.

Elizabeth ran to put on a fresh kettle.

Cassie's eyes roved from Nelda to Aemon. Then her gaze settled on Alrick.

"Would you help me with her, Cassie?" Alrick asked.

She nodded and took Nelda's other side, though her eyes stayed on Aemon's form. He mumbled obscenities under his breath, and his legs twitched as if he wished to fight them all, his mind raging at the unfairness of the fact that he could not.

They made it as far as the main hall before Aemon bellowed that he would be carried no farther.

"Let me go, you impudent dogs," he barked at George and Tredan.

They lowered him into Lord Drummond's seat, and he laughed bitterly. "Is this habit? Or are you humoring me."

Alrick and Cassie lowered Nelda into another chair.

Nelda whispered, her voice rapid, her blue lips hardly moving. Alrick couldn't tell what she said, but Cassie's face had grown paler since they'd left the sunlight of the lawn.

George stumbled away from his enraged temporary lord. He looked to Alrick.

"Brother," Alrick said. He wasn't sure where to find the rest of his words. From the air? The house? The last breath of his father, which surely circled him now? "Aemon, I understand why you did it," he said. "Why you both did it." He looked to Nelda, too, who did not return his glance, but stared intently into the space in front of her.

Alrick wasn't angry. He wanted to be. He tried to be. He called forth the memory of Merry's bruises, of losing Cassie to Aemon's ambition, of the way the lords all failed to even see him at Father's funeral. He tried to conjure his temper and failed.

"Finding this doesn't change anything. Not really." He pulled the will from his jacket. "The truth was always the truth, and the house has always known the truth." The candles guttered. "This house was never yours."

All at once, the candles melted and extinguished in their own pools of wax.

"She's cold," Nelda said. "Without her blanket of earth."

Aemon dropped his face into his hands. "Mother, I don't want this, anymore. I do not want his broken house." He struggled to lift himself out of Lord Drummond's chair, but failed and fell back against the wood.

"I think we've both put too much importance on chairs, Brother. Rest." Alrick set the paper on the table.

Aemon stared at the floor through his fingers.

Nelda stared at the ceiling.

The only light came from the kitchen doorway and the slim, high windows of the keep. Alrick's eyes struggled to adjust after the brightness of the lawn, but the darkness seemed to deepen.

"George, could you please ride to Cranston, then Oakbrook. Have the lords there summoned to affirm their witnessing of this will. It might be somewhat awkward, considering their unwillingness to come forward before now." Tredan leaned down by Nelda, examining her upturned face.

"I offered them land," Aemon said. "Yielding land—farms, if they would keep quiet."

Tredan sighed. "Well. Maybe we can offer to keep their transgression out of the papers, if they make this transition as smooth as possible."

George nodded, clearly relieved to leave the room, making swift progress to the door. He slammed it shut behind himself, and the light grew even dimmer. The tapestries rustled in the draft.

The rustling became a stir, a wave, and soon they bucked against the walls like ship sails in a cyclone.

Elizabeth shrieked and ran for the door, but it had stuck fast behind George, and would not budge. She ran, instead, into the dark corridor leading to the Lady's wing. Merry went after her.

Cassie backed against a wall, twisting the lace of her empty sleeve. Nelda made a choking sound. Alrick spun to her.

Her feet hovered inches above the flagstones, her head thrown back, hair trailing dirt and ribbons, hands clutched in claws.

There came a howling from the other side of the door as Fray threw himself against it, trying to return to his mistress. His nails clawed loud scratches in the ancient wood, as Nelda raked the air.

Her throat bulged. Burgrune's laugh burst from her open mouth.

Aemon lifted his head and stared at his sister, his eyes red and weary. "Enough of your laughter. It's over."

The chain above him snapped and the iron ring of liquid candles crashed to the table in front of him. Aemon fell back in the chair, head striking the flagstones. He moaned, and Cassie ran to him.

Alrick fished in his pocket for a vial of antidote as he reached an arm around Nelda's legs, trying to draw her back to the floor. Her nails scraped at his injured thumb, and he gasped and let go.

Tredan was there, then, with a bottle emptied over Nelda's gaping mouth. She choked and the laughter stopped.

Alrick grasped her again, and this time, he and Tredan we able to pull her down, holding her to the cold flagstones. She gulped rapid breaths scented with violets and tonic.

Alrick stood and searched the room for Burgrune's roving shadow. "It's over, Burgrune. All lines must end, sometime, and yours is over. There are only Aldanes here. This is House Aldane and you are not welcome."

The air grew frigid, and thin. Every breath starved of oxygen, though Alrick could see the fog of his exhalations gathering in front of his face. Vapor or frost breath everywhere, filling the corners of the room, circling the walls. Mist with small faces, whispering names.

"James?" Alrick whispered back to them. "Michael? Ella? Edyta?" He squeezed his eyes shut and recited all the names he could remember, from the long river of graves, from the lichen-covered stones, from his dream, from the wailing workhouse spirits. Small hands tugged at his clothes and he opened his eyes.

Cassie had pulled Aemon to the wall, where he sat against the broken plaster and wept. She did not look at him, but stared instead at the ring of spectral children that had surrounded her. Their scarred faces, tattered shifts, and cropped heads filled the hall.

Tredan shook, one hand pressed to his eyes, the other in his pocket, withdrawing vials of antidote. He chewed the seals open and poured them into his mouth, desperate to end the vision before him. "I tried!" he shouted. Medicine ran into his beard. He sank to his knees and wept, apologizing to the scratchlings who circled past him.

Nelda grasped Alrick's arm. "Brother," she said, "call your mother." She pressed her cold mouth to his ear. "Call her from the place you remember. She's been waiting for you there." She slipped her hand into his, and he felt a cold, wet weight there.

The weight remained in his hand as Nelda pulled away. He looked down. Berries. Dark and wrinkled, staining the fabric of his bandage a rusty purple.

Nelda pulled a ribbon-wrapped posy from her pocket. Flowers bright and dark, rich greens, thorn twigs. Nelda stretched her mouth wide and bit into the bouquet.

A shadow coalesced through the fog and the scratchlings scattered from it.

VERMIN.

SO MANY VERMIN.

The scratchlings flocked to Tredan and hovered around him as if protecting him, or seeking protection.

Burgrune's shadow advanced on Aemon, where he cowered against the wall. Cassie rose from his side and stood, facing the shadow, her face set in the same determined expression he'd seen in the hospital. A survivor.

VERMIN!

Cassie reached her hand out toward the shadow as if to touch its face, and as she did, it gained substance, till Alrick could see the fabric of Burgrune's dress, the locks of long, dark hair, her raging eyes.

The shadow of Burgrune looked past Cassie to Aemon. *"You planted the family seed in night soil,"* she shrieked.

Aemon struggled to his feet.

Cassie glared at the shadow, her eyes lit with a rage that further illuminated Burgrune's face. It was twisted with disgust.

"Perhaps that boy is right," Burgrune said. *"Better our line should end than be diluted with vermin blood."*

Cassie hissed and lashed out, and Burgrune's hand darted forward into Cassie's stomach.

Cassie screamed, doubled over, clutching at her middle.

Aemon ran for the door.

Burgrune pulled away from Cassie and reached for Aemon, overcoming him, yanking him by his hair. There was a loud pop as his leg twisted under him and he fell to the floor screaming.

Alrick leapt for Cassie, but Nelda held his arm tight.

"Call her, Alrick!" Nelda shouted around a mouthful of thorns. Her lips bled, her face pale and slicked with sweat, eyes black from corner to corner.

Burgrune turned on her daughter.

Alrick shook and felt the berries slick in his fingers. "Tredan!" he called, "Go to Cassie, now!" He heard a scramble and hoped Tredan and the scratchlings could help her. Would help her.

Alrick lifted the berries to his lips. They smelled bitter, like old memories turned into nightmares, and tasted as sweet as hope with an aftertaste of acrid despair. His mouth numbed, and then his throat. "Mother. Help." He managed to choke the words out before his tongue stopped obeying.

A scream filled the keep. One Alrick remembered, heartbreaking, desperate, and so far away. Everything seemed distant. Heavy. He let himself fold to the floor, allowed his face to settle against the ancient stones of his foundation, his fingertips slipped into the seams that held his house together.

Burgrune's shadow stood before Nelda, and Nelda rose, lifted, grinning down at her mother's shadow with a black and bleeding mouth. She laughed, in her own voice.

Burgrune snarled. *"Impudent little witch. You disgrace us all."*

"I'm not your little witch," Nelda said. Her voice came from the floor under Alrick's cheek. Her laughter the creak in the broad beams of the ceiling. The dry rasp of her voice the crumbling of plaster from the walls.

Nelda's eyes gleamed white, and her arms flung outward, scattering the empty stems of flowers. "I am the doorway of House Aldane and I am open."

The air rose into a cry around her, lifting her in a cyclone of ribbons and rags and tangled hair.

The distant scream neared, and Alrick felt a hand on his cheek, warm and soft, a gentle sobbing breath and kiss against his forehead. "What have they done to you, my little snapdragon?"

Alrick's heart fluttered at the voice, the touch. He couldn't see anything. He tried to lift his hand to touch the face in front of him, but it wouldn't move.

"Tredan! My baby needs you!" The hand on his face vanished.

"*Get out of my house!*" Burgrune roared.

Alrick felt other hands then, many, small, and cold, lift him from the floor. They held his head as a glass bottle pressed to his lips. A bitter liquid filled his mouth, and he felt fire rise in his middle. The hands spun him and held him as he heaved. His body twisted and wracked, muscles wrenching as his gut expelled the poison berries. The smell of them, mixed with his own acids, brought another flush of memories, of his mother screaming—her rage a force that would bring the whole house down if not assuaged.

"This is MY house," she wailed, "And MY child, and you will never touch him again, and you will never touch this floor again, and you will cross that threshold and never return!"

Light returned to Alrick's vision, and he peeled his eyes open to see the small figure of his mother grown large as if to fill the hall, bearing down on Burgrune's shadow.

Burgrune lashed at her, and his mother caught the shadow hand in her own. A pierce of light split from where their hands joined, like lightning.

Burgrune screamed and his mother howled. Nelda, suspended behind them, began to shake.

The scratchlings laid Alrick on the floor and rushed to the light that burst between the two women. They pulled at the skirts of Burgrune's dress, tearing it away in scraps of dark shadow that dissolved like fog in the sun. They tore at her hair, at her arms, till she bent and twisted low enough that they could reach her eyes.

The light from his mother's grip cut through the shreds of shadow peeling away from Burgrune's figure.

Burgrune's mouth stretched wide "A curse—" she screamed, but a scratchling grabbed her jaw and pulled and her chin came away in a spill of black smoke, so all that remained was a wordless cry and a stain of soot on the flagstones.

The scratchlings stood in a circle, their hands outstretched, their palms blackened with the ash of the fallen matriarch.

Alrick's mother lowered her empty hand and turned back to him.

His arms trembled as he raised himself from the floor, his head spinning still from the deadly berries.

Her eyes, long ago lost from his memory, burned him like a brand as he struggled to move toward her. "Mother," he said, his voice raw.

"I'm going to wait a while longer, snapdragon," she said. She made a motion toward him, but as she moved, her substance began to fall away. She squeezed her eyes shut, and the room grew colder as she drew on the air to hold herself together long enough to reach his side. She pressed a hand to his face again, and then was gone.

Alrick's hands searched the air for her, clutching at the last cool draft as it faded. He cried out, sounding to himself as the child he must have been to her.

Tredan grasped his hands and held them. "Calm, nephew. Still. Peace. She's never truly gone."

Alrick fell against his uncle and wept.

Soft cries sounded all around them.

Alrick looked up. Cassie rushed across the hall to Aemon, who lay collapsed half in and out of the doorway, where he had dragged himself. She leaned down to him, her skirt soaked in blood.

"Get away from me, wretch!" he shouted at her.

Cassie stood, stiffened. She looked back at Alrick, her jaw set in grim rage. She stepped over Aemon and ran out the door.

Alrick struggled to rise.

"Let her go, Alrick," Tredan said. "You cannot make anyone stay at House Aldane any more than you can make anyone leave."

The soft cries hadn't ceased.

"Nelda?" Alrick forced himself to stand.

Three scratchlings remained, corporeal, living. They stood around Nelda's fallen form. Alrick searched his pockets for more antidote but found nothing. He rushed to her side.

"Tredan, bring antidote, now!"

Tredan ran to them.

Nelda lay unmoving on the floor, her hands over her eyes. Her lips were white, stained russet blood brown.

"Nelda!" Alrick called to her. He pulled her hands away from her face, and they fell limp to her sides.

"What did she take, Alrick?" Tredan asked.

Alrick thought back to the ribbon-wrapped posy in her hands. To her open mouth, chewing through the flowers and leaves. "Everything. She took it all."

Alrick touched his fingers to her lips. No breath stirred. Her eyes motionless beneath their dark lids. "Oh, Nelda, no."

Tredan lowered the handful of bottles he had pulled from his pocket. "God, no, not again." He pushed Alrick aside and leaned over Nelda, lowering an ear to her chest.

He did not raise his head again.

The scratchlings pulled him away.

Alrick screamed.

Tredan shook his head. "I shouldn't have encouraged her. I should never have let her do this." He threw his bottles against the wall where they shattered, spilling pale medicine down the crumbling plaster.

"No, Uncle," Alrick said. "I could have prevented all of this if I had just let go…" He rocked back on his heels. A scratchling wrapped her small arms around his shaking shoulders.

"*Do something about it,*" she whispered in his ear.

Alrick's sob hitched in his throat. He squeezed the small hands, and struggled to his feet, turning, searching the room.

The blast of soot where Burgrune had been destroyed trailed across the floor. Aemon dragged himself through it, toward his fallen sister. His face now pale and limp, all trace of bitterness and anger abandoned, giving way to grief.

"Brother," Alrick said. He ran to Aemon, lifting him, holding him steady. Aemon clutched at him. "She's gone, Aemon. I'm so sorry. She took too much…"

Aemon let out a weak laugh. "You never learn anything, do you, Brother?"

Alrick pulled back.

"The Ladies of Aldane are never gone." Aemon's eyes roved over the floor and ceiling.

CHAPTER TWENTY-NINE

"Let's get you to bed, Aemon. Tredan, help me carry him. See to his leg. I will find where Merry has gone." He turned to the three scratchlings, then looked to the pale form of his sister on the flagstones. "Will you take care of her?"

"She's going to take care of us," they said together. A chill crept up Alrick's arms. He nodded.

He and Tredan carried Aemon to his bed, and Tredan inspected his injuries as Alrick rushed away to find Merry.

Merry, Anne, Martha, Susan, and Elizabeth had all gathered on the lawn, watching the house as if it were aflame, clutching each other's hands.

Merry cried out when she saw Alrick and ran to him, squeezing his face between her hands and pulling him into an embrace.

The bread and powder scent of her apron unlatched the hook in his heart and he wailed, buried his face into her shoulder, and let his strength fall away for a moment.

"Father never came. He didn't help us," Alrick choked between sobs.

Merry held him tighter. "It is no bad thing, if your father rests, lad. He can rest because he trusts you." Her broad hand stroked his back. She waited till his sobs had become deep breathing, then she lifted his chin. "What is to be done, now, my lord?"

Alrick didn't know where to begin. He had his house, at last, his land, his title. All else he had lost. He would have to build anew.

"There are carriages coming," Elizabeth said from behind Merry.

Alrick gasped. The neighboring lords were coming to verify their witness to his father's will. "I need the hall set right. Merry, find Mister Skillson and Shepherdson to receive our guests."

Merry nodded. "I'll get them ready. They're in the stables, calming the horses, after…Well, m'lord, Cassie rode off on Loki."

"Good," Alrick said. "She'll make it to the village quickly, then."

They scattered to their tasks, leaving Alrick on the lawn, watching the line of chalk dust in the distance, raised behind the wheels of two dark carriages. They'd arrive within the hour.

He crossed the lawn to Nelda's garden. Earth still mounded around the hole where they had dug, where they had found Burgrune and the missing will.

Alrick peered in. The bones were gone. Soft ash, in the outline of a small woman, clouded the dirt. There was nothing left of that hollow brow, no trace of satin or lace. Just an echo of her fire, there at the roots of her plants, among her murdered sons.

He grabbed the spade and turned the soil over, mingling the ash with earth, turning up the richer, darker soil. He heard a soft song behind him and turned to see the three scratchlings carrying the brightly bound body of his sister. Her body was wrapped in ribbons of every hue, her hair braided with them and coiled in an elaborate knot. They lowered her into the hole, where she curled softly against the earth, peace written across her pale face, so that Alrick felt he had only just seen the face of his sister now, for the first time. They spooned the earth back over her, where it didn't cover her so much as embrace her, until she was buried like a secret, like the long-distant past, like the old lords and ladies of House Aldane.

Alrick and the children stood around her, all whispering their own words, lost on the wind that made the dark flowers around them dance. He wanted to scream. He needed to shout himself inside out, as if his pain were air and he could purge it all. To howl so loudly that Cassie would hear him over the moor and hurry home. He wanted to tear down the hospital walls with his voice.

Instead, he breathed.

Fray came padding from behind one of the trees. He lay in the dirt, chin resting on the soft ground. Alrick bent to touch his shaggy head, but a low warning growl tumbled from the dog's throat, and Alrick stepped back.

When the scratchlings had finished their words, Alrick asked, "Can we bring the tree back?"

The children nodded and set out.

Alrick went inside, through the back kitchen door, where Anne and Martha set trays with cakes and tea. It felt too normal. It all looked too ordinary for a day that had ripped his heart from his body. The whole world should have stopped altogether. Normalcy felt indecent.

He climbed the stairs to the hall. All was set in place, as if it had not just been the scene of a battle, as if the floor hadn't just known death, as if the house hadn't played host to generations of pain. As if nothing could ever really change it.

The broken chandelier had been carried away. The table was set for receiving, with the will placed at its center in place of prominence.

He walked down the dark corridor to his wing—to Tredan's

wing—and climbed the stairs to his attic chamber. Alrick couldn't imagine leaving these rooms, now. They had become his home. He crossed to his pitcher of tea and washed himself in bergamot, cleaning away the residue of berries and sick, of medicine and tears, of grave dirt.

He put on a clean suit and brushed the dust from his shoes.

A spot of color caught his eye. He turned toward the bed. There, on the pillow, was a bright blue, round bottle, with a length of red ribbon tied round its neck.

Alrick's heart seized. He rushed to it, picked it up, and held it to his chest. It chimed as he moved it. He held the bottle up to the candlelight and saw, there in the bottom of the fogged jar, was his father's signet ring.

"Alrick!" Tredan's voice called up the stairs to him. "They're arriving."

Alrick set the bottle on his desk. He struggled to remember to breathe. His body seemed to think he had no need of breath, as if his trip—twice, now—beyond the threshold of life left him without a use for such trifles.

He drew in a long breath and went downstairs.

Aemon sat at the table, to the right of Father's chair. *My chair.* His leg was propped on a soft stool, wrapped in a wide bandage.

Tredan sat across from him, pouring him a cup of wine.

"You should go out to meet them, Alrick. We'll wait here," Tredan said.

Alrick stepped outside the front door, where Shepherdson stood waiting as the carriages pulled into the gravel drive of House Aldane.

"Where is Mister Skillson?" Alrick asked.

"He has left, m'lord. He said he's decided to retire after all."

Alrick nodded. "Well, Shepherdson, consider yourself promoted."

"Yes, sir."

"Do you know how to do this? To receive these guests?"

Shepherdson fidgeted a little. "I think so, sir."

"Good. I'll follow your lead."

Shepherdson flushed, and Alrick felt his own rosebuds bloom in sympathy.

George arrived first, on horseback. Concern crossed his face, and Alrick supposed he must be showing some trace, yet, of the last few hours' ordeal.

"George, please hurry to the village. See to it Cassie receives everything she needs and help her to get to wherever it is she wants to go."

George nodded and spurred off again as the carriages slowed and stopped in his wake.

The lords exited their carriage chambers and approached Alrick. They nodded to him, and he nodded back.

"Come inside. Merry has set refreshments." He turned to let them follow. It wasn't proper, he knew, but he was too tired for ceremony. These lords had betrayed their word to his father. Once their business was done, they could leave and never return, for all he cared.

Shepherdson tried to salvage some measure of decorum and seated the guests as Alrick took his place at the head of the table.

The lords glanced between Aemon and Alrick. Aemon kept his eyes shaded with a hand, not meeting any of their furtive glances.

Tredan cleared his throat. "Here is the missing will that we have been searching for, gentlemen. I know you have both seen it before, but perhaps it slipped your memory."

One of the lords pulled his face into a simpering smile. "I do recall this now, yes. I've signed so many of these. I keep no personal record—"

Aemon scoffed. "I already told them. There's no need to exhaust us all with an act. It's over. Lost. We lost everything. At least don't embarrass me and cost me my dignity, too."

The lords sat silent.

Alrick spoke. "Do you gentlemen acknowledge your witness of this document, the final will of Lord Drummond Aldane?"

"Yes," they both mumbled.

"Good. Then let's have some tea, and then you may return to your homes."

Shepherdson and Merry served, and all ate in silence.

The candle flames danced. Then grew, flames licking higher till they dwarfed the wax pillars, which shuddered, then collapsed into melted pools. Laughter tickled the air.

The neighboring lords scrambled back from the table, upending their chairs, then turned and ran from the hall.

Merry stood staring, the teapot clutched in her hands.

A ribbon tumbled from the chandelier above them and coiled in the sugar dish.

Aemon chuckled. Tredan shook his head.

Shepherdson set his tray down on the sideboard. "They've left the front door open, m'lord. Should I go and close it?"

Soft laughter sounded from under the table.

Alrick smiled. "No. Leave it. The door of House Aldane is always open."

The End

ACKNOWLEDGMENTS

I want to thank libraries everywhere for providing the resources that allow us writers to worm our way through research rabbit holes, giving a sense of life and reality to our fiction. Stories are born in libraries. They grow there, and bloom into the hands, minds, and hearts of readers.

I also want to thank my family, my lovely boys, for being my sweetest supporters.

I want to thank Doug Murano, John Coulthart, and Todd Keisling for making this book the beautiful object that it is. You can do a lot with a Bad Hand, and you're the best Bad Hands out there.

Very big thanks to all who read early bits of this book. There have been so many since I started this project in 2017, and some of you have been tireless champions of my work. Bonus big thanks to Lisa Morton, Rena Mason, Gwendolyn Kiste, Kate Grusauskas, Amelia Bennett, Alec Shane, and all my dears at PAWS—especially Kat Rohrmeier, who has the patience of a tortoise, the mind of an owl, and the heart of a whale. You delightful chimera, you.

SARAH READ is the Bram Stoker Award®-winning author of *The Bone Weaver's Orchard, Out of Water,* and *Root Rot.* You can find her online at authorsarahread.com.

Printed in the United States
by Baker & Taylor Publisher Services